Who is Diana?

Just a simple American girl who has flown to Italy to present her first collection of designer clothes to the waiting fashion world?

Who is Diana?

A smouldering woman of passion who drives young men to thoughts of suicide and older men to undreamed-of heights of power?

Let her tell you while her body still aches with sweet pleasure. Listen as she begins this most arousing account of sex . . . adventure . . . sex . . . laughter . . . sex . . . ambition . . . sex . . . and success.

Also by Lytton Sinclair

DIANA'S PARADISE

LYTTON SINCLAIR

Diana's Debut

Futura

A Futura Book

Copyright © 1983 by Warner Books, Inc.

First published in the US by Warner Books, Inc.,
666 Fifth Ave., New York, N.Y. 10103.

This edition published in 1988 by Futura Publications,
a Division of Macdonald & Co. (Publishers) Ltd
London & Sydney

ISBN 0 7088 4028 0

Reproduced, printed and bound in Great Britain by
Hazell Watson & Viney Limited
Member of BPCC plc
Aylesbury, Bucks, England

Futura Publications
A Division of
Macdonald & Co (Publishers) Ltd
Greater London House
Hampstead Road
London NW1 7QX
A member of Maxwell Pergamon Publishing Corporation plc

For Connie and Roz
They never stop

DIANA'S DEBUT

Preface

My first year in New York City was amazing. After quitting my job as a hostess for the local Howard Johnson's in my home town, Beavertown, Pennsylvania, I arrived by Greyhound at Manhattan's Port Authority bus terminal with nothing more than a suitcase full of dirty underwear and the phone number of a high school friend, who, after giving me a warmer welcome than I had any right to expect, turned out to be a highly successful actress in "erotic" films. She and her magnificently endowed film producer boyfriend mistakenly thought that I intended to make my living making love on camera. Even though I persisted in informing them that I was much too shy for, well, fuck films, they were not about to take no for an answer.

Thank God for the Mafia and organized crime! If there had not been a bloody territorial war between two crime families raging about my silly small-town head at that very moment, I never could have escaped into what turned out to be the central adventure of my young life. Yes, after being involved in a major bomb explosion, a gang-bang, a chauffeur-driven kidnapping, and an absolutely obscene murder in a secluded chateau in northern New Jersey, I arrived back in Manhattan in a full-length mink coat, several thousand dollars richer, ready for a career in high fashion. I must have looked sensational with my tawny mane, my oversized tits with caramel nipples almost always erect, always ready for some guy to roll his hungry tongue around—but enough! That's exactly what happened. Too many guys rolled their tongues around my tits. The sex got completely out of hand, I was victimized by an unscrupulous, jealous wife, and my money disappeared.

As I have often tried to explain, I am primarily turned on by a man's desire. When a man wants me, and only then, do I feel completely alive. Other women run away when confronted by a man's uncontrollable animal lust for them; they feel like they are being controlled. Not me. I feel it is my destiny to surrender to the dark mystery of desire. As my mother's beloved minister, who was my first great love, once told me, "Diana, you have so much to give!"

In New York, after the Mafia murder and the onset of extreme poverty, I was confused. I did not understand what my minister meant. So, desperate to discover a path of survival in the world's most competitive city, I made an honest mistake. I chose a life of celibacy. Yes, removing all makeup, putting aside any sexually suggestive clothing, wrapping my crowning glory in a plain kerchief, I began work as a humble seamstress in the basement workrooms of the House of Adoro, Italian designer Adolfo Adoro's international fashion empire of designer clothing, cosmetics, perfume, leather goods, and furs, which rivals Chanel, Pierre Cardin, Yves St. Laurent, Ralph Lauren and Calvin Klein in today's billion-dollar fashion industry.

And then Destiny intervened. Apparently I was never meant to lead a drab existence. Apparently, I was born for both pleasure and wealth. Try as I might, I could not prevent aroused individuals of all sexes from trying to seduce me. It seems like every time I turned around, hot, hungry lips would, without the slightest provocation or invitation, plant themselves on my surprised and frankly delighted mouth; ravenous hands would explore my upper thighs, climbing ever upward toward my purring pussy. Like I always say, I cannot resist desire. It is my undoing— and my destiny.

Inside no time at all, I had literally Done It All! There I was, a year after my arrival in New York, at my beloved Adolfo's funeral, tears streaming down my face. And, I might add, Maxey von Fuch's delicious honeyed sperm streaming down my thighs. Maxey von Fuchs is an international banker, the House of Adoro's general counsel and financial manager. Like I always say, thank God for small favors and big cocks. Because of Maxey von Fuchs, I was able to survive the psychological trauma of inheriting so much wealth and responsibility. Because of Maxey, I was to set my sights on Rome, where my beloved Adolfo, before his tragic and untimely heart attack during the biggest orgasm of his life, had made plans for me to present my first collectton in the world-famous Colosseum.

It was in Rome where, despite an international incident of unforgettable violence and bad taste, so many warm-hearted Italians with absolutely fantastic bodies would help me rejoin the living. It was in Rome, finally, where I would learn to let go of my small-town hangups about sex and *really* enjoy myself. For the bare truth is that it was not until I traveled to Rome to grapple with the ancient pagan gods of Lust and Abandon that I finally understood my own capacity for life and death and orgasm. *Diana's Debut* is the story of my awakening in Rome, the mother city of us all, with its great breasts, its tight, delicious cunts, its tumescent cocks, its not-to-be-equaled food and drink, from vitello tonnato and Agave '69 to its mouthfuls of overflowing come, its gorgeous women from contessas to whores, its studs, its ancient palaces, its many gods, its

11

brothels, its beds, its celebrity, its money, its blood. I realize that other American visitors, especially those who come to see the Pope, return with different memories. They describe greed, thievery, occasional squalor, a certain mean-spritedness in the inhabitants. Not me. Maybe it's what I brought to the Rome "situation"—I've been told my ass is the finest on five continents and my cunt worthy of worship. The Roman's lapped up every bit of me they could. I felt like I'd died and gone to heaven. Unfortunately, on a couple of occasions while I was there, I almost did.

Diana's Debut is the story of how a simple American girl went to Italy to present her first collection of designer clothes to the waiting fashion world and ended up as the star of a Roman orgy. Or is it *the* Roman orgy? All the beds in Rome seemed to be waiting for me with their magnificent bodies, male and female alike, every one warm, smiling, aching for me to join them in sensual pleasure. What can I say? I tried my best to accommodate everyone I could. People are so wonderful. My cunt is still aching with sweet pleasure as I begin this account of sex, violence, sex, laughter, sex, ambition, sex, and success. Fasten your seat belts, please.

Chapter One

Before his untimely death, my beloved husband Adolfo
Adoro had already informed me that as his widow, I was
to inherit a controlling share of Adoro stock as well as the
day-to-day running of the company. Quite a burden to
rest on the shoulders of a twenty-three-year-old whose
only business experience had been working as a Howard
Johnson's restaurant hostess. But Adolfo was a prime
motivator; he frequently assured me that not only were
my designs equal to his but my sense of fashion was
altogether superior. He admitted that he had often designed for skinny, bony model types, because they were
the only women he seemed to meet in the narrow world
of New York fashion; he insisted that I had more of a
sense of the "real" woman's body with her strong, solid
thighs, her broad hips, and rounded tummy. How could
I disagree with him? My own tits were disproportionately
large, my tummy was not perfectly flat; my vulva was so
fully packed you could see my slit when I wore a bikini,

and my ass made a statement all its own. Thank God for my showgirl legs; they served as a pedestal for my prime attributes. All my life I had bulged out of tailored clothes; I promised myself, when I started to sew, that if I ever became a designer, I would design clothes for the woman who liked to fuck. First things first, if you please.

Adolfo taught me that I should never expect to run a huge worldwide conglomerate like Adoro, Inc. all by myself. The secret of his fabulous success, he so often explained to me, was his ability to hire the most astute lawyers, accountants, and sales managers in the world. Adolfo had many fond stories of how some of the world's most successful designers had been back-alley seamstresses or struggling boutique owners until they hired the right financial managers. He himself had had a small dress shop in Rome with two seamstresses who executed his designs and provided other favors (mostly by spreading their legs). Adolfo's output had been small potatoes, with dozens of unfinished backup orders, until that fateful day in 1950 when he met a successful lawyer and investment

banker, originally from Berlin, German, named Maximillian, or "Maxey," von Fuchs, who had come into Adolfo's shop to pick up a cocktail dress for his Roman mistress. Maxey recognized genius when he saw it. He also recognized a fellow cocksman and saw the infinite possibilities for fun, glamour, profit, and sex. Most of all, sex. By using the devastatingly handsome, square-jawed Adolfo in American television ads, a radical departure from what had been the stuffy, upper-crust world of haute couture, and by convincing a few sex symbols like Sophia Loren and Jackie Onassis to be seen in Adoro, Inc. clothes, Maxey created a demand. By the time of Adolfo's death at fifty-six, it could be said that Maxey had, in truth, created an empire.

Now, with Adolfo gone, he promised to do it again, this time with me as the designer turned model.

"Darling," he said in his rich Teutonic growl, reminiscent of Henry Kissinger, "in five years' time, you will be one of the world's best-known women. You will be a top model, a leading designer, and a mogul. *And* a playgirl; that's the most important label of all. Because unless you are having fun, what's the point of looking beautiful; what's the point of spending money on clothes?"

"But, Maxey," I protested, "I'm just a small-town girl with hardly any education. What do I know?"

"You didn't get this far, my darling, without knowing something."

"But, Maxey . . . I wailed.

"Trust me, my darling. I will make you rich and famous," he promised.

Did I mention that this conversation was taking place in the back seat of the funeral limousine on our way to my beloved Adolfo's funeral, a conversation that ended with that stalwart blond German reaching up with his muscular hand into my special white mourning dress in a frenzied search for the pussy that was throbbing with grief and sorrow and a huge need to be comforted as soon as possible. Perhaps it was unconscious on my part, but I had forgotten to wear my panties, and by the time Maxey touched my inner thigh, the juices were flowing in my cunt. I was on fire. Thank God the limousine had darkened windows; thank God Maxey had paid off the driver in advance.

I have already sketched in this incident in *Diana's Desire,* but I never told the full story. Now that I am a person in my own right and have invested my savings in municipal bonds, I feel that I possess the emotional security to tell the whole truth. In the first place, despite rumors to the contrary, I am not a slut. Like any normal woman, I do not wish to be taken for granted. When Maxey stuck his strongly assertive hand up my quivering thigh and began to fumble for my super-sensitive little clitoris, I was outraged. Yes, outraged—primarily because I am very easily aroused sexually, a condition which too often can give a man the wrong idea, particularly

15

when he's got his hand or, better yet, his tongue wedged firmly into a pair of sweet, swollen labia dripping with hot, musky cunt-juice. At that particular point, no pun intended, it's too easy for a particular man to come to the mistaken conclusion that I'm looking for a fuck. Wrong. All it means is that on some subconscious level, far beyond my moral or ethical control, I am sexually aroused.

In the case of Maxey von Fuchs on the day of my beloved Adolfo's funeral, I guess it was my fault. Out of loneliness, I'm sure, I simply reached over to him in the back seat of that limousine and put one hand on the back of his strong, muscular neck to kiss him. Through sheer accident, it just so happened I let my other hand rest on the huge, throbbing bulge in his crotch just as I was giving him a little kiss on the lips. And if my lips were open when I kissed him and if the tip of my tongue was sticking out of my mouth, plump and pink and wet, that's really how I kiss everyone. The truth is, I don't have a very disciplined mouth. I have never, ever, been even slightly coordinated. So, of course, Maxey got the wrong idea, and before I knew what was happening, his strong, insistent tongue was exploring the soft inner flesh of my mouth, invading me, tasting me, sucking me.

When he finally retreated, I gasped, "No! No! Maxey, we can't do this!"

"But, my goddess, Adolfo of all people would want us to," he whispered. "Diana, I have waited for you since the first time I caught sight of you naked in the models' dressing rooms; you were bending over to put on your panties. I had made a wrong turn; I thought I was in the men's room. Suddenly I looked up and saw between your legs your big hunk of raw cunt-meat hanging down, your pink cunt-lips waiting for my mouth, your intoxicating hole waiting for my big cock to fill it up."

With that, Maxey passed the driver fifty bucks and slammed the divider window shut. By this time I was so turned on I was absolutely petrified. I had fantasies of

16

being arrested for disrespect to the dead. In my fantasies I saw the burly cops who stopped the limousine and dragged us out, pistols drawn; they had the stern faces of my mother, my grandmother, our local minister, our family doctor, and a psychiatrist I once fucked who used to talk and talk and talk about "feeling your feelings." Was I feeling my feelings for Adolfo? How could I tell? I was on fire between my legs. I wanted Maxey. He was alive. And he was the sexiest fucking fifty-five-year-old stud I'd ever met.

"But, Maxey," I continued, sounding as sad as I could, pretending life was very complex, "I am too upset to make love to anyone today." Again, damnit, without thinking, my hand was inside his shirt, exploring his hard, muscled chest with its male nipples as taut as pencil erasers. I can't help it; I am a person who finds it natural to touch. Isn't that what modern science has been telling us, that we must touch? Again, Maxey got the wrong idea. As I've already explained, his exploring hand was exploring my vulva. He was stroking my muff. His middle finger was already inside me, gliding in and out with sucking sounds, wet with my lubricant. It was too late; now he knew I was aroused.

"Unzipper me," he ordered.

"Maxey, I can't," I said. Again, his mouth was inside my mouth, tasting me, establishing passionate contact.

"Unzipper me," he begged, "or I'll get a blood clot."

"A blood clot?" I repeated, not understanding what he meant.

"I'm constricted," he went on. "These pants are too tight. I'm telling you I'll get a blood clot."

Well, I always feel helpless in the face of medical emergencies. What could I do to help him? I unzipped him and then spent three full minutes struggling to help him avoid a catastrophe.

"If you don't help me," he whispered, "they'll have to amputate." I didn't believe him for a minute but, great salesman that he was, he sounded so absolutely convincing that I decided to do whatever I could and argue later. After a certain amount of struggle with the elastic waistband of his jockey briefs, which would not admit the rising head of his erection, so that his cock was bent like a tree in a windstorm, we managed to solve his problem. His erect cock, as thick as a knockwurst, popped out, the skin on its broad head stretched so tightly over the erect tissue that it shone dully in the dim light of the back seat. I went down on Maxey like a predatory lioness, my glistening lips smacking and sucking. From that point, lust took over. I couldn't help myself. The situation was beyond my control. I was just there, an innocent bystander to my own overwhelming desire for sexual pleasure. I lost track of the time. I forgot who I was and where I was going. Was the sun shining? Who knew? Who cared? The car windows were deliberately darkened. We couldn't see out. No one could see in. It seemed like there were black thunderclouds in the sky, full of darkness and passion, just like us.

Now Maxey had an attack of the guilts. He insisted on making a point before proceeding further. "Diana, I just want you to know," he said, "that if we had been married and I had dropped dead, I would have expected Adolfo to do just what I'm doing, for your sake."

"What's that, Maxey?" I said, playing dumb, holding on to his thick German sausage with both hands. He didn't answer me. He couldn't. What was there to say? He was about to fuck me. He took my hands and put them over his hands, pushing down on his missile of flesh, positioning it for entry. Without warning, he did a brutal, wonderful thing. He cleaved into me, splitting through a mass of glistening labia into my hole; there was a tunnel there that opened willingly to receive him. Holding me precariously on the edge of the back seat, his two hands digging into my ass-cheeks, he brought me forward to control the angle of his thrusts. The head of his cock was so broad it touched deep spots in my flesh cave, causing mini-spasms of ecstasy that the jolting of

18

the funeral limousine only exaggerated. As I reached my first full orgasm, my legs, which had been wrapped around Maxey's classic Prussian head with its ice-blue eyes and chiseled jaw, my legs which had been locked at the ankles, suddenly unlocked.

My arms and legs flailed about, beating at Maxey and the inside of the car. I cried out in guttural sounds and syllables—"Aaaaaah" and "Uuuuuuuh." I was a wounded animal torn to pieces by the excess of pleasure; I was a rag doll dropped from a height; I was completely out of control. As my orgasm reached its height, my sounds became high-pitched, frenetic; I was loud and plaintive. Likewise, Maxey does not come silently. He brays; he gargles; he whimpers. My inner lips held onto his column of hard flesh, but when he came, he came with such raw violence I could scarcely hold on. He was a rodeo rider bucking me into the air. He unloaded so much come I could smell it between my legs. "Oh Christ!" I thought, "what happens if I smell like come at the cemetery?"

At this point, I can now divulge additional details about what happened during that trip between St. Patrick's and the cemetery in Queens (which must remain anonymous for the purpose of avoiding litigation).

When the limousine driver heard my orgasmic feet knocking senselessly against the divider window and heard our cries, he, who as it turned out was three months out of the Moonies, imagined we were calling for help and he opened the divider window just in time to see my magnificent Maxey withdraw his big white bratwurst and explode white globules of come all over my exposed honey-blonde bush and lower abdomen. With that brief vision of carnal sin, so forbidden to him for so long by the Reverend Dr. Moon, some center of his brain was pricked by the sharp needles of pleasure for the first time in his young life. The boy went slightly berserk. Unknown to us, at least until the end of the incident I am now free to describe, he reached down into his pants and began to feel his slug of a cock, once dormant,

19

now growing big and strong in the palm of his hand. Apparently, this was somewhere on the Whitestone Bridge connecting Manhattan and Queens. It took him a while to fully connect with the staff of life growing out of his groin. Mind you, he was also trying to drive a limousine. With his attention divided he proceeded to get lost. Maxey and I, by this time, were dozing in the back seat, unaware of time or geography. By the time our Peeping Tom located the front gates to the cemetery in question, Adolfo's coffin had arrived and had been set up under a tent, with chairs on either side of the open grave for our distinguished guests, who included the Italian ambassador, Senator Ted Kennedy (who has been so comforting to me and whom I am not free to discuss at this time), and the heads of most of the fashion houses in New York, Paris, and Milan. Adolfo's grave was at the top of a hill, in front of which a green meadow untouched by death or the hand of man sloped down to a woodland stream with willow trees on either side. The meadow was awash with wildflowers: buttercups, daisies, black-eyed Susans, lilies of the valley. When Adolfo had bought his burial plot he bought the entire meadow. He said he wanted nothing between him and the stream below. He said, half serious, that to him, as an Italian with his ancient pagan heritage, the stream below the meadow was the river Lethe which would carry his spirit to Hades, the Underworld. According to his wishes, the front of the sterling silver coffin, resting in its rosewood box, faced the stream. Off in the distance the Manhattan skyline, the triumph of Western civilization, rose proudly.

As the limousine entered the cemetery grounds, Maxey and I had revived and were now in the middle of our second glorious fuck. I had grabbed his fat cylinder and was rubbing it against my clitoris, pressing my blood-engorged labia and the folds of my vulva around the cock; we were exploring new ways of touching each other. Maxey was speaking in rapidly accelerating voice, "Diana, don't ever leave me!"

I was screaming, "Fuck me, Maxey! Fuck me!" Whenever I look into his white-blue eyes shining like beacons in his darkly tanned Teutonic face, I just can't help myself.

The driver, who had seen two lusty human specimens fucking their brains out and who had again decided to join the madness by jerking himself off, lost control of his limousine this time. He overshot his parking space, backed the car up against the back of the funeral tent, and, without intending to, bumped the end of my beloved Adolfo's casket in such a way that the casket was knocked into a standing position. To everyone's horror, the top of the casket, now functioning as a door, flew open with a bang. My beloved Adolfo, who at his own request had been wrapped naked in a linen shroud handwoven in Jerusalem, hurtled through the air like the man who's been shot out of the cannon at the country fair. He landed in the thick June grass of the meadow halfway down the hill and then proceeded to roll down the remainder of the slope, his shroud unwinding as he went. The funeral guests froze in embarrassment and terror. Maxey and I, who had jumped out of the back seat of the limousine when we felt the initial bump, ran down the slope after him. Maxey's zipper had gotten stuck; his half-erect cock was sticking out about six inches.

It was a circus! Adolfo rolled diagonally down the slope toward a clump of old willow trees which were growing on the bank of the stream where two young women—they couldn't have been twenty—had turned their picnic into a feast of love. One with silky red hair growing down to the pretty small of her freckled back was taking her sexual pleasure from the other one's black-bushed cooze. The redhead's feet were dangling in the stream as she licked her lover's cunt-lips and inner thighs. She had not a care in the world, no awareness of the burial at the top of the slope. The hot currents of summer and the cold currents of spring played tag around her perfect little ass. Then, of course, she heard voices, and, looking up, saw the corpse of a naked man with a fixed expression hurtling toward her. She screamed and grabbed her friend, pulling her out of the way just in the nick of time.

By the time Maxey and I got to the bottom of the hill, Adolfo was floating face-up in shallow water, wildflowers in his mouth. His dead body looked perfectly preserved in the crystal-clear water. The black animal hair on his body waved like seagrass in the currents of the stream. His cock was still tumescent, yes, still hard. I wanted to jump in the water for one last screw. I felt instinctively there must be a meaning in what had happened. I believed that Adolfo's spirit still hovered in his corpse, hungering for one last act of love before it traveled downstream to the Underworld where there could be no more sexual ecstasy, no more orgasm, no more arousal, no more sweet lips and hot cunt, no more Diana's ripe little ass. I knew that Adolfo wanted me while his flesh was still firm. Oh, shit, who's kidding who? I guess I more or less flipped out.

They tell me they had to pull me off of him. I was clutching at him, my skirt hitched up around my waist and soaking wet. They say I almost drowned. I don't remember any of this. I was in another place that afternoon, a dark night, with the only light coming straight from Adolfo's sightless eyes. I only know one thing: a woman's desire and a man's desire to be two in one flesh does not stop with death. My life is sometimes filled with madness; sometimes it has no more meaning than a three-ring circus. I have been labeled an irrelevant girl from the sticks, a slut, a first-class nut, a woman with too much emotion and not enough brain. Do not blame me for my excesses. Life is life. It must be lived. My brain is in my cunt; I like it that way.

After the funeral, it would soon be time for the reading of Adolfo's will. And then on to Rome where I would become notorious. And loved.

Chapter Two

Since Maxey von Fuchs, the House of Adoro's financial manager and my personal lawyer, had already informed me that, yes, as Adolfo had promised, I had inherited the Adoro fashion empire, I was chagrined when he asked me to be present at the reading of the will. "There will be some surprises," he said.

"But, Maxey," I protested, "I've already had enough surprises, starting with Adolfo's fatal heart attack. Please tell me what's the surprise?"

"Diana, my darling," rejoined Maxey, "Adolfo made me promise I would say nothing specific, but I will tell you this much: as you know, as much as dear Adolfo wanted and received his Bobby Kennedy-style celebrity funeral at St. Patrick's, he was pure Italian and saw no point in endless mourning. He always said that when he died, he wanted his loved ones to celebrate his life with the most extravagant party he could provide. So there was money put aside."

"How much money?" I asked. "How much of a party?"

"Never mind about the details," answered Maxey. "I'm your financial partner here. I'll take care of the money. I've been doing all right so far, haven't I? Now, you get dressed for the reading of the will."

"Oh, Maxey," I wailed, intent on inventing reasons for not attending such a dreary ceremony, no matter how much sherry and caviar was being served. "Oh, Maxey, I have nothing to wear!"

Maxey looked at me with that Teutonic smile that found it difficult if not impossible to break out into a grin. "Diana, my darling, have you already forgotten? You are now Adoro International and the main store right under your feet is filled with the world's most elegant clothing." I turned beet red. In my twenty-three-year-old mind's eye, I still pictured myself as the Howard Johnson's hostess who made her own party dresses with Vogue patterns and my mother's hand-me-down Singer sewing machine, and who, after work, had no responsibilities outside of decorating the Christmas tree and putting up the American flag on the Fourth of July.

Did I neglect to mention that Maxey and I were having our ongoing conversation about the reading of the will in the fourth-floor executive suite in the House of Adoro? Yes, the complex of four townhouses on Manhattan's Upper East side comprise the showrooms, workrooms, and business offices of our main store, which deals mainly in individually designed clothes for women who want the best. Adolfo's private apartment, now mine, was on the top floor. Maxey and I, needless to say, were in my bedroom, on my big bed, where we had spent the previous night in passionate lovemaking. This room, which had been my bridal chamber such a short time before, was a dark, warm place paneled in mahogany, with wall-to-wall Oriental carpets whose predominant color was red. There were brass sconce lights on a dimmer and eighteenth-century Florentine furniture from an old palace of the Medicis; the centerpiece of the bedroom was a canopied bed fitted with bloodred damask fabric. It was a perfect place to fuck.

Being a widow at twenty-three is not the easiest situation in the world, and Maxey made love so fabulously I decided early on I would not spend months suffering terrible loneliness if I did not have to. Why should I pass up Maxey? He was a German aristocrat, a millionaire, a combination stud and father-figure, exactly what I needed. If *I* had dropped dead, Adolfo would have immediately hired four terrific call girls to keep him from going over the brink. One of the prime functions of sex, something the psychiatrists and the various religions have not yet admitted, is its therapeutic value. Maxey was better for me than all the shrinks and clergymen I could possibly afford. He made me realize that I was among the living and that I still had basic emotional and sexual needs that must be paid attention to. But, yes, I also felt guilty about fucking my late husband's best friend and business partner, even though Adolfo, Maxey, and I had made it together on two occasions. I have to say that for a woman to have two studs fucking her, one up the ass and the other one in the royal cooze, is the kind of personal affirmation that's better than all the money in the world, especially when the studs in question are brilliant, accomplished, successful males who can't keep their hands off you. Or their mouths. Or their cocks. I mean, Maxey and I were practically family; if we couldn't sleep with each other, who could we sleep with?

Did I describe what I was wearing? My new Adoro wash-and-wear nightie, which I had designed myself. It's what made Maxey dive into my bed when he first saw it. It was high-necked and ankle-length, but there was nothing sexier between Baffin Bay and Tierra del Fuego. It was made of pink satin ribbons, occasionally attached to each other every six inches or so. That's all. No solid material. No lining. Just ribbons. Every time I moved or shifted my weight, it was peek-a-boo time; a different patch of skin peeked through a piece of the whole (and the hole), a glimpse of nipple, a part of my resplendent ass. Sometimes, if I bent over to pretend to pick up something on the floor, my incredible crimson gash showed through with its magnificent lion's mane of dark orange fur in back and its mouthful of ripe, hanging fuck-flesh. I hate to brag, but I have more than a mouthful of cunt, front or back. My cunt is full and luscious, my labia like ripe orchids hanging in the jungle of desire, a flesh-eating lure for the big piece of male meat it hungers to devour, first by taking it into its dark coral walls, then by sucking it in a furious spasmic struggle until the brute in question releases its animal soul to me, its animal soul and its love. My cunt, you see, has devoured many a man, so I make it a point to dress for the kill.

The question is, who is the killer and who is the killed? I seduced Maxey as soon as I could because I needed to be impaled on his warrior's sword. I needed to thrash about and die, so that I could rise again in the night under the light of the moon, to love again, to die again. Such is life. It is the ongoing rhythm of sex and death. They are one and the same, bigger than me, bigger than Maxey, bigger than Adolfo. I could never have responded to death by withdrawing into the dark and weeping myself into a black widowhood. Do I sound too philosophical? I absolutely must be; I need to convince myself that the events at Maxey's townhouse following the reading of Adolfo's will were better than staying home and watching something positively uplifting on "Masterpiece Theatre."

We gathered together at Maxey's on East Seventy-Fifth Street, in his upstairs suite, to be exact. The rooms were a play in lavender: lavender Ultrasuede walls, a mauve carpet, purple velvet furniture, and draperies that were almost white except for a wash of lilac. Maxey was wearing a black Moroccan caftan trimmed with gold braid, a strange choice of garment for him, I thought. "Good ol' Glorianna," Adoro's top model and my late husband's one-time lover, was there, too, all six feet of her, her proud Cherokee bloodlines showing in her high cheekbones, her perfect aquiline nose, and her slanted almond eyes. She was wearing a sheer white satin pants suit without underwear that emphasized her nipples and the crack in her ass. I absolutely couldn't stand Glorianna. She was too proud, too cold, too imperious. Besides, she'd stolen my first great passion in Manhattan, Angelo O'Shaughnessy, the one-time king of porn flics, a soul-wrenching situation I describe in detail in *Diana's Desire*. Maybe, in truth, Angelo two-timed me; maybe it wasn't really Glorianna's fault. If not, then why did she try to get me arrested for giving him a blow job in his hospital bed, especially when Angelo said it was the best he'd ever had?

Looking at her now, I felt confused and upset. Why was Glorianna at the reading of Adolfo's will? I prayed that my beloved had not left her a single sou. Some of the other Adoro models were there, too, most of them frankly irresistible. Adolfo had a thing for enormous brown eyes and small, tight asses which rode high and proud when their owners walked across a room. He liked small, pointy tits, too. "The ballerina look," I called it, wondering what some of these "ballerinas'" cunts looked like. Backstage at any major fashion house naked tits are in abundance as models change quickly from one costume to another. Nipples range from tiny, inverted push buttons of pleasure to big chewy teats the color and texture of dark caramels, with aureoles spreading creamily like fudge for a couple of inches across a breast. Who can say what is preferable? Sometimes sex is good when the other person is small and tight and cold and we feel totally in charge. Sometimes we want excess flesh to invade us; huge cocks, heavy balls, breasts that hang heavy and ripe, cunts that are so big, so dark, so rich and meaty they require a horse to satisfy them. Yes, sometimes a horse with its dumb, sullen, barely feeling heart is exactly right; its foot-long cock all that's required. This is why it's always good to have a stable of young models, male

27

and female. Because when you want to fuck, you really need a choice. It all depends on whether you want to control or be controlled. This need will vary from day to day.

I've never been a lesbian or considered spending my life with women; after all, God created us male and female, right? There is nothing more fulfilling to a woman like myself than getting fucked by an attractive man who wants me badly enough to rip the clothes off of me. But every now and then there appear on the scene certain women of a certain age that even a normal heterosexual woman like myself cannot pass up. Yes, it's true; there are some girls who were made to be fucked as frequently as possible by men, women, and children. I'm talking about certain women between, say, seventeen and twenty-seven who possess bodies that beg to have your hands and mouth, I mean *my* hands and mouth all over them. The sight of a plump little vulva, its mound rising gently and provocatively from the lower abdomen, its firm, ripe shape apparent even under the most luxuriant, thick, black bush, the suggestion of red slit impossible to disguise even when she's standing up, leaves me speechless. And when she bends over to pick up a room key or, heaven forbid, when she sits on a silk sofa, her legs akimbo, which is to say, spread, breaking all rules of etiquette, a wave of desire passes over me and a demon spirit possesses me. The word "lesbian" has nothing to do with it. It is pure, simple animal desire, and society should accept it as such. Sexual categories are not my cup of tea; any poor person who thinks in terms of them has never experienced the full power of sex, which overrides categories.

Anyway, having stated my case, let me now describe my two choicest models (Glorianna, that cunt who changes her underwear three times a day so she won't smell like a woman doesn't count) who were present that evening at Maxey's at the reading of the will: Belinda and Rosemarie. Christ. Just looking at them standing there against a lavender wall pretending to be shy, I knew at once that beneath their clinging black satin dresses, above their sheer black stockings, there was no underwear. No, nothing but a garter belt that snapped onto the top of those stockings, those black stockings that hugged and sucked those milk-white thighs. Besides, I could smell their cunts from the other side of Maxey's lavender living room. Who was kidding who? I'd bet money those cunts were naked, bare, open, and steaming with juicy lubricant. Belinda and Rosemarie.

Yes, but something was wrong. They were too contained. I could feel their restrained passion under their careful surface. They stood by themselves. Were they nymphomaniacs afraid of anyone finding out the truth? I certainly hoped so. I suddenly felt shackled by my small-town upbringing. I craved to go over to Belinda and Rosemarie, engage them in polite conversation, and then, without asking permission, put my hands up their dresses, fingering one cunt and then another until my hands were steaming wet and my cunt was ready to explode at the touch of a tongue. But there was nothing I could do except sit there with my hands folded in my lap, the loyal widow, and long for what was forbidden to me in that particular time and place. Belinda looked like Snow White with her raven mane, sapphire eyes, and chalk-white skin. She had fires under her cheeks. Her full-skirted "mourning" dress in fitted black satin was cut so low in front I swear I could see the edges of her aureoles peeking out over the top of her dress. Or was I just imagining things, hoping that was the case? Rosemarie I don't even want to talk about. With some women, you just know they never wash the underwear they don't even wear in the first place. They douse themselves in Chanel No. 5, knowing full well the mingled odors of sweaty flesh and French perfume will repel the Puritans and drive the sensualists half-insane with erotic arousal.

Anyway, I was not about to get aroused. Not then. I sat in my chair examining the polish on my nails.

Glorianna sat across from me, looking down at her lap, which I decided was an appropriate gesture for the closet slut of all time. I still couldn't imagine what she was doing there, since unlike the younger models she was too headstrong to lend herself out as a party decoration. Something was clearly afoot. Glorianna hardly spoke to me when she came in.

Finally, after what seemed to be several hours of waiting, Maxey read Adolfo's will. It was a personal document written in longhand after his bypass operation, a month before his death. The first part I already knew about. He left the bulk of Adoro International to me, his widow, with the express hope that I retain Maxey von Fuchs as my business partner and financial manager, and that I serve as both Chairman of the Board and President of Adoro, Inc., until I found some marketing genius to take over as President. Adolfo also hoped that, just as we had discussed, I would inaugurate my design career at the Roman Colosseum. So far so good. We were in perfect accord every step of the way. Then came the shocker. I could hardly believe my ears! My beloved Adolfo was bequeathing to Glorianna, that cold-hearted cunt, five percent of Adoro, Inc.! "For all her many years of devoted service, both personally and professionally!"

I wanted to hang a sign with the word "whore" around her elegant neck, but fortunately for me, I decided not to. I had too much to be thankful for to be mean-spirited about someone else's good fortune; besides, there were more than a few observers ready to hang the same label on me. Adolfo never had to marry me in the first place. Who was I to be entertaining such negative thoughts now? I had never been the jealous type. I had never demanded exclusive love from any man; it too frequently became claustrophobic. I finally had to admit to myself that Glorianna was there; she was going to be a continuing presence in my life. There was nothing I could do about it. She would not go away. If I fired her as head model, if I barred her from board meetings, she was too close to

Maxey, too intimate with too many Adoro employees not to be always hanging around. And certainly, whether I liked it or not, she would be a continuing part of the New York fashion world. But I didn't like it. I knew myself too well. There was a battle on the horizon. Indeed, by the end of the ensuing summer, in Rome, Glorianna and I would come to blows. Because of Glorianna, I would seem notorious to some, a saint to others. Because of her, I would be forced to understand the passion that was to be central to my destiny.

As I sat in Maxey's lavender living room mentally battling the woman I perceived to be my rival, the reading of the will continued. It was the surprise Maxey had promised me: "I have bequeathed the sum of twenty-five thousand dollars for a gala celebration to be held after the reading of the will, a party so splendid that every guest there will enjoy the absolute best time in his or her life. When you think of Adolfo Adoro, remember the party I have given for you. I love you very much. Adolfo Adoro."

With that, Maxey finished the reading of Adolfo's will. There wasn't a dry eye in the house. But not for long! Maxey pressed a button, which opened a wall panel. Then, he pressed a series of buttons on the panel. Instantly, his living room was lighted with a theatrical drama. Where before there had been expanses of lavender and glass, there were now islands of darkness and deep shadows ready for intimate scenes to be played out. There were hiding places for those who wanted privacy and bright islands of white light for those who wished to be seen. What else? Music, of course. Mood music. Mantovani; violins and romantic overtures. For a girl from Beavertown, Pennsylvania, Mantovani, that maestro from the fifties, was more than enough to suggest making love. But what am I talking about? Again, almost against my will, I was obsessed by fantasies of fucking. Wherever I turned, whoever I met, my imagination turned to fucking. "What is the matter with me?" I thought. Adolfo clearly wanted his

31

best friends to have a marvelous time sipping the best champagne and acting civilized. There would probably be filet mignon and jumbo shrimp. And fresh strawberries and creamy cheesecake, with cognac after dinner. A very New York meal. Nothing more; what else is there? Food, wine, soft music, and old friends. What more did a party need? I had to get a good grip on myself. Except, where were the old friends? Who was this party for exactly? Maxey, Glorianna, Belinda, Rosemarie, me, and a few of the newly hired girls. Twenty-five thousand dollars just for us?

Maxey must have been anticipating my next question. He pressed another button. The sliding doors to the two bedrooms adjoining Maxey's living room slid open. I was in absolute shock! At least ten studs, all first-string on the New York area's leading professional football team (no names mentioned,) walked out of that bedroom grinning from ear to ear. They were starkers! From the other bedroom paraded what I found out later were the "top ten" call girls in New York. They were naked, too, of course. Without a moment's hesitation, Maxey flung off his black caftan to grandstand a rising erection, and when I turned around to catch Belinda and Rosemarie's reaction, I discovered that they had joined the party. They weren't wearing a thing! Their black bushes were like coal on virgin snow, so white were their thighs. Their cunts were just as I had fantasized, hot pink gashes, flesh magnets in the night. From the kitchen came a crew of "servants" bearing hot hors d'oeuvres. They were as naked as the guests. There were cocks, cunts, tits and asses for every taste. I got so excited I could barely breathe. It seemed like everyone was drinking champagne, making toasts "to success!" "to life!" "to love!"

From out of nowhere, hands began to undress me. Many hands! I had to stop and catch my breath. I felt like a kid in a candy store. The football players were lined up in a conga-line row in front of me, six of them anyway. Could it be they were waiting to fuck me one by one?

32

The one in front, a stocky redhead with a bushy beard and a mushroom-shaped cock and enormous egg-shaped balls, said, "Hello, babe, what are we waiting for?" I wasn't sure what to say. Was I confused or was I pretending to be confused?

Glorianna had taken the star fullback and two of the call girls to the library and shut the door where they remained for most of the evening (thank God). Belinda, who had remained behind, had had her cunt-cave stuffed with pâté de fois gras. She was being eaten out by a black stud with the swagger and authority of an Othello. I could see his long muscular tongue snaking its way inside her as his horse-cock grew in length and girth, and his hips and ass began to undulate out of instinct, rehearsing what was to come. At this point I didn't know what I wanted. Did I want to be gang-banged or did I want to get to know Rosemarie? Somebody had to make my mind up.

That's exactly what happened. It's difficult when you're a young, grieving widow to take sexual initiative with a gorgeous stranger barely three weeks after your husband's death. These great athletes, thank God, were also gentlemen. They understood my emotional needs perfectly, which is not to say my body did not make them crazy. I kept hearing, "Christ, look at those knockers! Wow!" "Christ, Jerry, I never saw a cunt with lips hanging out like that!" "Hey, Bronkowski, how come she's not a hooker?" "Because hookers don't look that good! Christ!" "Shut up, Brad, you talk too much; we're supposed to give her a fucking good time." "Hey, Brad, have you forgotten how to fuck?" "I think we should shut up and fuck." Everything was "Christ" and "Jesus"; they were a very religious group, all things considered. It was appropriate for the ecstasy to come.

A note on these guys. They weren't your frustrated suburban husbands with potbellies, skinny arms, and desperately well-mannered penises. They weren't your average run-of-the-mill porn stars, either, with boring faces, emaciated limbs, and foot-long cocks—what I call "the cart leading the horse." These guys were *men* in every sense of the word: strong, barrel-chested, thick-necked, massive physical specimens with sturdy legs, taut, muscular stomachs, great knotted calves, and full-bodied rumps that were hard and full of fight. Their skin tone ranged from pure creamy white of vanilla pudding to black fudge waiting for a hungry mouth to devour it in great slobbering gulps. I looked at the six of them. There wasn't a concave chest in sight. Every guy was built like a brick shithouse.

I didn't know where to start exactly, but figured the guy in the front of my little conga line would do. He was a blond, hairy animal with dense golden wires thick and matted on his sturdy barrel chest, his rugged redneck frame equipped with raw muscles of a farmboy, not to mention what else it was equipped with, an uncut piece of red meat that rose to greet me with its plum-sized glans dripping drops of pearly ooze. He looked me straight in the eye and said, "All right!" At my invitation, he was the first of the evening. He dove for my muff, sank his strong fingers into my flanks, and, kneeling before me, began to eat me out, sucking on my clitoris until I vibrated with shuddering ecstasy, my inner lips unfolding like a rose and shimmering with dew. I was ready to be rammed. I didn't have long to wait. My farmboy football player spread-eagled me while my five other studs and two of the most luscious girls I'd ever seen decided to do something constructive with their time rather than chew their cuticles waiting in line. (I must say that as a young widow I was treated with the utmost caring and compassion. Adolfo knew exactly what I needed. I plan to do the same thing for the friends who survive me when my will is read.) My football-playing farmboy let that big mushroom-shaped tool of his cleave into me, dividing my succulent cunt-lips, pushing deep into my cunt-cave through my tight coral flesh. Then he began to fuck me, pounding back and forth, screwing the bejeesus out of

34

me. As my pleasure grew, my widow's grief began to wane.

At my side, a Scandinavian Amazon with a big blond bush and inch-long nipples was doing her best to make me feel good. I could feel her labia sucking up and down the sides of my body, cunt-kissing my flanks as she nuzzled my upper arms and the muscles on the side of my neck. Then my Amazon stuck my fingers deep into her glistening meat. What a treat! I was beginning to come alive! I wanted more! And I got more from the men; those guys had terrific team spirit. From every direction, it seemed, compassionate hands and mouths were pinching my nipples and stroking and sucking my tits and my stomach. Big sausages of cock-meat were fucking my armpits and the insides of my elbows. One rugged blond stud kept saying, "I can't believe this! I can't believe this!" as he lifted me up and wedged himself under me, making himself a down-covered mattress. He nibbled the back of my neck. Then, suddenly, from underneath, I felt this fat, greased, knobbed column of flesh, his engorged cock, entering me up my ass, or trying to. I was such a small-town prude I gave him resistance. I felt so constricted; that is, until he showed me how much he really cared. I could tell by the tone of his voice and by the fact he took chances that he meant every word he said.

He cried out, "I love you, baby! You don't know how much! I'm crazy about you! Crazy!" That's when I realized my blond stud wasn't some hired fuck. This man really did care. I wasn't just a piece of meat to him, a pickup, a job. After all, he was a professional athlete, in the top one percent of salaried professionals in the United States. I decided that if he cared enough to say he cared, I could care, too. So I opened up. I relaxed my anal track. I let his greased pole with its big probing knob push its way into me, thrilling me with its raw power, as his hands grabbed me from every side. There were wonderful mouths, too, all over me, kissing me and sucking me. I smelled cheap perfume and come, sour sweat and champagne. My orgasms came so thick and fast I could neither count them nor tell where one began and another left off. I was drowning in muscles, pectorals and biceps, mounds of hard flesh everywhere I touched. These guys were so good to me; they must have sensed my loneliness. They took turns with me, front and back. For all the subtleties I've mentioned, this was basically a gang-bang, make no mistake. It was the beginning of my return from the dead. It was thrilling beyond belief.

My second stud was Tyrone, the overdeveloped black with the dark flashlight between his legs. Tyrone didn't waste time with eating me out. He liked openmouth kissing and straight fucking. And all he said was, "White bitch. White bitch. White bitch." Tyrone opened me up wider than I'd ever remembered; my labia stretched to accommodate that great tool of his, which felt like it was reaching all the way to where I breathed. I could hear my heart and his cock pounding together in unison. "White bitch! White bitch! White bitch!" I loved his anger. It was part of his sexuality. When he came, he pulled out of me and gushed a river of white come in the channel between my tits. Instantly, my attendants massaged me all over with the sticky lubricant. I loved being treated like a sex object. I loved men waiting in line for me. At that point in my life I did not have the emotional strength to deal with interpersonal relationships. After all, I was a widow. I was thinking about Adolfo all the time. If I had to establish an interpersonal relationship every time I had sex, I would have remained celibate for the next five years, and we all know the terrible damage that can do.

My next lover-stud was one of those short, compact athletes with dimples and twinkling blue eyes who smiles like a cute kid, except that there's a cold killer lurking somewhere underneath the surface. His name was Butch; he kept looking at me with those dimples and that grin. They were his peacock feathers, his masculine lure, and he knew how to use them. His cock was the proud cock of what's called a phallic exhibitionist. It wasn't all that big, but on a short man a fat cock can look enormous. Unfortunately, I couldn't give him all the attention he needed, I had so many admirers paying attention to me. Butch really got angry. His anger wasn't a black rage, which can be a kind of disguised love. His anger was the ice-house kind. This dimpled running-back hammered away at me like the little monster he was, saying, "What's so great about you, huh? What's so great about you?" He withdrew his pork meat just before he came and splattered his volley of cold cream in thick pools around my belly button, leaving it for my Scandinavian Amazon to lap it up, ignorant dear cunt that she was.

If it hadn't been for my, let's see, my fourth fuck in the gang-bang, I have to say that this party would have definitely been my last gang-bang. My "fourth fuck" of the night didn't look so great at first. He had graying hair, a bald spot, and thick glasses. When I asked him about his glasses, he told me he'd just won the Most Valuable Player of the Year award for running forty yards in the wrong direction due to bad eyesight; then, once he realized his mistake, for running all the way back to score a decisive touchdown. And now he said he was going to score with me. He apologized for wearing glasses in "bed," but explained that without his glasses he couldn't see the cunt in front of his face. I found out later, like me, he was a widower—of sorts. Turns out his wife, a former Dallas Cowgirl, had run off with a former Rockette from Radio City Music Hall. The two of them had checked into a motel somewhere near Albuquerque, had both caught Legionnaire's Disease, and were dead by morning. From the neck down, my "fourth fuck" looked just like Burt Reynolds, my favorite movie star, with his moustache and hairy stomach and easygoing smile. I decided to let him be compassionate. He spoke to me so politely after he'd sucked on my clitoris and tenderly kissed all the orchid petals of my labia. Only then did he presume to introduce himself.

"Hello, Diana, I'm a guard. My name is Joe [last name

37

withheld to avoid lawsuit]; I'm so pleased to meet you."

"Thank you," I said.

"You're such a lovely, well-bred young woman."

"Thank you," I said.

"It's rare to meet women like you, especially in New York these days."

"Thank you," I said.

"Your clitoris has me throbbing with pain. I'm so hard, I'm practically black-and-blue."

"Oh, Joe, thank you," I said.

"Diana, thank you for letting me do it. That's really great of you."

"The pleasure's all mine," I said, dreaming of being with Burt Reynolds, wondering if he had anything on four-eyed Joe, whose sizeable balls thudded quietly against the front of my ass.

"I can't wait to give it to you, you lovely thing," said Joe.

"Why are you waiting?" I asked.

"I can't wait," he repeated, sounding a little bit paralyzed.

With that, something in me snapped. I had had it with good manners. "Fuck me!" I screamed. "Fuck me! Fuck me!"

That broke the ice. The whole room was watching. I didn't care. This time I gave myself completely to the Act of Love, grasping his cock by its base and pulling it inside me. "Burt" pressed his mouth down on mine and drank my kisses like rare vintage wine, savoring each moment. his mouth was inside mine. That's all I cared about. He was happy. I could tell. He did not pump me. His motions were slow. I could tell his soul was in his cock. And, believe me, this was a soulful man. All my vaginal muscles were holding on tight to his male organ. There were loud sucking noises as my ass grew soaking wet from the heat of the room and the heat of desire. Like Mae West, I like a man who takes his time. He took ten minutes, at least, ten glorious minutes of easy fucking, with him saying to me, "Hey, you're great; you fuck better than any woman I've ever fucked; you got a cunt on you that doesn't stop!"

"Forget your eyeglasses and your bald spot, Joe," I said. "You got a cock like a python. Whatever you do, don't stop." When he finally came, it was a celebration and I loved him for it. I cradled him in my arms for a few minutes. He was tired, so I helped him to lie lengthwise on the couch while I got up to take a breather.

A progress report: Glorianna was still behind closed doors. Maxey was tit-fucking one of the call girls who had the right equipment for it. She was sucking on his nipples as he fucked the glistening channel between her voluminous globes. Two of the men were performing sixty-nine on each other; no one seemed to mind. There was enough of everything to go around, including coke, which at that moment I didn't need; I was too high on sex. Belinda, kneeling on all fours, was getting fucked up the ass from behind by a very white stud with coal-black hair on his chest. That's when I snapped. I figured if all the guys wanted was her ass, I'd take her cunt. Her cunt, as I've explained, was adorned by a very dark bush. I wanted that bush in my mouth; I wanted that cherry-red clit. I wanted a mouthful of white vulva and juicy pink labia; raw meat has always been my favorite. I wanted to run my tongue in the folds and grooves of her sexual flesh and make her whimper. I wanted to make her squeal.

Yes, I was on a power trip; to hell with it, this was my party! I was beginning to come alive again, beginning to let go of the grief and self-pity that comes with death. Adolfo knew what he was doing. Thank God for Adolfo and his terrible death. Death can be wonderful, you know, as long as it's someone else's, and when it's your own, so what, you don't even know you're dead. Without Adolfo's death, I ask you, where would I be today? I kissed Belinda, nibbling on her lower lip and sucking it. God, I was bold and getting bolder. Like I say, to hell with conventional morality! I maneuvered myself under her on my back, then raised myself up, resting on my elbows until that sweet ripe cunt was hanging right above me, ripe for my hungry mouth. I lunged. Not far enough. I lunged again. This time: target zero! My mouth was full of ripe cunt, its juices streaming all over my face onto my tongue. I eagerly lapped them up, those bittersweet nectars of this sexually aroused adult woman. Sensational. She did squeal. "Eeeehhh!" I was so turned on I was in agony because I needed my hands to lock onto Belinda's legs. How could I get satisfaction myself? My pussy was dying for someone to pay attention to it. Thank God one of the football-playing studs noticed my predicament and within seconds was eating me out, his fat middle finger greased with mayonnaise from a platter of hors d'oeuvres, stuck up my ass, his lips fondling my clit, his tongue sending volts of electricity throughout my system. Finally, I had the combination I was looking for. Finally, I felt past my grief. I was back on the track, ready to roll toward Rome. I owed it all to Adolfo, that saintly Italian husband of mine. He knew the value of sex. He knew the meaning of love.

Better yet, the party wasn't completely over. There was more. White Lady was being passed around on an antique sterling silver tray with an engraving of a unicorn on its surface. It was so classy-looking this time I couldn't pass it up. I cut one long line of the white powder. Actually, I'm not sure what it was. It was probably just sugar, which some people think is worse than cocaine. Again, I don't believe in drugs, anymore than I believe in lawsuits, but how many times do you have to get through a reading of a will? In these days of high taxes and cutbacks in essential services, let's have a little tolerance for those of us who have tragedies to deal with. I took it straight up the nose. I felt an immediate crackle in my head, a little electric charge. And then, I found myself in paradise, the gold skin of one particular stud changing into moonlight.

There was a sea of penises, tropical fish slowly swimming through the underwater kingdom, searching for exotic prey. They didn't have far to look. Cunts, coral, pink, ruby-red, like a new species of sea anemones open to whatever food floated by, open to the predators intent on devouring their warm meat. The sounds in the room were the basso sounds of deep groaning, orgasmic wails, soprano, staccato, beeps, grunts, falsetto; a symphony of every sound possible by man. It was all there and I remember opening my legs for all the fish to come and feed. The sea snakes came and entered my cave, to caress me and to be kissed in return. I was wrapped in a sea-grass shroud and carried along by the tide. Wave after wave of hurricanes blotted me out, then brought me back from the black depths into the glittering surface sun, then back to the black. Christ! I thought I had died and gone to heaven, animal heaven at least, which ain't half bad.

When I awoke, the room was back at lavender and mauve. Everyone had gone. The sea snakes had gone. The football team had gone. The girls had gone. Glorianna, gone. I was in Maxey's double bed and he was in a silk dressing gown with an ascot; he was holding a breakfast tray. Black coffee, o.j., and croissants, plus a little silver dish of currant jam.

"Where's the butter?" I said groggily, thinking heaven comes in too small a dose to be worth its advance publicity.

"You don't need butter on croissants if they're made right," said Maxey.

"Oh," said I, taking one. He was right. They were so flaky on the surface from all the butter in their basic ingredients it was hard to avoid spraying grease-laden croissant crumbs all over the crisp blue and white bedspread, but who cared! I hadn't come this far from Beavertown to worry about spots on bedspreads. I felt completely at peace and finally beyond my grief. Adolfo had reached across the grave to extend a comforting hand to me.

"Maxey, crawl into bed with me and just hold me," I said.

"Are you okay?" he asked.

"I've never been better, Maxey. I just want to be close, to talk to you, to hold you." He did as requested, first removing his bathrobe. "Maxey, don't try to turn me on," I said. "My cunt is sore from fucking every available stud in Manhattan."

"Everybody had you," he said.

"The women, too?" I said, amazed. "People are going to think I'm some kind of lesbian."

"Don't worry," he said, "as far as your sexuality is concerned, people don't think; they go straight for your cunt. And that includes the women."

"Everyone?" I said. "I thought I was making careful choices; a little bit of this, a little bit of that . . ."

"At two A.M.," announced Maxey, "you sat on my purple velvet hassock, spread your legs as wide as you could, and leaned back your head into my lap. They came one at a time to pay homage to you for the next two hours." His news horrified me. I had this image of this passive cunt, half-asleep, receiving my admirers in lack-luster fashion.

"Oh, God!" I cried, "I must have been terrible! I can't even remember a thing. I'm going to have to write letters of apology! Oh, Maxey!" I wailed, "I can't even apologize. I don't even remember their names!"

"Don't worry," he said, "you have absolutely nothing to apologize about. You were absolutely wonderful.

"What do you mean, Maxey?" I asked.

"Your cunt-muscles practically reached out and grabbed every cock and tongue that came within six feet of you," he answered. "You have a brain inside that box of yours. I swear you've got two sets of muscles in there; one that licks at a man's glans in one direction and another that pulls at his shaft in another. The guys said that if you were a hooker, you'd be making a thousand dollars an hour."

"And what about the women?" I asked. "What did they say about me?"

"Now, listen," Maxey said, his hands simultaneously kneading and stroking my breasts, "those women are, for the most part red-blooded American girls, naturalized citizens or otherwise, and I'm sure they don't want the world to know they craved your body from the minute they saw you naked." His right hand was fondling my bush and he was rubbing his engorged member up and down in the crevice of my ass.

"Maxey, what do you mean when you say those girls are 'for the most part' red-blooded American girls? Who isn't red-blooded. What do you know that I don't know?"

"I wasn't going to tell you if you didn't remember," said Maxey, by now fingering my clit, his glans feeling as big as a small apple, its skin tight and polished as it rubbed against the tingling skin on my ass. "Your two models, Belinda and Rosemarie, had a knockdown dragout fight over you. We had to gag them and tie them up. We couldn't take a chance on someone in a nearby apartment calling the police."

"You had to tie them up?" I said, slightly shocked. "What happened?"

"Belinda was kneeling in front of you; she had her two hands planted on your inner thighs while her full face was stuck in your cooze for about twenty minutes. I'm not exaggerating. Rosemarie was beginning to get impatient. She kept saying, 'Enough already!' Then, it got to be, 'Okay, Belinda, you've had enough. Leave some for me!' After about five minutes of this she was shouting, 'Belinda, you pig! You rotten pig!' and she started beating Belinda on her back with a sterling silver peppermill, creating huge welts. Belinda got so upset she couldn't eat you out anymore. She was in tears, sobbing, screaming about how every time she wants something, somebody takes it away. It was a terrible scene. We had to ask a couple of football players to take them home."

"Where are they now?" I asked.

"Who knows?" answered Maxey. "Maybe the football

players got lucky. As if they weren't lucky enough to begin with."

"What do you mean?" I asked.

"What do I mean?" said Maxey." I mean, first we paid them a thousand dollars apiece to come to the party; then, they take a crack at you; then, it's Belinda and . . ."

"A thousand dollars apiece!" I shouted, dumbstruck at the idea. At this point I really was shocked. "Maxey, you paid ten guys a thousand dollars apiece to fuck me?"

"Yes," he said, "plus five hundred apiece to the girls. I must have paid fifteen thousand just for the sex."

"Fifteen thousand dollars for sex!" I choked. "Oh, no! Maxey, no!"

"Maxey was adamant. "Adolfo left twenty-five thousand for a high-class orgy. What was I supposed to spend it on, the starving poor of Calcutta? Please, Diana, have you no idea of what things cost these days? The caviar alone was fifteen hundred. The champagne cost two grand."

"But Maxey, fifteen thousand just for the sex? I kept repeating. I couldn't get that figure out of my head. I felt vulgar. I felt cheap. "Oh, Maxey," I said, "don't you see? All that money spent on sex—that makes me some kind of super-tramp; I'm just a whore on wheels!" By now, Maxey's large hand, coming from behind, was on top of my vulva, gently squeezing it, his stiff cock between my legs, stroking me under my pubic bone, a special delight of mine.

"Diana, Diana," he said soothingly, "you always get things backward."

"Like your cock," I said teasingly, anxious to change an unpleasant discussion.

But Maxey insisted on making his point. "Diana," he said, "when you pay men for sex, that makes them the whores, not you!"

"But how can men be whores when they're getting rich off sex?" I asked.

"Diana," Maxey insisted, "you don't understand.

44

You're not a whore when you pay someone to have sex with you. You're what's called 'lucky.' " Well, Maxey was sure right about one thing; I didn't understand his point. And I still felt like a whore. If I'd known beforehand he was going to pay that football team to come to our little orgy I never would have opened the door. I know plenty of football players who will come to my parties for nothing, men with no need to sell their bodies. I've never had to pay for sex, and I never will. I believe in giveaway love.

After the reading of the will, I made a firm resolution to keep my sex life and my bank account completely separate. If I met someone in the fashion industry in my line of work whom I felt like fucking, I would do that, but only if my groin told me to go ahead. There's a brain in every man and woman's groin that tells us who to fuck and who to stay away from. Anyway, I took my own advice. I have never fucked anyone, male or female, where money changed hands; although I have to say that my one big exception to my own rule, my three days as a hooker in Mrs. Boothby's whorehouse in Rome two months after the reading of the will, had nothing to do with money—even though it's true, I quickly threatened to become the highest-paid hooker in Italy. My three days at Mrs. Boothby's had nothing to do with sex, either, and everything to do with proving to myself I was a complete woman. This was in response to "Good ol' Glorianna," the employee who almost ruined me. (See Chapter Six). In any case, in the end, Glorianna got hers and I went on to take part in front page headlines. Before I left Rome at the beginning of August, I had fucked more people than the Emperor Nero and Cassanova put together and I was, allegedly, responsible for murdering three members of an international terrorist group. (See Chapter Nine.) All I can say at this time is that they had it coming to them.

By now, Maxey had entered me from behind with his pile-driver cock and was driving me to ecstasy. He sunk his mouth into the side of my neck and was sucking me voraciously as he pressed his body against mine as close as he could and twisted my nipples. "Oh, yes, Max, yes!" I cried, taking his hand and guiding it to my clit. I wanted him there, wanted his strong fingers fondling my most sensitive piece of fuck-flesh. I preferred to use my hands to reach down under my legs and grab his big balls, squeezing them gently and rubbing the heels of my palm against the broad base of his undershaft where his skin was loose and his veins were thick with blood. I loved to stroke that ragged seam of skin that runs down the middle of his undershaft. He shivered with pleasure when I hit the right spots. Max was never so ferocious. He fucked me like a Bowie knife slicing into a raw peach. In and out, in and out, he screamed animal sounds of abandon and pleasure, his hands clutching at my thighs with the force of a man who is about to drown hanging onto the branch of a tree.

I looked down at the massive column of muscle which moved in and out of me with an almost technological perfection. Imagine, a night of orgy and Maxey had saved his best for me! With a final frenzied shout he began to shudder with an orgasm that grew in intensity until, shaking violently, he exploded inside me. His eruption triggered my own climax, a full-sized spasm. My teeth rattled. My eyes rolled back. My tongue lolled. I completely lost muscle control. My brain drained into my cunt and dribbled down my legs. I was awash with come and drenched in sweat. Maxey and I were melted into one. For several minutes we could not pronounce words. He moaned softly. I whimpered and made breathing sounds. His fingers stayed in my cunt until he began to suck on them and savor the taste he loved so much.

"Maxey, don't ever leave me!" I cried. "Let's stay here in bed forever. I don't want to go to Rome."

"What?" he sighed in mock protest. "Don't you want to be a famous designer, Diana?"

"Maxey," I said, in dead earnest, "with you for my

lover at night, I could work as a cleaning lady in an office building and still be happy."

"Cleaning ladies in office buildings work at night, you ninny," retorted Maxey. "You'd be fucking the work-aholics who never go home."

"Oh," I said, "in that case, maybe I better go to Rome. If I have to be a famous designer to get you, Maxey, maybe I'd better be a famous designer. I guess sex isn't everything, is it?" Maxey looked at me and smiled. Then, he drew me into his arms. In no time we both fell asleep. After all, we had to be rested. There were many preparations to make before the promised trip to Rome.

Chapter Three

When royal families travel by air, they usually split up into two groups and use different planes, so that in the event of a crash, one party will survive to run the country. In a nutshell, the crowned head takes one plane, the consort and/or heir apparent another. This is why Maxey and I took separate planes to Rome, with plans to meet for dinner the night of the Fourth. Just imagine, I was an American girl-made-good who would be spending the Fourth of July in Italy with my German lover. That's called making your own fireworks. I couldn't wait.

My bête noire and arch-rival Glorianna took yet a third plane. She said it herself: "In case you two guys die in plane crashes, I want to be somewhere else when it happens. Don't forget, guys, I own five percent of the Adoro International stock. Don't get yourself killed or I might have to take over the company, ha, ha." Glorianna's great ego never considered that she was just as likely as we were to crash into a mountain. She figured she was the child of Destiny. The fact that I'd gone from hostess at a Howard Johnson's to head of a fashion empire in less than a year made no impression whatsoever on her. As she told me later, I was the exception, she was the rule. With me, she explained, my success was more accident. I had no sense of taking command. I was too nice, too sweet, not a trace of the natural-born ruler. As a triple Leo, she could never settle for second best. Someday, somebody, no names mentioned, would make a mistake and, like a lioness, she'd be right there to attack and kill. When she asked me my astrological sign, I said, "Libra," figuring I'd throw her off the track, as Librans are supposed to be bright and charming but not particularly predatory. In point of fact, I am a Scorpio. Scorpios are the most sexual sign and the most powerful in terms of worldly success. Scorpio women, especially, are driven to success. Princess Grace, my favorite movie star of the 1950s, is a Scorpio. She acts like a lady, but she put Monaco on the map. How? Simple. She gave great head to a prince. Scorpio.

My plane was a 747. I sat up in First Class. The movie for the day was *The Blue Lagoon* where these two blue-eyed blond castaway children grew up on a South Pacific isle as brother and sister until they reach puberty, at which time they fling off their loincloths and fuck their brains out—underwater. Do I sound cynical? Perhaps. After all, I was a lonely young widow, the tears of grief not yet dried up on my cheeks. All the sexual interludes in the world could not make up for the loss of True Love. Do you think a hundred orgasms could touch my heart even once? After all, at root, I was grounded in the All-American nuclear family, with both parents absolutely dedicated to one another and to their grateful children, a family committed to love of country and worship of the Judeo-Christian god. I have always believed in this kind of life, even though I must admit that at times it has seemed as remote and inaccessible as a fairy tale. Besides, I wasn't alone in First Class; I had something better than *The Blue Lagoon* to occupy my time, (Note: The Undersecretary of State has advised me to delete the story of my plane trip to Rome and, more precisely, how exactly I landed, but I have decided that the public has a right to know.)

Let me start at the beginning, when I arrived at the TWA Terminal.

It had been beastly hot in New York that July 3rd night. I had no choice but to dress as lightly as possible. The only reason I wasn't wearing panties is because the day before I had packed all my clean underwear and sent my trunks to Kennedy Airport with my assistants. I expected my clothes to be hanging in my hotel room closets when I arrived. It wasn't until after I was already on my plane that I realized I'd had a whole lingerie department of my own in the Adoro store underneath my quarters. Why I didn't just run downstairs and grab a pair of panties is beyond me. Sometimes I just don't think.

In the meantime, a terrible thing had happened. As I was walking from the cab into the TWA Terminal at Kennedy, a sudden gust of wind blew up, and in an instant my sheer silk print skirt was up over my face. That's what happens with silk. I figured, "What the heck?" I decided it looked sexy, like that famous picture of Marilyn Monroe with the air from a subway grating blowing her skirt up over her face.

It wasn't until I was halfway through the line at the check-in that I realized that everyone, and I do mean everyone, had been staring at me since I walked into the building. Some of the men, particularly the middle-aged men, had glazed and haunted eyes. Luckily, I'm not vain. I figured I reminded them of some dead relative or maybe their wives when they first started dating. That's when I first met Ali Ben Gonadi, a tall dark Arab dressed in a sheik outfit complete with white headdress, flowing robes, and a knapsack on his back. "Odd," I thought. "What Arab wears a knapsack?" But this dark hunk was no imposter. He had the hooked Arab nose, eagle-beaked like a great warrior; his sensual lips were full, almost Negroid, suggesting illicit ancestral liaisons between masters and slaves; his skin was burnished and his eyes were like burning coals, black, penetrating, and full of fire.

He stared at me for a full minute before he opened his mouth. "I saw you when you came into the terminal," he whispered in a husky voice. He sounded vaguely English, like he'd spent some time at Oxford. Christ, do I flip over intellectuals!

"What do you want?" I inquired.

"Possession is nine-tenths of the law," was his reply.

"I don't understand what you mean," I said. "Are you a mugger? What do you want?" This is called playing dumb. I figured he was used to silly girls who were so attracted to him they didn't know what to say except, "Please take me home with you; I'll do anything you want." I, on the other hand, was a business executive. I was about to be sexually harassed. I looked at this man with a most fierce and steely expression. The only trouble was, I kept running my hands back through my hair and wetting my lips with my tongue. I couldn't help myself. At that moment I was looking at the God of Sex. As far as I was concerned, he was Lust Incarnate. I would sell my soul to have him. No, I wouldn't. Yes, I would. No, I wouldn't.

Slowly, but surely, as I stood there on that white marble floor, I was going insane. I was absolutely petrified I would go berserk from sexual repression and either stab him in the face with my felt-tip pen or lie down in front of him and crawl up under his robe where I would give him the best blow job of his life, and for my efforts probably be beheaded right there on the spot by one of his two bodyguards, who lurked in the shadows about ten yards away. Besides, although I am pro-Israel, I adore Arab men. But what subsequently happened is now part of history, so it must be told.

52

"Are you traveling to Rome?" he asked, bringing me back to reality.

"Yes," I said, trying to look virginal and chaste. That's when it struck me with the force of revelation. I wasn't wearing any panties! No wonder every man was staring, no wonder this Arab warrior was making a pass at me. I'd been too nervous to notice the cool breezes from the air-conditioning playing around my thighs. I immediately put my hand up under my dress to feel my pussy. Jesus! My soft, thick bush grazed my hand. With a hair-trigger reflex, no pun intended, I looked down at myself; what I discovered made the situation twice as bad; My dress was practically transparent! My dark blond bush was identifiably dark blond through two gauze-thin layers of the most expensive silk in New York. No wonder I was being ogled. No wonder so many men and lesbian types were accidentally on purpose brushing up against me and muttering, "Excuse me" with a leer on their lips as they grabbed their crotches and made for the rest rooms where they could jerk off in a locked stall.

I began to tremble from embarrassment. Morality had nothing to do with my feelings, mind you. If I had forgotten my panties in a candlelit supper club in Montmartre, I could have enjoyed my mistake with the stud of my choice. But here, at the TWA Terminal in New York with its gleaming white marble floors and sweeping walls composed almost entirely of plate glass a hundred feet high, all lighted like the blazing midday sun, I kept thinking how I'd disgrace Adoro International and the pristine memory of my recently dead husband Adolfo. I held my head in my hands and began to weep. The Arab snapped his fingers; one of his bodyguards, scimitar drawn, was beside him in an instant. "No!" I shuddered, fearing the full brunt of harem law, as frequently reported in bloody detail in my favorite newspaper, *The National Enquirer*. Ali muttered something in Arabic and snapped his fingers again. With that, the bodyguard's scimitar went back in its sheath and his headpiece came off. *Voilà!* A makeshift white apron to wrap around my waist. How ingenious.

How could people be so anti-Arabs?" I thought. "Arabs care so much for people's feelings." Well, now, at least, I was safe from further scandal. "How can I ever thank you?"I gasped. Ali had a wonderful Third World way of answering my question. He took my hand and placed it squarely on the familiar protrusion on the front of his robe below his waist.

"Sit with me on the plane," he said soothingly, nibbling my left earlobe, "and we will tell each other the story of our lives. By the time we arrive in Rome, I guarantee you we will be old and dear friends." What sensitivity! What compassion!

Of course, being from Beavertown, I had to joke, "Is that an oil well in your pocket or are you just glad to see me?" Ali didn't answer my silly joke. He was above that sort of thing. The man had class. He took my head in his finely manicured hands and began to suck on my tongue. His mouth tasted wonderful. I liked everything about Ali, especially the fact that he desired me so much. He must have known instinctively how much I hate to travel alone. All things considered, I surrendered to him completely. I don't mean we fucked on the terminal floor. I mean I gave him my mouth in such a way that he knew he could have the rest of me. That's all a woman ever has to tell a man.

There were certain complications; after our 747 for Rome took off with the two of us, Ali Ben Gonadi and I, sitting together with our hands in each other's crotches, our conversation took on a darker tone; at least, his did. After four Scotches, which Muslims are not supposed to drink in the first place, he informed me that his body-guards were not on the plane. "I paid the check-in clerk to deliberately make a mistake and book them on the next plane."

"All because you want to sit alone with me?" I asked, naive young thing that I was.

"No, silly girl," was his terse reply.

There were twenty dead minutes before we spoke again. He kept his distance, drinking more Scotch, and brooding. The dark mystery of this Arabian steed inflamed my desire for him; I was positive that if I could go down on him, I could bring him out of his deepening depression. However, it was not possible to engage in sexual activity at that time because of the stewardesses, who refused to leave us, especially Ali, alone. Strange thing, if you talk to these girls about their reputations as pussy-on-the-wing, they protest that they have a bum image; they claim they never fuck either passengers or pilots in the air or on the ground. If that's true, then they're fucking them underwater at some as-of-yet-undisclosed aquarium. I think I know a hot cunt when I smell one. One of the stews, a little redhead with a British accent named Marilyn Wood, whose last name should be spelled "Would," stood over Ali at least five times an hour saying, "Can I get you anything, sir"

Finally, Ali snapped; he stuck his right hand up Miss Wood's dress and fondled her. Apparently, she, too, had forgotten her panties. Mind you, his left hand was gently squeezing my clitoris. "I love you," he said to Marilyn.

"Here's my phone number and address while I'm in Rome," she said, handing him a card she'd been keeping in her brassiere.

I was so outraged I wanted to order him to take his hand out of my cooze immediately, but I had second thoughts about that. After all, my hand was on his sizeable shaft, with a huge swollen knob and a nest of egg-shaped testicles in a soft, hairy sack resting underneath waiting to be fondled. I didn't want to give that up. I decided that no matter what I thought about Ali's playing around, it was okay; because, one, he was honest about it, and two, I, and not Marilyn Wood, had my hand on his cock. "I can't wait till the lights go out," I told him.

Ali's response startled me. "Here in this airplane there is not sufficient room to perform copulation."

"Have I got a surprise for you!" I thought. I leaned over

and put my head under his robes. His cock was slung under him like a loading ramp, with a knob so big I could barely get it through my wide-open mouth; my teeth could not help but scrape him as I took his first six inches and, holding the base of his broad shaft in one hand and his loose and heavy balls in the other, began to pump up and down using my teeth to lightly scrape the ultra-sensitive tissue on the underside of this impressive organ. In no time he came in my mouth with several thick spurts of that protein-rich seed-bearing cream I love so much. By this time he had my head in both hands underneath his robes.

When I reemerged, Marilyn Wood was standing over us, glaring. I just looked at her, jism dripping over my lower lip and down my chin, and said, "There's plenty left for you in Rome." Ali kissed Miss Wood's hand and stuck a fifty-dollar bill in it. She smirked and walked off, wiggling her ass as she walked. I figured her cunt-juices were already spilling over her labia and down her luscious milk-white redhead's inner thighs. I knew it—she headed straight for the bathroom!

Then, caressing me and stroking me, Ali told me the story of his life. He was just barely a prince, he said, the twenty-seventh son of the fourteenth son of the ninth son of the one-time Lion of the Desert, Ibn Saud, ruler of all Arabia in the first part of the twentieth century. With the discovery of oil, the royal family became stinking rich, but being so low down on the totem pole, Ali himself was worth only a few million. He had no real power and, as comedian Rodney Dangerfield says, "no respect." Ali claimed to have earned a doctorate in Italian Renaissance art history from Harvard, but nobody in Arabia cared. The royal family considered him a ne'er-do-well, if they considered him at all. His plans to desalinate the Red Sea produced only salt; his gold mines in the desert yielded a low-grade tar. His opera house in Mecca was a disaster. The fact that the prima donnas had naked faces was bad enough; he almost got beheaded for that. His only movie, intended for Third World audiences, with himself playing an Arab Tarzan in a leopardskin loincloth, got itself laughed out of the movie theaters—Arabs don't take to half-naked men, although some make an exception for half-naked boys, but that's another story.

The upshot of Ali Ben Gonadi's life, in the final analysis, was that nobody paid him any attention. "I am determined to become a world figure even if I have to resort to becoming notorious," he kept saying throughout our conversation. Finally, as the night wore on, the cabin lights dimmed and dinner was served, by the horny Miss Wood, of course. Dinner was breast of squab, petit pois, hearts of palm salad, lemon mousse and fresh strawberries. Ali kept passing Miss Wood fifty dollar bills, although throughout most of the meal he kept fondling my labia and clitoris, running his fingers up and down my delicate raw cunt; never once did he make a move to put his mouth or his cock in the general direction of my pussy, so that he or I could get full satisfaction.

My "stud" was clearly sexually inhibited; it must have been his Muslim upbringing or something. His behavior was driving me bats. I was beginning to feel raw, almost violated. Finally, with tears in my eyes and a choked-up voice, I got the courage to ask him, "What did I do wrong?"

He stroked my head with his free hand. *"Ma chérie,"* he said, "what do you mean?"

"Ali," I began, devastated that he didn't even know what I was talking about, "don't you want to fuck me?"

"I promise," he said, "I will fuck you before we land in Rome," and then he laughed the oddest laugh. If there was meaning in that laugh, and there was, I was not to know the meaning of it until several hours later, when, after fitful sleep, as we crossed one time zone after another, we met the rising Mediterranean sun.

When we were over the island of Corsica, Napoleon's fabled birthplace, several hundred miles to the west of Rome at about nine A.M. on the fourth, Ali finally took his hand out from under my dress and excused himself to go to the bathroom. Apparently, unbeknownst to me, that moment was when he padlocked the door to the pilot's cabin and handcuffed the stewardesses, all except for his great and good friend, Miss Marilyn Wood. As it turned out, he kept his equipment in his knapsack, at least that part of his knapsack that wasn't a parachute. On his way back from the pilot's cabin, he threw me a ski mask and an empty sack.

"Here, put on this mask," he ordered.

"But, Ali," I squealed.

"Put on the mask!" I did as he commanded; he was carrying a machine gun. The gun must have been in his knapsack, too. Miss Wood was given instructions to tell the captain over the intercom to land in Rome at the Leonardo da Vinci International Airport (the Romans call it Fiumicino), as planned, after first circling over the City of Rome, and particularly over the Vatican, to the east. The captain was to make all the usual announcements, and, in addition, he was ordered to inform the passengers that there was an air robbery in progress by Prince Ali Ben Gonadi of the Arab Republic on behalf of the Palestinian refugees. Prince Gonadi and his hostage, an American prostitute" (I was absolutely shocked when I heard that) would parachute out over Rome from the left exit door in the tail of the plane.

Ali then grabbed the intercom microphone and made his own announcement to the passengers. He had a gun, and, if necessary, he would use it. He had nothing to live for except Allah; if he was going to be killed, he planned to take as many people with him as possible. His orders continued: all passengers were to place their wallets, purses, and pocketbooks on their laps. His assistant, the American prostitute (me, who else?), would collect only cash for the Palestinian refugees on Israel's Left Bank, victims of Jewish and American "capitalistic devils." The passengers' "contributions" and the publicity resulting from the air robbery would be enough work for one day. Furthermore, the passengers were informed, if any passenger harmed his prostitute assistant (hello, there!), we would both be shot on the spot, and he didn't have to explain what a hole in the fuselage would do to the passenger air supply. It was at that moment, I think, I finally realized what a male chauvinist pig was.

The passengers did as ordered. If any person withheld money stashed in their shoes or money belts, I didn't have time to look, and neither thank God, did Ali. His personal wealth, I later found out, was something like fifty million dollars. This man was clearly looking for the attention of the world.

I began to think I was enjoying my last hour of life on this planet. A smart-ass New Yorker with a goatee grabbed my arm and screamed, "I'm holding her hostage!" Instantaneously, Ali's bullet whizzed through the man's shoulder and lodged in the seat behind him. As red blood spurted over the man and me, passengers shrieked in pandemonium. The smart-ass with the goatee, not seriously injured, fainted.

Ali's voice boomed out, "Passengers, be warned, if I shoot a hole in your plane, you will be doomed! I have but one parachute!" Then Ali handed Miss Wood what looked like a thousand dollar bill, which she hurriedly stuffed into her brassiere. He ordered her to move all the passengers away from our exit door, and then, when he gave the signal, to push him and me (me????) out over Rome, then to quickly shut the exit door before the rest of the passengers followed us.

"But . . . but . . . but . . . I," I stammered. "I can't go; I don't have a parachute!" I tried to explain to him I hadn't finished collecting the passengers' cash; my sack was only about half full. It was no use. Miss Wood gave Ali the word that we were now directly over Rome. With his help, she pushed open the exit door as ordered. It was a horrible moment. The morning wind was sucking us with hurricane force. The 747 had trouble keeping its balance. The passengers, herded into the front section of the plane, were for the most part hysterical as the wind sucked off their scarves and shoes and jewelry.

"I haven't got a parachute!" I yelled at Ali as I clutched onto the arm of a seat for leverage.

"Come with me," he ordered, lunging forward and grabbing me. He took the money sack, zippered it shut, and attached it to a special hook on his belt. The belt also had a special extra loop, which he unbuckled and wrapped around my waist like a windowwasher on a skyscraper. Then, to my utter shock, with one quick motion, Ali ripped my skirt off. Without comment, he held me under my buttocks and jumped out the exit door screaming, "Fuck Western Civilization!" I was screaming so loud I was incoherent. It was an absolute nightmare. Even in the best of times I have always had an irrational fear of heights. I prayed to be dead. I prayed to be blotted out, I was so afraid.

Well, Ali must have pulled his rip cord, because within a couple of minutes we were floating over the City of Rome into a bright summer morning, the sun was a giant crystal in a robin's egg sky, under a huge white parachute, which, I later found out read "ALLAH" on both sides in fire-engine-red lettering. With both hands, Ali cupped me under my buttocks. Did I say he ripped open his Arab robes? He must have, because as he cupped me under my buttocks and drew me to him for a prolonged and lasting kiss on his sensual lips, I felt his plum-sized glans press against my slit and cleave into me, dry as I was. At first, I have to say I was not in the mood to make love. I was scared out of my mind. My vagina felt like sandpaper.

"I love a dry cunt," he murmured, nuzzling me. "I love the challenge of its saber tooth." I found myself, almost against my will, warming up to this monster. I realized I needed the warmth of his mouth and the insistent intrusion of his invading cock to reassure me I was not alone in that awful void. Then, something happened. I surrendered. Surrendered to the moment. Surrendered to the awfulness, the strangeness, the violence of it. Surrendered

60

to the man himself. I am that way. I do not fight my circumstances. I marry them.

In the next three minutes before we landed in Saint Peter's Square, I had the most incredible fuck of my life. I met his thrusts as he buried himself deeper and deeper into my ripe wet cave. He pulled my buttocks toward him every time he plunged, but I set up a countermotion, pulling back, creating a tension and a suction that made the loud slurping noises of hungry animals eating for the first time in days. My moaning came out of pleasure and terror. It was the best kind. I was coming now. Ali's middle finger was up my ass, releasing me further from the tension which kept my intestines practically glued together. He came just as we were level with the top of St. Peter's Basilica, the head church in Christendom. I could see its familiar green copper roof out of the corner of my eye, since, as is my wont, I never miss a trick, no pun intended. Ali came, boy, did he come, with volleys of come, so much glistening white come, running through my labia and lacquering my naked legs.

When we landed, safely, thank God, the omnipresent photographers in Rome, the so-called papparazzi surrounded us like flies at a picnic. Needless to say, they had just spent the previous five minutes photographing the picture of the decade, an Arab and a gorgeous blonde fucking under "ALLAH" as they parachuted down over St. Peter's in Rome. Finally, Ali stood up and withdrew his mammoth cock, not a bit embarrassed to have it photographed; it was his pride and joy. Need I point out that, as I lay on my back under the gorgeous Roman sun, they were photographing me, too. I had a silly grin on my face. I was so happy to be alive and so grateful for such a daring and ultimately satisfactory fuck. Imagine, here I was in Rome! At last! Never mind how I got there; I had arrived in one piece! Then, oh my God, it struck me! And this was worse than no panties and a see-through silk dress at TWA—I was stark naked from the waist down! The papparazzi hadn't been photographing *me,* they were photographing my *cooze!* My legs were wide open, my bush was glittering gold in the noonday sun, and I was showing pink! One of the sleeziest of the papparazzi was lying on the ground in front of me with his camera wedged up between my legs! What shame! What ignominy! I went white from terror!

It got worse. I heard the sound of marching feet. Then, like in a picture book, I saw the Swiss Guard, the Vatican security force, marching toward me carrying long-handled pikes called halberds. There were six of them dressed in their familiar armored breastplates and wasp-striped uniforms of orange, blue, and red. "Oh, Christ," I thought, "so this is the end of Diana Hunt from Beavertown!" I could see it now; I was to be speared to death for lascivious conduct in the Vatican! All my life I had heard stories about what the Pope does to people who enjoy sex outside of marriage. "This is what I get," I thought, "for leaving the good ol' U.S. of A!" With that, I promised God that if I got out of this alive, I would definitely show my next fashion collection, probably the beachwear collection, wthin the confines of the continental United States under the good ol' red, white, and blue, the only flag for a free-thinking girl like me. My prayer finished, I waited for the first sword blade to penetrate my soft, yielding, feminine flesh. I waited for the instrument of death to enter me. I waited for six inches of masculine steel to invade my soul.

Chapter Four

A miracle happened. With the force of religious revelation I saw a way out—Monsignor Giovanni "Vanni" Caro, my beloved Adolfo's best boyhood friend, the gorgeous northern Italian ex-hockey-playing priest who had celebrated Adolfo's funeral Mass at St. Patrick's and who had treated me with such tender affection afterward. "Vanni," as he insisted I call him, was on the Pope's personal staff at the Vatican. "Vanni" would help me, I knew it. I could still see his sea-blue eyes peering into my soul and staring down my dress as he offered me consolation; I could still feel him gently stroking my hands with tears in his eyes. "If you ever need me, you beautiful, gorgeous, saintly, young woman, you come to Vanni," were his last words to me in New York.

Ali Ben Gonadi, whom I now decided I definitely did not like, was regaling the papparazzi with a prepared speech on the rights of the Palestinian refugees. Repeating our earlier scene at the TWA Terminal at Kennedy Airport, I grabbed his headpiece, wrapped myself with the white veil and ran like a jackrabbit toward the first open door I saw across St. Peter's Square, screaming, "Monsignor Giovanni Caro! Monsignor Giovanni Caro!" Only because I was barefoot and only because I'd run track in high school did I outstrip the two Swiss Guards who were hot on my heels.

I ran across the cobblestones, past the ancient Egyptian obelisk in the center of the square, down the seventeenth-century colonnade, into the open door of a yellow stucco building marked "Administration" in several languages. Two Italian nuns were typing away at some IBM word processors. They looked up at me impassively, but not too impassively; one of them pressed a button under her desk. I kept saying, "Monsignor Giovanni Caro!" Just as my two Swiss Guard pursuers arrived breathless in the doorway, I was handed a telephone.

"Hello," I said, gasping for air. "This is Mrs. Adolfo Adoro; I must see Monsignor Caro; it's a matter of life and death!" Luckily for me, Vanni was in his office getting a special spinal massage from his chiropractor the very minute I called. He picked up the telephone and said hello in Italian. I had no trouble recognizing his sexy movie-star voice.

"Vanni!" I shouted, "it's me, Diana Adoro! I must see you immediately; I'm in terrible trouble. Please tell your police I'm legitimate!" With that, I handed the phone over to the Swiss Guard, who, after listening to Vanni read him the riot act, turned beet red and started stuttering in German.

He hung up the phone and spoke in Italian to one of the Italian nuns, who then said to me in English, "This boy will take you to Monsignor Caro, but first you must cover your arms."

"Cover my arms?" I exclaimed, tightening the Arab veil around my waist to make certain my cunt was not visible. That's all I needed, to be caught naked inside the Vatican itself! From out of a metal locker the nun produced a white cotton jacket, similar to what a dentist or doctor would wear in a clinic, and had me put it on. High fashion it was not!

The Vatican, for the most part, except for St. Peter's Basilica and the Sistine Chapel and some of the private quarters, which I will describe later, looks like plain business offices with plain beige walls and plain fluorescent lights. Most of the clerical help are nuns and priests from all over the world who man computers, Xerox machines, and IBM Selectrics. The Church runs thousands of schools, orphanages, hospitals, and clinics, not to mention the vast paperwork involved in Catholics seeking annulments of their marriages and priests trying to be formally released from their vows. On my way through these ordinary corridors to see Vanni, everything seemed a little too pat, too ordinary, too everyday. Where was the mystery and the glamour of Rome? I couldn't believe the boring, bureaucratic look and feel of the Church behind closed doors.

The elevator leading to Vanni's fourth-floor quarters was a little more elegant; it was a tiny, two-person gilded rattletrap of a cage. Very nineteenth-century upper-class. Perfect for Audrey Hepburn and Cary Grant or Peter Sellers and Sophia Loren. Halfway between the second and third floors, the elevator got stuck. That's when my guardsman made his move. He leaned over and, without warning, stuck his tongue in my mouth and grabbed a handful of ass. How could I blame him, considering he first saw me in mid-air over the Vatican fucking my brains out? Lucky for me, I wasn't locked in a jail cell. Lucky for me, I wasn't dead.

The guardsman's tongue was huge and muscular; it filled my mouth with warmth. But I had an uncomfortable feeling accommodating this man; not only did I not know his name, I could not see his face under his medieval iron hat. There was no way in that crowded elevator we could possibly lie down and make love properly. Vanni, moreover, that dear, concerned priest, was waiting for me a few feet away. Yes, that was it—Vanni. He gave me a reason to refuse my guardsman, who was feeling humpier and humpier every minute. I kept thinking that if I fucked this strong, self-sacrificing Swiss mountain boy, I could make up for my sleazy encounter with my Arab prince, about whom I was beginning to have second (and third and fourth) thoughts. I became possessed by the idea that one good fuck could cancel out two bad ones. But how could I? There was Vanni upstairs waiting for me. Vanni, so pure, so perfect, so undefiled. How could I present myself to the priest who buried my beloved Adolfo if I had Arab come streaming down my left leg and Swiss German come streaming down my right?

The Swiss Guard wasn't waiting for an answer; he was dry-humping me in that channel between my buttocks, that crack in my ass some men find so irresistible. I felt his big pipe rubbing against me. Sure, I wanted to turn around and grab his young cock and push it hard into my pussy, but at that moment something in me snapped. I just couldn't continue my insane pace. "Am I a nymphomaniac?" I thought, "or am I just burning my candle at both ends? How much longer can this go on? Do I possess any clear sense of self that knows the difference between one man and another?" My only sense of men was that those men who wanted to fuck me were studs and those who didn't had serious personality problems.

"Nooo" I cried out in anguish and pain. I was so confused. I felt polluted. I felt used. "I have to talk to a priest! I have to see Monsignor Caro! Pullease!" My outburst so frightened the young Swiss Guard that he stopped on the dime. I no longer felt the weight of his lead-pipe penis; I no longer felt his hot lips on the back of my neck. It was over. He pressed another button. The car moved upward. Within the space of one minute we had arrived at the fourth floor. The gates opened. Vanni was standing there in his black cassock and bedroom slippers looking like the balding ex-soccer champion he was. Behind me the gates to the charming old elevator closed shut and my guardsman descended into his own version of hell without saying a word.

A week later, I heard that he had committed suicide the following day. What the hell, I can't fuck everyone, right? The official report was that he had slipped on the edge of the roof to his apartment house while feeding the pigeons. If I had not had Vanni to comfort me, I would have felt responsible. In fact, if I had not had Vanni to protect me while I was in Rome I would not be alive today, mentally, emotionally, or financially.

When I first saw Vanni again, I had forgotten his absolute male beauty, so extraordinary in a man of fifty-six. His face was craggy and deeply tanned; his facial muscles were tough and sinewy with just the hint of dissipation so typical of European men who have lived through so much bloodshed and so much love. Above all, Vanni was a great, strong man with a brilliant mind. Of course, I knew that under his cassock was the overdeveloped body of a great athlete: stocky, chiseled, and massive through the loins and thighs. I also knew, through sheer instinct, that there was a big plump cock under that cassock ready to spring into action at a moment's notice. But what was I thinking? This man was a holy priest of high standing. He clearly had no interest in sex. And if he had, he would probably have yielded to temptation only once or twice in his life after months of torture and self-recrimination. Obviously, I was on the verge of a nervous breakdown, fantasizing about a priest. Diana Adoro, indeed. I was well-named, wasn't I? It seems that I was fast becoming the all-time slut of the Western world, fucking everybody I met, right after my beloved husband's death. Arriving in Rome under "ALLAH"! on my parachute! I could not bear to remember; it was too painful. Everything was too painful. Arabs and orgies and cameras up my cunt! I just broke down, falling on my knees in front of him, choking back tears, sobbing without cease. "Oh, Vanni, I'm so bad! I'm so bad! I must be the Anti-Christ! I'm no good! I'm just a slut!" And with that outburst, I inched forward and clasped him around his knees, pressing myself for comfort and protection, against those strong treetrunks of his legs with their rock-like calves. "*Carissima,*" he said, soothingly, "my dearest Signora Adoro, I see your gentle spirit is troubled by so many things. Come with me to my special quarters and we will talk about you and about the many burdens that weigh down your soul." Vanni lifted me up with his strong arms and looked me straight in the eye. His eyes were ice-blue, almost white, yet they seemed so warm and caring. In fact, they seemed to burn with a white-hot heat. "What a holy man," I thought. In his august presence I felt naked to my soul, but not a bit ashamed. Although I am not a Catholic, I think I can tell a good priest when I feel one—I mean see one.

By this time, two of his aides had arrived on the scene, Vanni introduced us. Both apparently were priests. One was about thirty-five, fat, swarthy, and sweating like a pig. He nodded and bowed to almost everything Vanni said. The other priest was tall, rail-thin, with an enormous Adam's apple sitting in the middle of his throat. "Mutt and Jeff," I thought. After they'd left, I found out that they were lovers. When I expressed shock about homosexuality in the Vatican, Vanni explained to me that as much as the Catholic Church condemns a specific sin, it invariably embraces the sinner, as long as there is no public scandal involved. "Hmmm," I thought. "Interesting." Besides, he explained, the two priests in question were good administrators and protected him from gossip and prying eyes. "Hmm," I thought. "Interesting." I wondered to myself what kind of gossip Vanni could possibly be subjected to. He was a perfect specimen, just like Jesus Chirst. A perfect specimen.

Upstairs, in his private apartments, Vanni explained to me that, except for the installation of modern plumbing and electricity, things had not changed much in three hundred years. I could see what he meant. The hallways were long and narrow and dark. The walls were covered in burgundy satin brocade; on them hung large, heavy photographs of long-dead cardinals and popes in ornate gilded frames. About every twenty feet was an ancient oil painting of either Jesus with his heart exposed with a little burning cross on top of the heart or the Virgin Mary with the same heart condition.

"Why are their hearts exposed?" I asked.

"Because," Vanni began to explain, "because even God is on fire with burning, passionate love for men and women."

"Oh," I said, not completely understanding. "But, Vanni, Mary is not God. Why is her heart exposed, too?"

"Because, *carissima,* my dearest Diana," Vanni explained, "Mary and Jesus her son are, in truth, twin souls. In God there is both masculine and feminine."

I was absolutely astounded. "Vanni," I said, "you mean that in God there is sex!!!" As I say, I was astounded at the strange way he explained religion. In Beavertown, the Reverend Dr. Tumble, my grandmother's pastor, certainly never ...

Vanni interrupted my thoughts. "My lovely Diana, we are coming into a new theology," he said. "This theology has not yet been approved by the Holy Father. In fact, he may condemn it. But eventually, it will constitute the True Belief, because every theologian I know is coming to the same conclusion."

"What do you mean?" I said.

"I mean that God is love and love is physical. Even when we die for one another, that is physical. Giving gifts to another, that is physical. Sex, too, that is physical."

"Oh," I said, playing dumb. I wasn't sure what he was leading too. He continued his theological explanation. "You see, my Diana, God is physical in Jesus Christ, and Jesus Christ, who is in agony because he loves so much, he is inseparable from Mary the Woman."

"You mean Jesus and Mary fucked? I mean slept together?" I asked. (I almost blew it, didn't I?)

"No," Vanni answered, "that is the tragedy. Jesus and

Mary could not sleep together because they were mother and son."

"Is that why they were in agony?" I asked.

He ignored my remark. "We must find our own conclusions. We cannot expect the Church to do all our thinking for us, can we?"

"No," I said, "but, Vanni, I'm not even a Catholic, so . . ."

"Ah," he said, a little bit surprised, "then, I must be especially good to you, so that you do not think badly of us."

By now, my curiosity was getting the better of me. There was one question I had been dying to ask ever since I got off the elevator. "Vanni," I whispered, "where does the Pope sleep?"

"His rooms are next to mine," he answered matter of factly. "But do not worry. These old walls are thick. Sounds do not travel here. There are many secrets in these walls." Presently we came to high, dark mahogany doors with intricate carvings. On one door was a scene of Jesus on the cross. He looked absolutely terrible. I figured that must be the old religion Vanni was so concerned about. On the other door was a scene of Jesus standing on a cloud with what looked like rays of light sticking out of his body on all sides. I wonder if that was supposed to be the new religion. I asked Vanni about it, but he gave me a rather strange answer; he said his secret ambition was to burn all the art in the Vatican. Then, he unlocked the door on the right and ushered me into his two-room suite. The outer room was high-ceilinged with large windows.

Flesh-colored raw silk shades covered the windows, giving us some privacy. The draperies were coral-red watered silk. Seeing them, my first thought was that they were the exact shade of my labia. I had to force myself to stop fantasizing about sex; it would destroy me. And moving right along, the room's walls were polished brown tooled leather; they reminded me of an African prince I'd once known. His skin had had highlights of gold, just like the walls, and he was "tooled," too, but in a different way. I was becoming furious with myself. I just couldn't keep sex out of my mind. Most of Vanni's furniture was modern Italian, probably Milanese; banquettes and modules covered in raw canvas with slabs of pink marble for occasional tables. There were a few carved wooden chairs that had been stripped down to their pale, naked wood, their cushions covered with the same cunt-colored watered silk as the draperies. The room's lighting was controlled by a small wall panel. Vanni could dim any of the lights, mostly hidden, by a turn of his wrist. The floors were highly polished dark parquet with a large Oriental rug in the center. It was a pale rug with a flesh-colored ground, Teutonic flesh to be exact, not unlike Vanni's own northern Italian complexion. A large, eighteenth-century, cherry-wood armoire, embraced his stereo equipment. He pressed a few buttons and suddenly, it was my favorite conductor, Mantovanni, playing "Strangers in Paradise," right out of my favorite decade, the Fifties. What more could a girl from Beavertown want?

Vanni's sitting room so overwhelmed me with its fresh, naked beauty that once the dark mahogany doors closed fast behind me, once I felt completely safe, I abandoned my attempt at chitchat about religion and a certain tourist's curiosity about the Vatican. In short, I stripped myself of all pretension and for the second time broke down sobbing. What else can a young widow do when she's all alone in a strange new city? Vanni was the perfect priest. He absorbed every ounce of my considerable pain. He led me over to his beautiful banquette, the one covered in raw canvas so I could sit down, and then he cradled me in his arms because he didn't want me to be left alone. What an absolute saint!

"Tell me the trouble, my dear, sweet Mrs. Adoro," he intoned in his priestly voice, so deep and gravelly, kissing my neck with all the concern of a long-lost best friend.

"Oh, Vanni," I cried, "I was, I was, well, *ravished* by this Arab prince, he was really a fanatic; he made me

71

jump out of the airplane with no parachute except his arms and he fucked—I mean we had intercourse, I mean *he* had intercourse, with me, that is, on the way down. That's how I got here!"

His reply startled me. "Did you enjoy it, Diana?"

"Did I enjoy what?" I said, taken aback.

"Fucking him in mid-air," Vanni replied. I couldn't believe my ears. He said "fuck." I had forgotten the brutal reality of men like Vanni; I had forgotten he was once a soccer pro; I had forgotten he heard the sordid confessions of the entire world day after day after day. Why wouldn't he say "fuck?" What other word could he use, really? He held my trembling fingers in his massive hands and stroked me like a dear, concerned father. Well, why not? That's what he was. I felt so safe. I snuggled even closer to him than before. Then, with a wonderful human gesture, this man of God kicked off his bedroom slippers, so I felt free to kick off mine. Then he helped me wriggle out of my lab technician's coat. My boobies were really jiggling under my see-through silk dress, but, thank God, he only noticed my arms.

"This is medieval clothing," he said, referring to the tight white jacket I had been wearing. "After all, God created your arms for his pleasure and everybody else's.

"Oh, Father Giovanni," I wailed, "don't say that!"

"Don't say what, my pretty flower?" he asked.

"Don't say I belong to everybody else," I wailed. "That's my trouble, I'm just a slut!"

"A what?" he said, sounding genuinely shocked. I couldn't help but tell him the whole truth.

"Vanni," I began, "I'm available to every man who finds me attractive. I'm what's called an easy lay! Tell me what I should do!" I don't know why I was sounding so dramatic. I was beginning to feel his masculine energies coursing through me like a current of electricity. "Vanni!" I insisted, "tell me what I should do! I'm beginning to feel used and dirty."

His answer was absolutely profound. "You must ask

yourself if you enjoy sex. If your answer is that you do enjoy sex, then you must not punish yourself for enjoying it, for if you do that, your self-flagellation is the real sin because you are sinning against life itself."

"Oh, thank you, Vanni!" I cried. Suddenly, like a lightning bolt from heaven, I saw the wisdom of his words and a great burden was lifted from my shoulders. I drew his magnificent bronzed head down to mine and kissed him on his craggy cheek. "What would I do without you?"

But Vanni wasn't satisfied with a kiss on the cheek. Who could blame him? He had posed a question and he wanted an answer. "Then I can assume you enjoyed your Arab up there in the air?"

"Yes, it's true," I admitted. "I loved his outrageous personality." I did. "And I loved his passion," I continued. "I kept thinking, I don't agree with this Arab. I'm pro-Israel. Besides, he's clearly got a severe personality disorder, but you're right, Vanni, as a man, he intoxicated me. I'm a sucker for 'take-charge' personalities. Oh, Vanni! Thank you for making me tell the truth about myself. I'm crazy about making love. I love sex and most of all I love men! But forgive me! I shouldn't be burdening you with all this sex talk!"

"Burdening me?" he said, genuinely confused.

"I mean, because you're a priest," I said, "and you're not allowed to have sex."

"Not allowed to have sex?" he said, repeating my statement. "Diana, we are not allowed to get married."

"But, but, but I thought the Catholic Church prohibits sex between unmarried persons," I exclaimed.

"Yes," he admitted, "that is true. That is the law on the books. But we are also free to follow our conscience and disobey a given law when there is a higher good."

"A higher good?" I asked.

His answer was profound and to the point. "Ecstasy! Ecstasy is the higher good! Ecstasy is the highest good of all!" And with that, the paternal arms that had been

73

comforting me tightened their grasp and extended their reach, and suddenly, I was under him and his mouth was on top of mine, delving into me, exploring the crevices behind my soft, warm tongue. He felt so protecting, so caring. Then he got off me, knelt down beside the couch, picked me up and carried me into his bedroom, a semi-dark room with a king-sized water bed occupying most of the floor space. He deposited me on the bed and, like a butcher unwrapping a loin of pork, peeled off my make-shift skirt, gasping with delight as he viewed my exposed cunt. Then, with one continuous gesture—what a consummate pro he was—he ripped off what was left of my dress. I was so grateful to be there with him. Standing beside the bed, he disrobed. Once he had unzipped his cassock, which featured about a hundred nonfunctional little black buttons up the front of it, he was completely naked. We were so exactly alive, I thought, neither one of us believed in underwear! He told me later he liked the feel of his long cock swinging over his naked thigh as he walked through the Vatican corridors.

"The Vatican is so antisexual," he said later, "I have to keep reminding myself I am a man. The easiest way is to remember my cock. Dispensing with underwear is the best way to do that." His body awed me. I had never seen a man in his mid-fifties with such a strongly muscled stomach. No flab, not really, just that same hint of decadence that was on his face, a decadence born of sensuality and too much enjoyment of the flesh.

"But, Father Vanni," I cried, suddenly stricken by memories of lust in the worst possible places, namely, the memory of my perversion on the way to my beloved Adolfo's funeral with Maxey von Fuchs in the back seat of the funeral limousine. "I made love to a man I barely knew, and, yes, I enjoyed every minute of it, because I was alive and feeling anything but dead!"

His eyes narrowed. His pupils were pinpoints as he fixed his intense gaze on me. "It is you who do not understand," he began. "All through the funeral Mass at St. Patrick's, as I tried to pray for my poor, dear friend, my best friend from the age of four, my poor dead Adolfo, I kept looking down at you, the poor young widow Diana, and I kept seeing you naked, completely naked, your incredible big breasts, your skin like apricots, gold from the sun. You tormented me, Diana. When, at the consecration of the Mass, I lifted up the Host, the body of Christ, and said, 'Take ye and eat,' I was torn apart by suffering and desire, because when I said the word 'eat,' all I saw was your vagina!"

"My cunt," I interrupted.

"Yes, your cunt," he continued, "your sweet, tight cunt, and when I ate the body of Christ, I was completely possessed, because in my mind I was eating your cunt!"

What could I say? I spread my legs open and thrust my pelvis toward him, thrust that cunt he loved so much, thrust the tight rose petals of my salivating labia toward him, hoping he would invade those petals with his battering ram and open me up to the love of a deeply caring man. Did I forget to describe his cock? It was just what I expected, long and dark and mushroom-shaped, growing thicker the closer it got to his outsized glands. Yes, he was erect. In fact, he was rampant, He had the power to impale me. But not yet! First, it was preprandials—drinks before the feast. Vanni climbed on the water bed, which is like a huge vat of Jello, sank to his knees, and pulled me toward him by my inner thighs. Then, in a flash, his large-boned head dove for my quivering pussy. The poor man was starving for cunt. My heart went out to him.

"You are the finest wine in Rome," he groaned. "I want to drink every single drop of you."

I could not wait for him to quaff his thirst. My skin was wet and flaming with the tingling sweat that comes from sheer excitement. My luxuriant mound rose and fell to the rhythm of his breathing; with a serpent's power his tongue went directly for my clit, slithering through the passion petals of my tempting coral flesh. "Eat me, Daddy! Eat me! Eat me!" I screamed.

With that, he went for my meat like a savage dog. The priest was gone. The scholar had fled with the gentleman. This savage muscle-head devoured me ravenously. He sucked my inner thighs black and blue, his strong fingers grasping onto my ass with the power of a vise. He buried his head in my raw meat and ate me out indiscriminately, grunting and snorting without control. Foaming at the mouth he attacked my clitoris, lathering it with his saliva, sucking it, rimming it with his tongue, making fierce animal sounds of enjoyment and satisfaction. Finally, I could contain myself no longer. By clawing and wrestling on the open seas of that water bed I finally managed to grab a handful of the rock-hard flesh on his athletic torso. The constant screwing motion of my trying to turn myself around increased my pleasure to such a degree that before I could grab his throbbing shaft of cock-meat I went into the familiar convulsions of orgasm. The more I bucked, the harder Vanni rode me.

"Fuck! Fuck! Fuck!" he screamed, exultant. The tension that comes from being restrained by a powerful man sent ceaseless spasms from the top of my head to the bottom of my feet. My sexual tension, despite my Arabian interlude such a short time before, had been greater than I realized. I tingled. I burned. I kept letting go for what seemed like forever.

In the middle of our orgy-for-two something unbelievable happened. On the far wall of Vanni's bleached mahogany chamber, a large panel that comprised the middle section of the wall came crashing down! It missed the edge of our bed by about two feet; it missed my outstretched foot by about two inches! Because the room was so thickly carpeted, the only sound was a muffled thud. Startled, I looked up to see what had caused the thud. Since the wall panel was now on the floor out of sight I saw only the small room beyond where the panel had been. In the middle of that small space, seated on a leather chaise longue, was a large gray-haired man in a white cassock and white skullcap with a look of absolute terror on his face. No wonder. If he had caught us in the act, we had caught him in something far worse—it was clear we had a voyeur on our hands! His cassock was bunched up around his waist, his BVDs were down around his ankles, and his stout cock, now beginning to waver, was visibly erect.

"Oh, Kiki!" Vanni exclaimed. "Kiki, Kiki, Kiki, what are you doing?" The man in the white cassock and white skullcap looked ashen.

"Maybe he's having a stroke!" I exclaimed. Vanni then did a wonderful thing. He stood up, buck naked and still rampant, walked over to the man in white, kissed him first on the head of his cock, then on his forehead, and finally on his hands. The man's right hand had a huge gold ring on the ring finger.

"What do you have all over your hands, Kiki? Vaseline?" Vanni asked in a kindly tone. "There are better things, my friend." "Kiki" maintained his look of terror. Vanni kissed him on his cock again. He was clearly trying to lessen the man's embarrassment by implicating himself in a borderline gesture of bisexuality, or something. Italians are so symbolic. I couldn't begin to guess at the traditional meaning of the gesture. Finally, Vanni took the man in white by the hand and led him to our bed. By now, his cassock was draped around his wonderful spear of a cock. It was so long and languid, obviously shrinking from embarrassment.

"We must comfort him, Diana," Vanni explained. "He's had a terrible shock. Let's get these clothes off him." So we undressed our voyeur, unraveling what seemed like yards of white watered silk, in the process unbuttoning and peeling off an undershirt that smelled of lilac water. The man's body was massive like Vanni's, but softer, more like a wrestler's, and in startling contrast to Vanni's burnished gold skin, this man was chalk white with the supple, overdeveloped muscles of a shot-putter. By the time he was completely naked, his cock looked like a plump white slug. It didn't move; the man himself was clearly emotionally and physically paralyzed. Vanni, that compassionate man, was stroking his friend's head, kissing his cheek, trying to comfort him. I have never seen a grown man so embarrassed as our shot-putter. Tears were rolling down his white cheeks.

"There, there, Kiki," Vanni intoned, stroking the other man's nipples and nodding at me to do my part. I tried to help. I began to kiss his chalk white flanks, making sure my overhanging breasts stroked his naked thighs as they hovered over him. Finally, "Kiki" spoke in a thick Slavic accent that sounded like Russian.

"The vall (wall) fell down, Vanni," he said.

"That's all right, Kiki," answered Vanni. "It doesn't matter."

"But I vasn't (wasn't) using birth control, Vanni," said the other man.

"I know you weren't," said Vanni consolingly.

"I never use birth control," said Kiki, who then turned to me. "You never use birth control, do you?"

"Oh, no," I replied, smiling and lying through my teeth like I always do when I suspect someone is a psychopath. Thank God for IUD's; they've always worked for me. By now Kiki was beginning to talk, so much so I was afraid he'd never shut up.

"If Monsignor Giovanni make you pregnant," he said, "it is no matter, ve (we) have special home for children of priests. Good Catholic home!"

Vanni, smiling, said, "Diana's not Catholic, Kiki." He meant it as a tease.

Kiki did not get the joke, as they say. He began to wheeze, gasping for breath. "Vat! (What!) Vat! Not Catholic! This girl not Catholic!"

"No," said Vanni. "She's a Protestant."

"Protestant," Kiki repeated, like the word referred

to someone from another planet. I thought he was going to have a stroke.

"Don't worry, Kiki," I whispered, "don't worry. If I have Vanni's child, I promise you, he can be raised a Catholic." I thought that would shut him up. Not quite.

"Young voman (woman)," Kiki said, "you do not call me 'Kiki'; you call me 'Poppa.' 'Poppa,' you understand?"

"Yes, Poppa," I replied, trying to sound like the obedient child he seemed to want.

A strange thing happened; from the moment "Poppa" started giving orders, his cock began to rise again. He also became less and less shy.

"And now, young voman (woman), you will sit on Poppa's face."

"Yes, Poppa," I said, looking to Vanni for support.

"It's all right," Vanni said. "Go ahead. Sit on Poppa's face."

So I did exactly that; I sat on Poppa's face, as a silent, wet tongue devoured me for two or three minutes. There was another order. "Now, you must bend over, Protestant voman (woman)," he said, chuckling at his own joke and adding, "and perform fellatio on Poppa."

"Perform what?" I asked, having no clear idea of what "fellatio" meant.

Vanni, who was so educated, came to the rescue. "Blow job," he said.

"Oh," I said, always grateful for new sexual vocabulary. I bent over as Poppa held my cunt squarely over his mouth. His cock looked like a big white sausage. Frankly, I was beginning to feel like a stranger at my own orgy. I decided to pretend I was back in Beavertown with my beloved family dentist, my First Great Love, who first fucked me while he was drilling my third molar. But Vanni, who knew I felt uncomfortable, saved the day. He mounted me from behind, doggy-style, slipping his golden rod into me from behind as I sat on Poppa's face so that his balls rested on Poppa's eyes and the

79

undershaft of his cock stroked the tip of Poppa's nose. Poppa, for his part, seemed extraordinarily pleased.

It was almost like Vanni and "Kiki" had performed this ritual before. Apparently they had. As I bent down to take the big, white mushroom-head of his cock into my well-practiced mouth with its warm and luscious tongue (if I do say so myself), suddenly, without warning, there was an obstacle. The big gold ring, heavy and ornate, on the ring finger of his right hand was staring straight at me. What did Poppa want me to do, compliment him on his ring, or what?

"Kiss his ring," ordered Vanni.

"Kiss his ring?" I asked, not comprehending. "Kiss his hand, yes, but kiss his *ring*?"

"I'll explain later," said Vanni, who clearly was impatient to shoot his load. "Oh, Diana," he groaned, ramming me with his banana, "you're so, how do you say, you're so fucking terrific!"

"It is the symbol of my spiritual authority," said Poppa, interrupting Vanni and bringing us back to the subject of his ring.

"Whatever you say, Poppa," I replied, kissing the dead gold ring, hoping my conciliatory gesture alleviated such a perverse need on his part. "Christ," I thought, "I'd rather rim his asshole than kiss his ring!" My gesture seemed to please him.

"Now, you may perform fellat . . . blow job," he said, laughing for the first time since he had so unceremoniously fallen through the wall. "Blow job!" he repeated. "Blow job! Blow job!"

"Diana," Vanni groaned again, groping for my tits, which he loved. "Oh, Diana, please let's move!" Christ! I love that man! What a wonderful priest, so willing to accommodate other people's problems! First, there was me, and now Poppa. Because I loved Vanni so much I went down on Poppa, as he had requested. Vanni's cock, deliciously rammed up my twat, began to pump, began to drive home like the powerful piston it was, ramming, driving, back and forth, back and forth, while I sucked and stroked and tongued the great albino sausage in front of me, fondling and stroking his enormous balls, as he cooed and sighed, from time to time calling out in Russian, which I later found out was Polish, to some lost dead love, I guess, for what seemed like hours. For a long time, I held back any real emotional involvement with this strange intruder. Finally, I too, surrendered. My woman's heart went out to this lonely man who had first seen me through a hole in the wall! I surrendered to my golden god, Vanni, whose hot hands were continuously stroking my breasts, squeezing them in circular motions, pinching my nipples until sharp jabs of pain excitement flashed through my body and my cunt was bursting with the ache of sexual pleasure. And Poppa! Even he began to act more like a human being, simultaneously stroking my sides and Vanni's arms, caressing my hair, massaging the back of my neck. As Vanni's orgasm came closer, he began to groan with intense sexual pleasure; his thrusts bordered on raw violence as he drove harder and harder, inflaming my cunt-meat while Poppa sucked my clitoris with a loud, infantile, smacking pleasure. He knew exactly where my pink pleasure-bud was and, with an expert's practiced tongue, he kept it exposed and throbbing. I raked the pubic hair around the base of his thick cock with my perfectly manicured nails, causing him excruciating pleasure. And then the unthinkable happened! Poppa went berserk! He began screaming American obscenities in his thick Russian (Polish) accent. Where he learned them I have no idea, but he was certainly familiar with how they are used.

"Fuck you, you fucking piece of pussy meat! You cunt, you cunt-lips, cocksucking whore! Fuck me! Fuck me! Oh! Oooh! Oooh, babeeee! Fuck! Fuck! Fuck!" With a little encouragement, the paralyzed man in white had become a sex maniac! My own orgasms came fast and unexpected. My head thrashed back and forth as the waves of orgasmic release made me practically uncon-

81

scious with delirium. Thank God, the Great White Cock was still in my vibrating mouth, because with all my involuntary thrashing, my constant spasms, my teeth grazing the tender skin, I brought him into an orgasm that bordered on an epileptic fit. At the very same moment, Vanni, whom I'd been neglecting badly, finally came. Vanni withdrew from me at the last minute with a wonderful, loud sucking sound and spent his considerable load all over Poppa's face. I got the same idea and let go of Poppa's rampant cock just at the exact moment that enormous swelling exploded in a shower of pearly globules all over his abdomen and all over me. Without planning it, Vanni and Poppa and I smeared the sticky sperm all over us like the precious ointment it was. Then we rubbed our lubricated bodies all over each other like children deriving the last possible ounce of sexual satisfaction and sensual pleasure, touching and stroking as much body surface as we could before our ointment dried and our lust ebbed. I used Vanni's nose and chin and ears to fuck myself, rubbing my fuck-flesh over all the knobs and protuberances of his glorious head.

Finally it was over. We were spent. The three of us lay in each other's arms. I kissed Poppa tenderly. "Poppa," I said, "you're a dear, sweet guy and a wonderful fuck, and I really mean that."

"You, you are not Diana," he replied, "you, you are the angela. Angel, that is you. Angel cunt. Angel fuck. Fuck fuck." I kissed him again, this time straight on the mouth.

He turned to me and with deeply feeling gray-blue eyes, he looked straight into my soul. "You see, how vonderful (wonderful) it is to make luv (love) sex, fuck, vhen ve (when we) do not use birth control?"

"Yes, Poppa," I answered obediently.

"Vith (with) no birth control, ve (we) touch the true power of sex, the true power of life!"

"Oh, Poppa!" I cried, "what a beautiful thought!"

thinking how much better I liked him when he was thoroughly obscene.

Then Poppa burst into tears. "Oh, Giovanni, I do it again!" With tear-filled eyes, he looked up at me. "I do not blame you. It is me. I am sinner. I am terrible sinner! Excuse me now." And with that, he gathered up his wardrobe in white and walked back through the broken wall into the darkened room beyond. I heard a door slam, and then another. Poppa was gone. Finally I felt I could talk to Vanni alone. I had questions. Many questions.

"Was that the Pope?" I queried.

"You mean the Holy Father?" was his august response. "I'm not sure I can tell you."

"I thought the Pope was Italian," I said. "This one's Russian."

"I don't really know—Russian, Polish, Lithuanian. Something like that," was Vanni's overly cautious response.

"Vanni," I said, "I'm sorry if I sound impossibly ignorant, but when I was a little girl, my mother dragged me to her church, the Tabernacle Witnesses, three and four times a week, so I more or less blank out when it comes to organized religion. That was the Pope, wasn't it?"

"Diana, he's really very well-intentioned when it comes to Third World politics, the living wage, the rights of the poor, the need for workers to educate their children . . ."

"Vanni," I interrupted, "I'm sure you're right, but . . ." Vanni was clearly on a Vatican soapbox, determined to defend the Pope to the death. God, what a body he had! His muscles knit together in classic perfection, his still tumescent cock, perfect in its straight, cylindrical shape, swung in front of him. I got the sinking feeling that this magnificent male had no idea how beautiful he really was. Men are not supposed to think of themselves as beautiful,

I guess. "And, Diana," he started to continue, "the Holy Father is brilliant, absolutely brilliant, when it comes to Polish, I mean Russian politics..."

With that, I could take no more. I hadn't come for politics. As far as the Pope was concerned, I figured I "gave at the office," as they say. I grabbed Vanni's perfect cock, pushed my warm cooze up against him, and embraced him with a kiss that said "I love you completely, you sexy man!"

"Diana, you take my breath away," was his husky reply. I pressed against him, trying to rub as much of my naked skin against as much of his naked skin as was humanly possible. Our bodies seemed to ignite each other and in no time we were two in one flesh, rising up and down in perfect rhythm as we fucked and fucked and fucked, until finally we fell asleep. The pale afternoon sunlight filtered through the closed louvered blinds of the Vatican. They tell me the Catholic Church changes slowly. If life at the Vatican is any indication of how the Church muckamucks spend their time, I can understand why. No, I'm not criticizing the Church. I have absolutely no use for lowbrows who criticize the clergy; it's what I call a cheap shot. Monsignor Giovanni Caro, my "Vanni," was one terrific fuck. Besides which, as far as my Arab stuntman was concerned, Vanni saved me from a fate worse than death. To be sure, there were complications that I will discuss as they presented themselves in the course of my Roman holiday, complications that brought back both my Vanni and the irrepressible "Poppa," the man they call "Kiki" into my life again.

After I promised I would ask no more questions, especially "who?" and "how?" Vanni, only five minutes after making a phone call to the Vatican supply rooms, produced a stunning if conservative Harris tweed English walking suit in soft gray for me to wear with an Irish rain hat in the same fabric. Yes, and alligator pumps. All round, a perfect fit, if a little warm for the Roman July. Vanni gave me the sensible advice to pull back my thick blond hair into a plain knot and to wear the rain hat and maybe a pair of dark glasses to avoid the papparazzi who had photographed me starkers. On that score, at least, I was safe; the Italian mass media were still prohibited from publishing or broadcasting open cunt shots!

As a parting gift, Vanni handed me more than enough money for a cab trip to my hotel, where, presumably, my bags, Maxey von Fuchs, and a hundred policemen would be waiting for me. He advised me to state that I had been raped, traumatized, forced to rob passengers, stripped of my clothes, and virtually pushed out of a jet plane without a parachute, but that, thank God, I had had close friends in the Vatican; and no, I did not wish to press charges. I did not wish to talk about the matter further. I was opening my first couturier collection in the Colosseum in three weeks and I needed my energy for that! Vanni said that if I followed his advice, by the time the Colosseum show opened, every journalist in the Free World would be there.

"Never act like a victim," he ordered me. "Never. Never. Never." As soon as dusk settled, he ushered me out of the Vatican, down a back stairs, and through a secret tunnel which let into the basement of a small parish church. From there it was out a side door and into the Roman streets where he hailed me a cab near the Castel Sant'Angelo, an old fortress which sits on the Tiber River next to a bridge by the same name.

I waved Vanni a polite good-bye. I did not dare kiss him, not in public. But I wanted to. He had been so good to me. My cunt still tingled with a sweet ache.

It was not the last I was to see of Vanni in Rome that month.

Chapter Five

In the dying light of dusk, Rome was a blur of first impressions. I was unprepared for the perfectly manicured gardens, the trees and shrubbery routinely sculpted into square boxes of solid green; I was delighted to discover the ancient stone fountains and centuries-old marble gods and goddesses, thick streams of water gushing from their open mouths, water fed by mountain streams, carried down to Rome by stone conduits known as aqueducts. As I was soon to learn in my month there, however, modern Rome is far more than a shrine to antique monuments; the suburbs boast gleaming white apartment houses and office buildings more starkly spectacular in their design effect than anything I had ever seen in the States. For the moment, however, I was in the old city of Rome, the historical arena of a schoolgirl's fantasies, so breathtaking in its beauty, especially in the subtle interplay of light and shadow on thousand-year-old walls of churches, palaces, and the crumbling ruins of antiquity that my face was wet with tears. The truth is, I've never been the greatest appreciator of architecture; I really can't tell a basilica from a bank. Even in New York, I have to carry a map with me at all times to tell me where I'm going. People are what really grab my attention, and I have to say that the people of Rome, even on that draggy, dog-eaten summer's eve, had me mesmerized. I was transfixed by those half-clothed physical specimens of all ages and sexes. There was intelligence in every face, style in every outfit, and appetite in every crotch.

When most Americans think of Italians, they think of the descendants of Neapolitans and Sicilians who comprised the majority of Italian immigrants at the end of the last century. These people, generally golden-skinned with nut-brown eyes and black hair, are clearly southern Mediterranean with its Greek and Arab influences. I have always found these particular Italians to be an acquired taste, one whose beauty grows more stunning and satisfying with each encounter. My beloved Adolfo was in this southern Italian category. His passion, his lust for beauty, his peasant strength made him the most attractive man I have ever known, period. But I cannot say either about him or about other southern Italians that, generally speaking, on the basis of physical appearance alone, they ever knocked the wind out of me the first time I laid eyes on them.

The Romans are another matter entirely. As Maxey explained to me in one of his many history lessons, they have been an international melting pot since Day One, with every conceivable tribe or ethnic group, mostly in the persons of merchant princes and Roman Catholic clergy from all over the world leavening the basic Roman stock, which is called Etruscan. Little is known about the Etruscans except that they were already established when Aeneas, the so-called father of Roman civilization, arrived from points east about eight hundred years before Christ. To look at the average Roman of today, the Etruscans were clearly a tall, fine-boned people with strong, intelligent faces, flawless skin, and bodies that out-did the Greek statuary in perfection. Two thousand years of intermingling with Vikings, Mongols, Syrians, Egyptians, Prussians, and Poles, who were in Rome for schooling, merchandising, or saying Mass, have produced a master race of beauty and style. Given the best food in the world and the most benevolent climate—except for July—these people, these Romans, have become a gorgeous breed, each successive generation outdoing the one that preceded it.

Walking through the streets on the way to my hotel, I was absolutely goggle-eyed. I passed one beauty after another, the men, lean and muscular, in perfectly tailored silk pants much tighter in the crotch and ass than the average heterosexual male in New York or Beavertown would dare to wear—he'd be too afraid he'd be mistaken for a screaming fag. The Roman male of either persuasion is first and foremost a male animal, with his masculinity on prominent display. "If you've got it, flaunt it," is an old Roman expression. The women are the same way. No matter how tall and willowy, they enjoy ample bosoms, otherwise known as big tits, and rounded backsides that make the Creator look like the Prime Pornographer. To put it crudely, I never saw one flat ass in Rome; Roman tummies are rounded, too, as nature intended. Their thighs may be a little too rounded for American tastes; maybe the problem is these well-fed loins look like they were made to support pregnant bellies and grapple with big cocks. Their sexual heat is almost visible in the way they walk, the way they prepare food and eat it, the way they look at strangers with eyes that are, at once, penetrating and warm. In short, these sophisticates are sexual without apology, especially when they're millionaires wearing expensive designer clothes, which I decided augured well for little ol' designer me.

I was surprised that not one Roman Romeo made a pass at me, but who makes passes at a girl who wears glasses and a heavy tweed suit on a hot summer's night?

Besides, hadn't I had enough sex for one day? Why was my appetite for lovemaking, otherwise known as fucking, inexhaustible? My sexual hunger was much more acute than it had ever been in New York. Maybe because I had never been abroad before, for the first time in my life I was confronted with the lure of the stranger and the mystery of the person who speaks another language, in other words, someone who is virtually inaccessible. They were all around me.

As the moon rose, the shadows in the streets lengthened until night had overtaken day. The city did not glitter like New York at night. The lights were softer. Rome seemed to glow.

The Hotel Hassler, the home for Adoro International's personnel during our stay, sits on the Via dei Monti at the top of the fabled Spanish Steps close to the seventeenth-century Borghese Gardens. This spot is considered the hub of Rome, the very center. The Hassler, with its 1930s ambience, is the small hotel where European kings and American presidents love to stay when they visit Rome. No wonder. The marble-pillared lobby with its curved and gilded ceiling, its indirect lighting, its blue-velvet chairs, its Oriental carpets, its silk curtains and freshly cut flowers gives the place a hushed smartness.

I walked by a square-jawed hunk of a sexy doorman into the Hassler lobby. For the moment, the place had clearly lost its famous hush. There was absolute pandemonium. At least fifty papparazzi, photojournalists with flash cameras and note pads, and several television crews were waiting for the one and only Diana Adoro, celebrity of the hour. The hotel staff was up in arms; the regular clientele, the type that prefers its movie stars to stay in the movies, seemed grim-jawed and humorless as they came and went between coffee shop, elevator, front desk, and front door. My first impulse was to bolt. Then, I realized that with my baggy tweed suit and unmade-up face, I was unrecognizable. The only question was, how to get to my room and/or find Maxey von Fuchs without giving myself away. From overhearing the gossip in the lobby as I searched for a familiar face, I deducted that Ali Ben Gonadi, my Arab terrorist, had been taken to a local jail for questioning and possible charges of hijacking, kidnapping, air piracy—you name it, but with the help of some friends bearing bombs he had apparently escaped, at least for the time being. The gossip about me ranged from the sublime to the ridiculous: I was in Rome to star opposite Paul Newman in a film about a fashion designer and a cop; I was an ex-prostitute suspected of murdering my husband Adolfo Adoro, whom had I had blackmailed into marrying me; I was Jackie Onassis in disguise!

Finally, I spotted one of my assistants, little Lena Pansky, who, as it so happened, was scurrying out to find Bufferin for another assistant. Plain aspirin wouldn't do. Thank God for me, someone had a headache. As Lena rushed by, I grabbed her. She wasn't too pleased.

"Hey, lady, get the hell away from me!"

I had to be quick. "Lena," I said, "don't say my name —it's me. I need your help. How do I get to Maxey?"

Lena stared at me for a long minute. Then, at last recognition. "Di . . . !"

I clapped my hand over her mouth. "Lena, if you value your life or your job . . . let's calmly walk outside and talk." And so we did. Lena had a letter for me from Maxey. Upon arriving in Rome he had left immediately for Zurich. There were snags in our bank loan. He'd return as soon as he could. Happy Fourth, etc. So that was that. For the time being, at least, I was on my own. Maxey knew nothing of my arrival in Rome. I had to think fast. My major concern was my reputation. I couldn't afford to be known as a playgirl or, worse, a jet-setting slut. If that happened, American women would assume I didn't know very much about how to cut and assemble a cocktail suit (which I didn't) or sew a straight seam (which I did).

I took the bull by the horns, walked into that overcrowded lobby, shouted for quiet, introduced myself as Gertrude Makeme (my mother's maiden name), Diana Adoro's personal assistant. Mrs. Adoro had returned to New York immediately under an assumed name to consult with her doctors and lawyers. She would be back in Rome the following week to begin work on her fashion show, at which time she would be happy to meet with the press. The questions were legion, but I kept them short. No, I had not traveled to Rome with Mrs. Adoro. Her staff had arrived a couple of days earlier. No, Mrs. Adoro had not known Prince Gonadi before her trip. No, she had not been accused of murdering her husband Adolfo Adoro; they were absolutely devoted to each other. Yes, it was true she was planning to transform the Colosseum into the world's most extravagant fashion show because she thought Rome was the world's most beautiful city. End of questioning.

During my press interview, Lena, as I had directed her to do, went to her room to fetch the publicity packets we had put together in New York. The glossies of yours truly bore absolutely no resemblance to the plain young woman in the Irish rain hat and English country walking suit. The press seemed satisfied. So far, I was safe. Within minutes, the papparazzi had left the Hassler; that is, except for one or two who stayed, obviously because they suspected something was a little fishy, although Diana Adoro's story, as I told it, bore scant excuse for intensive investigative reporting. Still, I had to be careful. I resolved to disguise my appearance as best I could till Maxey returned. I hoped that by the end of the week my untimely entrance into St. Peter's Square on the Fourth of July would be a dim memory for the general public.

Through Lena's intervention, I met with the Hassler manager, who had been privy to the press conference. He was a crusty old Englishman who seemed to like me. I told him flat out who I was, apologized for unintentionally, causing, the ruckus in his lobby, and asked for absolute anonymity and complete privacy. My name, for the time being, as far as the hotel staff was concerned, would be Miss Makeme. I asked for a different room than the one initially assigned to Diana Adoro, in case there were still reporters snooping around. All telephone calls and correspondence to Diana Adoro were to be forwarded to me. The manager seemed to appreciate my quiet laid-back style, although I had warned him that I intended to disguise my appearance as much as possible, whenever possible, to outwit the loyal opposition, whoever it was. I don't think the dear Englishman had the slightest inkling of what the librarian-type girl engaging him in matter-of-fact conversation could do for a pair of skin-tight hot-pants cut below the navel, with a crescent of ripe ass bulging off the bottom of each cheek.

An hour later, my staff had transferred my clothes and personal effects to my new room on another floor, which overlooked a formal Renaissance green-and-white garden with fifteenth-century statues of saints crumbling to pieces in the twentieth-century smog.

There was another letter from Maxey. To sum it up: he was delayed in Zurich another day; no serious problems. Yes, he had seen the newspaper photographs of my flamboyant arrival in Rome; where was I? I hadn't answered my phone.

I instructed Lena to call Maxcy in Zurich and explain who Gertrude Makeme was without giving away her true identity to the CIA, who was undoubtedly listening in. I was standing by.

"Hello, Maxey, this is Gertrude Makeme."

"Darling, you realize Mrs. Adoro's style of arrival may cost us our Zurich loan. As it is, the whole kitandkaboodle, i.e., Adoro, Inc., is in hock . . ."

"Maxey, Diana Adoro went back to New York for the week. Everything is very quiet here now."

"What did the police say?"

"To whom? Maxey, this phone may be tapped."

"You realize American housewives won't buy a call girl's clothes . . ."

"A call girl? Maxey, have you ever been kidnapped and raped?"

"If I was, I blocked it out."

"Maxey, there are reporters all over the place."

"I hope Mrs. Adoro is well disguised."

"Absolutely. I hope Baron von Fuchs remembers that Mrs. Adoro is in New York and that all mail and phone calls go through Miss Makeme."

"*Achtung!*"

"I miss you, Maxey."

The phone call finished, I went to bed. Alone. I missed Maxey. In my fantasies and dreams he was beginning to take the place of Adolfo. Maxey was warm and comforting. I could rely on him most of time. I wondered what he was doing in Zurich in his late hours. Was he alone, too? Was he dreaming of me? At least I had one constant fear in my life besides clothes.

I fell asleep, proud that I had outwitted so many monsters in one day. I wondered how many more monsters were out there waiting for me. How many lovers? With so many unanswered questions, I fell into the dark abyss of my dreams and dreamed of me and Maxey making love. For a brief time I was at peace.

Chapter Six

The next morning, the sun was shining brightly. Breakfast on the roof garden with espresso and croissants couldn't have been more elegant. My crew was already up and out on the job pricing trailers to use as changing rooms at my Colosseum show and, wonder of wonders, the papparazzi were gone! A major Italian film star from the Sixties had been found dead from a drug overdose in a motel near the airport. Terrible for her; a reprieve for me.

I decided that as far as the general public was concerned, if I kept my mother's name for another day or two and continued to dress incognito, I would be safe from scandal and corruption. My only problem, as usual, was that I tended to let my heart rule my emotions. Before I knew it, I was "in over my head," as we used to say in Beavertown. Sex was forever my undoing, even when it wasn't exactly my doing.

I had allowed myself a free week at the beginning of

my Roman stay. I wanted to soak up the Mediterranean atmosphere; I especially wanted to observe the women of Rome to see if I could find fashion ideas to steal for my collection. Already I had noticed their liberal use of large fringed scarves over their shoulders and around their hips. I wondered how the shapeless black cotton shifts the Roman widows wore would look on long-stemmed American girls if they unbuttoned them to the top of their tits and added a necklace of lustrous, lumpy freshwater pearls, which had always reminded me of fresh come. Lulu Touché, my woman in charge of pins and needles, would arrive in four or five days. I couldn't wait to hold a design conference with her. One particular bright spot of my first week in Rome was that Glorianna, my head model and now (curses!) my rival five-percent owner of Adoro, was, thank God, sunning her "stunning" stick figure on the French Riviera. I told her to take as much time as she wanted. I figured I was free from her catty, competitive remarks for at least a week.

When I first saw the Colosseum in the clear light of morning, I decided that Adolfo must have been off his rocker when he persuaded me to hold my fashion debut there. It's a pile of stones! Admittedly, by moonlight it's a romantic ruin, especially after a bottle of Chianti, but by day, even from its "good side," it looks at best like a huge public stadium in a state of extreme decay. So many of our own sports arenas in America have used it as their architectural model that it's hard to realize how special it is, or was. Most of its original white marble facing was stripped for various Renaissance palaces like the Palazzo Farnese, and the Colosseum's original floor has long since disappeared, leaving the interior walls of the basement exposed. From the highest rows of seats inside the Colosseum, those walls, depending on one's tolerance of confusion, resemble either an interlocking grid or a labyrinth. Adolfo's big idea was to install a new floor made of transparent Lucite (Plexiglas) over the basement walls, a floor which could be lighted from underneath as well as above, all lighting to be monitored by a computerized lighting board similar to one used at a rock concert where any light of any color can be dimmed, focused, spotlighted—whatever is necessary for whatever effect. Admittedly, if we could transform the Colosseum, once the stage for bloodshed and extreme cruelty, into a super-chic setting for high fashion, we would have the world's attention.

There was so much work ahead of us! The sound system had to be equally as sophisticated as the lighting. There could be no accident blaring while the wrong knob was being tuned. Static was absolutely out of the question. Then again, specially made electrical generators would have to be brought in to supply our power needs. Maxey was the producer-director-financial manager of all these basic structural concerns, which I have only touched on. My job, understandably, was the fashion show itself. I was responsible for the music, the lighting design, and the stage direction. I was also responsible for every model, from her runway choreography to her makeup. Maxey showed me how to hire experts and how to delegate authority for every technical aspect of the show. I wasn't particularly worried about coordinating professionals who knew more about their specialties than I did. After all, when I was hostess at the Beavertown Howard Johnson's, I coordinated waitresses, cashiers, short-order cooks, and cleaning women. I had to cover for our night manager, who spent half of every night in a motel room across the parking lot with Beverly, the hatcheck girl. He was also the night manager for the motel; it was whispered that Beverly made fifty dollars an hour in her motel room. Someday, I'll write the story of my three years as a working girl in Beavertown, especially the tale of how I got myself fired as a restaurant hostess because I wasn't willing to earn fifty dollars an hour, too. This is no reflection on Howard Johnson's, who run excellent restaurants and motels. At least, ours was, as long as I was covering for the night manager, who, as it so happened, was summarily sacked two weeks after he fired me. In any case, I arrived in New York with more than a little business experience. With Maxey at my side directing me, I really had no fears about my ability to pull off my big fashion show. There was only one draw-back, however, one overwhelming risk factor—money! As it turned out, my fashion show was going to cost me two million dollars! Aside from salaries, bribes, rents, travel and hotel expenses, there were the basic facts of life: the electrical generators I've already mentioned, plus the lighting and sound systems, the Lucite floor, and a hundred thousand dollars worth of polished, varnished pine boards to create tiers of bleachers for my audience. Yes, Virginia, there is a Roman Colosseum, but never, never underestimate the ruinous extent of a Roman ruin! We needed ushers, guards, and telephone operators, mes-sengers, and a corps of roustabouts. We needed rehearsal space in the Hassler, plus trucks, trailers, and buses to transport goods and personnel to the Colosseum on the appointed day, Sunday, August third! Two million dollars! This pile of pennies meant one giant loan from the Bank of America, with Adoro International as collateral. In other words, if my fashion show was a bust, it was back to Beavertown for me. My life depended on my capturing the world's imagination with a collection of clothes that would make the average woman feel well dressed, smart, sexy, friendly, and sensual—at half the price. In other words, I wanted to create a look called "The Adoro Girl!" that every ordinary American house-wife with or without a job and/or career would want to emulate. Chanel created her look in the Twenties and Thirties; Dior did it in the Forties; McCardell in the Fifties; Klein in the seventies. Now it was my turn.

There was some good news. A leading documentary filmmaker named Buck Johnson, who was also a legendary black California stud, had come into town with his crew to make an hour-long documentary called "Diana's De-but" to be shown on Public Television all over America. I couldn't wait to get started—on the documentary, I mean.

On my second day Maxey had already arranged for me to meet Buck Johnson, who, I was told, was staying with friends in the oldest residential section of Rome called the Trastevere, which literally means "across the Tiber." Buck was more than willing to meet me at the Hotel Hassler, but I was intrigued by the Trastevere, after having learned so much about it in the travel books I'd been reading. There were intimations of medieval gold mosaics, inlaid marbles, and saffron-colored buildings. According to legend, Trastevere's street brawls are the most riotous in Rome, their songs the most lascivious, their women the most sensuous, their capacity for alcohol the most amazing. Trastevere is not too far from the country; I was told that the smell of the barnyard mingled with the odors of the best cooking in Rome. So many contradictory impressions; I couldn't wait to see it. Besides, I figured that Buck and I should have some time alone at the beginning, since later in the week chaos was bound to ensue and we might not have a chance to talk, to really talk.

Of course, I was probably asking for trouble on that steamy summer day. A disguise is a disguise is a disguise, but why I wore my black satin hot-pants with the four-inch gash on the right cheek I don't know, since, typically, I'd forgotten my panties again and a mouthful of soft pink ass bulged through my gash. Then, too, I wore black patent leather high heels. A poor choice, admittedly. As for the rest of my outfit, I must have been hung-over. That's my only explanation. Why I chose to wear, instead of a blouse, a flesh-colored brassiere with a floppy silk red rose pinned to each point I just cannot explain. I guess I thought I was starting a new style. The year before, white lace camisoles and full-length slips from the Victorian era had become popular for summer party wear. I thought I was taking the "underwear as outerwear" idea one step further, but in this case, that one step took me over the side of the cliff, so to speak. In my own defense, I have to say I tried to be classy. I wore a picture hat of the finest straw and carried a matching bag. My watch was a Rolex. It was brand-new, my beloved Adolfo's final gift. Finally, on that ill-fated morning in Rome, I wore a twenty-four-carat charm bracelet worth fifteen thousand dollars around my right ankle, and, oh yes, I sprayed myself with a whole bottle of Chanel No. 5. Fuck it, I looked like a first-class tramp and smelled worse. That's what I got for experimenting with a new look. But my appearance had nothing whatsoever to do with Mr. Buck Johnson. In fact, as I was walking across the Castel Sant' Angelo Bridge on my way to meet Stud, I mean Buck, and four men had propositioned me in the space of ten minutes, I seriously contemplated returning to the Hassler and cancelling my appointment. Maxey could deal with him better than I. There was nothing to negotiate anyway. But I had second thoughts. Even if too many television and movie cameras got in the way of my fashion medleys on the Lucite runway, the presence of so much media would confirm the event in the world press. Without that confirmation there would be no event worth mentioning.

I was not completely prepared for Mr. Buck Johnson. He was my generation's answer to Harry Belafonte, that perfect blend of African and the Mediterranean, with iridescent eyes as green as emeralds, skin the color of dark caramels, and a whiskey voice, husky, sweet, and riveting. He greeted me at the open door of a sixteenth-century townhouse painted terra cotta. The outside of the house seemed to be crumbling. The street, made of cobblestones and brick, was cracked; it was a streambed for discarded laundry water and cooking water. I could smell animal urine and, somehow, the faint, acrid odor of sex. "Where was I?" I wondered; I felt a long way from Beavertown. In truth, I felt like I had finally come home.

Then there was Buck. He was dressed in faded American jeans so tight I could see the outline of his glans lying halfway across the top of his left thigh. In the fashion world, this is what's known as a "horizontal crotch," although I have my own definition for that. His faded alligator shirt hugged a weight-lifter's torso. As every American girl knows, when a black man is built, there is no competition, and when a black man is hung, get ready for bed. Racial generalities?? There was nothing to prevent Mr. Buck Johnson from wearing an Oxford-cloth shirt with a button-down collar and a three-piece Brooks Brothers suit with boxer shorts. After all, this was a business meeting, wasn't it? Didn't I have two million dollars at stake and wasn't he America's leading documentary filmmaker, a Pulitzer Prize winner, to boot, for his riveting documentary on group sex at Harvard? Hadn't his autobiographical novel about his three illegitimate half-Vietnamese children been at the top of *The New York Times* best-seller list for three months? Hadn't it prompted a congressional investigation of American servicemen abroad? Hadn't his centerfold picture in *Playgirl* with his half-erect cock caused him to be asked to leave the President's Prayer Breakfast, even though he had, as he put it, been making a political statement to the Third World about "Black Majesty." Mr. Johnson was a controversial figure with almost religious connotations. Very serious business, indeed. If he expected to fool around with me, he was on dangerous ground.

His opening remarks, I have to say, were not in the best of taste.

"Holy Moly! Somebody's sent me a hooker for breakfast! Okay, Momma, how you like it?"

"Mr. Johnson," I said, ignoring his remarks and trying to sound as British as possible, "this is strictly business."

He replied with an annoying chuckle. "Momma, I wouldn't have it any other way. Just tell me who paid you to welcome me to Rome."

The light dawned. He had no idea who I was. When he called me a hooker, I thought he was making a joke at my expense. It never occurred to me he was being serious. I dug down into my straw bag for my business card, which, of course, it turned out I'd forgotten, along with my underpants. Besides, Buck's physical presence had thrown me off balance. His glowing emerald eyes were as much a distraction as his growing cock. I felt terribly confused. How could I possibly convey to this man my true identity? How could I make him realize I wasn't there to shimmy out of my hot-pants and spread my legs for his big black tool? I could tell immediately that he was one of those men with nothing but fucking on his mind. How? By the way he was holding onto his crotch and running his thumb back and forth over the blackjack in his pants. I could tell by the way he was licking his sensual lips with his wet pink tongue.

Finally, out of desperation, I decided to tell the truth. I decided that maybe if I introduced myself, he wouldn't want to go to bed with me. My plan was simple; I would describe my fashion show to him. He could take notes with his thick black pen. It would be a formal meeting of two American business people. Yes, that was it. We were going to mix business with pleasure, I mean pleasure with business, or something.

"Hello, Mr. Johnson," I said, extending my hand for him to kiss. "I'm Diana Adoro. I'm experimenting with a new fashion look. I guess it doesn't work, does it?"

Immediately, my hand was lifted up and taken to meet his warm, moist lips. My knees buckled. Buck seemed so warm and comforting. It's not that I had been neglected since my beloved Adolfo died. Maxey had been a wonderful lover, and I could always count on Monsignor "Vanni" Caro, and, as I have described, there were occasional unexpected, well, "fucks," for want of a better word, but meeting Mr. Buck Johnson made me aware of what I'd been missing. Just because I've had steak for dinner doesn't mean I'd pass up chocolate mousse for dessert, does it? Who can live on steak alone? Variety is not just the spice of life, it is the prerequisite for mental health! Which is not to say that I am always thinking about sex, but as Buck picked me up and carried me over the threshold, as a joke, of course, I could feel my breasts heaving and the juices in my cunt start to flow. When Buck put me down on a mink-covered sofa that somehow seemed immoral, although I don't know exactly why, he grabbed at that slit of pink flesh protruding through the gash in my black satin hot-pants.

"Mr. Johnson," I said, "I realize that you don't have to know the logistics of my fashion show."

"That's right," he interrupted, "all I have to do is follow you around, Momma."

"That's right," I continued, "as long as we have a good working relationship . . ." I had to stop. I was dumb-struck by what happened next. What can I say? The man didn't touch me; he just undressed in front of me, first peeling off his alligator shirt to reveal his sculptured torso with its tight black curls across the mahogany chest with its medallion-sized coffee-colored aureoles with their sweet, chewy nipples that stuck out like a woman's when she's aroused. His stomach was rippling with muscles; the word "washboard" was not far wrong. Of course, muscles are irrelevant. I am rarely turned on by naked men. Personality is all I'm looking for, sort of. Then Buck stepped out of his jeans. Instantly, I could smell his cock. I could smell his balls. I could smell his meat. I was almost delirious, I was so aroused. He had one of those black asses that, unfortunately, Greek sculpture never got around to.

Let me explain. Somehow or other, in a well-developed black, male or female, but especially in males, their genitals are so complex, not only in size but in the number of nerves and blood vessels, and they are such masters of the sex act that they need extremely developed ass muscles to support their genitalia. When these latter-day Nubians fuck, it's not just in and out, in and out; they can actually move in two directions at once, practically rotating their cocks as they pump up and down. In the best of them, their glans can expand and contract in opposite

103

rhythm to their penile shafts. My mother told me this. She also said that if it's a middle-class white woman (like herself, presumably) who's "getting it," she can go stark, raving mad right in the middle of the sex act; her nervous system can just plain burn out. I don't know what to say. This never came up until Buck. Some people say that saying black men are super-lovers is a racial myth which oppresses the majority of black men, which is why I have to stress that only the top ten percent have "it." Buck was definitely in the top ten percent. Buck was probably in the top one percent. And now I will reveal a fact never before known to the general public. My mother, who was super-religious when I knew her, almost to the point of fanaticism, spent her whole adult life repressing an all-consuming lust for blackass; it was she, who, one night on a drunken binge after her favorite minister had been stabbed to death by his wife's sister, confessed that she was going to burn in hell for having fucked every black man in western Pennsylvania before she was twenty.

Mr. Buck Johnson must have been able to read my mind. He stood by his sofa, as his Anaconda cock grew fatter and longer, until, finally, it looked like a small treetrunk sticking out. This man reminded me of the magnificent black stallion on my grandfather's farm who had the kind of physical presence that defies death. Like I say, I'm not particularly into bodies. If I had a mad urge to climb that "tree," and I did, it was only because I wanted to plant a kiss on his mouth. I figured he must be lonely in Rome all by himself.

"You don't look like the Diana Adoro I expected," he said. What was I supposed to say? I invariably say the wrong things, anyway.

I said, "Well, I'm wearing Adoro clothes," as if that proved something. "Adoro doesn't make hot-pants like those," he said. The truth is, my hot-pants were made to be worn under a skirt made out of the same material and slit up the side. "There's no way Adoro makes pants like that," he said, continuing his attack. I looked down at my poor hot-pants. Oh Christ! The way I was lying on the couch was absolutely obscene! My satin pants were stretched even tighter than before; the slit in my vulva was most apparent; my vulva looked fat and round and smothering in its tight black prison.

"These are the Adoro label," I said.

"No way," he continued. I was so upset by his callousness that I burst into angry tears.

"All right, I'll show you!" I stammered. "Nobody believes me anymore!" I quickly shimmied off the couch, kicked off my high heels, pulled the hot-pants down over my feet, and handed them to Buck. "Adoro label, see for yourself!" I said triumphantly. Buck grabbed the pants and held them to his nose. By this time, I was already out of my brassiere. "Adoro label," I said, handing him the bra. He hung my hot-pants on his treetrunk cock while he smelled my brassiere the same way he smelled my pants.

In the meantime, I was so upset to be called a liar I lay on the sofa sobbing. Unfortunately, my simmering cunt-juices betrayed my feelings that I was a victim of Mr. Buck Johnson. I couldn't help myself. I seemed to be carried along by a tide of passion over which I had no control. In any case, I was profoundly upset. Was I a nymphomaniac? I seemed to be fucking almost every man I met. "There's something wrong with me," I said suddenly.

"What?" he asked, "venereal disease?"

"No, no, it's just that here we are naked together and we're not emotionally involved. I only met you five minutes ago; there has to be something wrong."

"Wrong?" he said. "Wrong? Did Momma say wrong? Honey, just take a good look at you."

"Look at me?" I repeated. "What is there to look at?" Before the sentence was out of my mouth, Buck was lying beside me, our two flanks burning into each other with intense heat, his long brown finger the length of most men's penises encircling my taut nipple, driving me wild, as he savored my skin.

105

"You are the goddess of the moon, Diana; you glow in the white man's dark," he whispered.

"But it's morning!" I cried.

"Then, you glow in my African sun!" He laughed. "Your pussy glows with the special glow of raw red meat; your big tits glow, too; they are tropical melons for my mouth," and with that he mouthed my big golden globes with their silken aureoles that felt like "rose petals" and my nipples that seemed like "miniature caramels." The poetry was bad enough. The more aroused he got, the more he spoke in a kind of fake jive talk: "Oh, baby, I ain't never had it so good; you is honey sweet." Did Mr. Johnson realize that his body and not his soul was all I cared about? It's true. Finally, I saw the naked truth, no pun intended. I was a second-class slut. He must have read my mind. He pulled me forward and, cradling my ass, brought my cunt-meat forward to meet the penetration of his big black cock. I hoped to heaven he liked a tight, wet cunt. I hoped he liked raw vagina-meat with strong lips that could drain the semen out of his testicles that hung like hard rubber handballs in his black-velvet sack. I hoped he liked a cave that had all the power of a vacuum pump, yet could caress his tender glans as sweely as it worked his loose outer flesh over his steel-hard shaft. In other words, I hoped he bought what I had to offer. I wrapped my legs around his mahogany torso.

Buck was so clearly excited about fucking me, he gave me the works; everything my mother had described! Yes, it was true; that cock could move in three directions at once, expertly guided by the computer in his ass. His speech became simple and direct—from out of nowhere, it seemed, poetry appeared. "Hey, Pussy, fuck! Wow. Motherfuck! Pussy, Pussy, Motherfuck! Eeeeeh!" and "Momma, Pussycunt, Mommacunt, you are so sweet, sweet to taste, sweet to fuck. Oooooooh, Momma!"

At that moment I felt like the most desirable woman in the world. To think I could make an established filmmaker become a fool over me! There's many a repressed woman who would have turned beet red at the sight of Mr. Buck Johnson looking at her and called the cops the instant his gaze dropped below her collar bone. Not me, honey. I felt like the finger of God had entered me and was caressing my cunt in a divine effort to pleasure me and make me happy. Yes, I was *loved,* loved by all that is black in this world; the soft southern nights, the bedroom with the lights turned out, double fudge chocolate cake, Kaluha, black beans, and the billion black eyes of India and the Far East. There was a column of living flesh connecting me with the sweetest, most molasses-voiced genius stud I had ever met. He was the best of mother and father. His fucking touched spots so deep in me that my juices streamed out of me, my inner lips made loud sucking sounds as we bucked and heaved on the thick fur couch. I stuck my middle finger into his chocolate ass to discover the feel of the sweet nougat inside. As I worked it in deeper and deeper, he, too, began to groan from ecstasy. I was thrilled to think that I could give pleasure to a super-stud. For a few minutes, this wonderful man allowed me to forget I was the head of an international business empire. For a few minutes I was just a piece of ass—and I loved it!

This man was crazy about my tits. He kept fondling great handfuls of my golden globes, yes, definitely the award-winning kind, and murmuring, "Mmmm." Before long, his awesome instrument had brought the two of us to the verge of orgasm. My vagina was flushed with hot blood, my nerve endings on the brink of explosion. I felt Buck's cock swell and the sweat pour out of him. As the morning light shone on his rich brown frame, he became golden and godlike. We were both golden, really, both shimmering, both warm. We exploded together. His gush of thick creme de come triggered my orgasm. I lost control and thrashed about insensate, unconscious to everything but a golden blur and a humming sound. Every nerve in my body from my toes right through my spinal cord tingled as the pleasure ripped through me. My man kept murmuring "Momma" as he held me close, nuzzling me, stroking my stomach with the full weight of his classic Egyptian head.

Afterplay? A morning spent together exploring the shadows of Trastevere? You've got to be kidding. As Jack Kennedy said so well, "Life is not fair." As it so happened, my arch-rival Glorianna, who was supposed to be on the French Riviera feeding her pet shark and fucking herself blind, the same Glorianna who had stolen my first obsession, porn star Angel O'Shaughnessy with the matted gold hair on his big barrel chest, just happened to be upstairs in Mr. Buck Johnson's rented villa at the very same moment that I was downstairs making very loud animal sounds of passion and entanglement. Had our sounds somehow wafted up to the second floor? Apparently. Glorianna certainly wasn't dressed for any occasion but getting up in the middle of the night and going to the bathroom. In fact, at first I didn't recognize her; she looked like an enraged librarian. She must have been taking a shower. Her face was devoid of makeup; her wet hair was slicked back like a rat in New York harbor. She was wearing a floor-length terrycloth caftan the color of babyshit. In short, without her false eyelashes and blusher, her preternatural strength was more than apparent. This was no glamour girl; this was a monster! When she caught sight of me with Buck's semen trickling down my ravishing thighs, she was a demon gone berserk!

"You pig!" she shrieked. "You fucking animal pig!" Not one word against the man of the house; all her rage was directed at me. Buck at least tried to protect me.

"Hey, Glorianna honey, stay away from this girl; she's one terrific fuck!"

"That's right, she's one terrific fuck," screamed Glorianna. "She fucks anything that's wearing a cock! She's a fucking nymphomaniac, that's what she is!" I, for my part, was trying to remain calm and at the same time protect my perfect complexion from her two-inch claws, which she normally kept filed to razor sharpness.

"Leave her alone, Glorianna; it was all my fault!" shouted Buck, continuing with, "Hey, baby, I thought you were upstairs asleep."

"How could I sleep, with the all-time 'tramp champ' downstairs having orgasms with the first real man I've met since Angelo moved to the West Coast!" wailed Glorianna.

"But, Glorianna . . ." I protested, "I thought you were on the French Riviera."

"Oh, Jesus, Diana, what do you want?" said Gloriana. "You've got Maxey any time you snap your fingers, and from the looks of yesterday's newspaper, you've been meeting a few Arabs."

"How can you say that!" I replied. "That Arab tore my dress off in front of all the passengers and forced me to jump out of a 747 without a parachute!"

"Right onto his cock, no doubt," hissed Gloriana. "You're always being forced to fuck, aren't you? Always falling on the wrong cock, isn't that so?"

Then, Buck put his foot in his mouth: "Hey, come on, Glorianna, honey, we're not married or nothing; we just met last week!"

"We have a *relationship*!" screamed Glorianna. "I gave up my vacation in Cannes so I could spend a week with you in this, this place, this godforsaken fucking tourist trap!"

"Rome is a godforsaken fucking tourist trap?" said Buck, amazed at her conception.

Glorianna took another track; in her condition she was ready to try anything. "Buck, I have to talk to Diana; you've got to leave us alone. Please, baby."

Buck, with his cock dangling in front of him like a giant licorice stick, seemed unperturbed. "Just as long as one of you girls is still here alive when you finish tearing each other's tits off." With that remark, he went upstairs. I assumed that I would see him again shortly. The truth is, I would not see him again for several days, at which time I would be a different woman, sadder, wiser, and twice as sexy or, rather, "sexual." You see, it was Glorianna who forced me to make the change from sexy to sexual, although at the outset I think she would have preferred that I go from sexy to dead.

"I want to talk to you, Mrs. Adoro," was how she began, spitting out my name like an obscenity.

"You've been talking to me for ten minutes and I haven't tried to stop you, have I?" I said, holding my ground. I was still stark naked, mind you. I figured my best defense to anybody's blitzkrieg was my gorgeous 1940s movie-star body. Frankly, it drove women rivals to foam at the mouth. Yes, I had a body like Marilyn Monroe's. I still do, except that unlike Marilyn, God rest her soul, my hair is a natural honey blond and my skin has a golden Scandinavian glow inherited from my mother's mother who came to Philadelphia from Denmark as a pastry chef. Tradition is very important as to how a given woman acts and behaves in bed. Certain things are handed down from one generation to the next. My maternal grandmother not only made the best cream puffs in Philly, she also gave the best head at a time when proper American girls, black or white, wouldn't do such a thing. I go into my family background in an upcoming book on my search for roots. My point is, I always think of my sensual grandma when I behold my golden skin. I could see Glorianna eyeing my tits. They really are unbelievable. They're so big, you'd think they'd sag, but they don't. My breasts sort of "waft" in mid-air. And my aureoles! Even I marvel! Unlike most women's they are not pasted flat; they are delicate little cones of white-gold silk, on the ends of which are attached my caramel teats, perfect for sucking, pinching, or nuzzling. My stomach is so smooth it seems molded as it descends in sloping mounds and valleys into my dark-blond mink muff, that triangle of silky fur that guards the entrance to my cunt, the cunt that the world's most virile men have been known to punch each other out for. No, I can't say that, as of yet, any gentleman's been killed over my cunt, although I wouldn't be surprised if that happened one day, because my labia are as smooth and silky as a blooming rose, yet have a wondrous muscular strength. The best of all possible worlds. I can grab a cock with my cunt-lips and bring the man off without touching him with my hands. My ass I've already described many times before; it continues to amaze even me. It's a classic black woman's ass, small and high and tight. It rides up when I walk. I have to have my dresses especially cut. I'm very proud of the fact I give a man a big solid handful of "grabass," a handle to hold onto when he drives his piston home.

Glorianna must have sensed how much men crave my body as she stood there staring at me; she was positively bug-eyed. I decided to act superior; why not, I was paying her salary.

"Do you want me to fire you?" I asked, as coolly as I could manage.

"Fire me?" she said. "I own five percent of your company, remember? I got it the same way you got the other ninety-five percent, by fucking Adolfo Adoro; except by the time you came along, Adolfo had gotten tired of me. Like he always said, he could take a woman for about four years. When he died, I had less than six months to go."

"What are you implying?" I said, astounded at her boldness. "That you and Adolfo were getting it off while he was married to me?" Considering Adolfo and I, singly or together, believed in fucking everyone from the cleaning lady to the delivery boy, sometimes both at the same time, my bourgeoise housewife routine did not have a chance of being credible and Glorianna knew it.

Otherwise, my dear Diana," she continued, ignoring my protest, "I wouldn't have gotten a tenth of a percent. You see, Diana, your greatest advantage was that Adolfo had known you less than a year. All you really had on your side was timing. Just timing. But in this case, timing was everything!"

"Adolfo loved mc more than any woman he'd ever met!" I retorted, repeating what he himself had told me frequently.

I guess Glorianna couldn't take the plain truth. She got vicious. "Except Adolfo was too blinded by his animal lust for you to realize you aren't really a woman!"

"I'm not a *what*?" I responded, somewhat taken aback by this strange turn in her argument.

"I said 'woman'! You know damn well what I said: 'Woman!'—exactly what you aren't!" She didn't stop there, either. "My God, Diana, a common whore on the Spanish Steps knows more about being a woman than you do! You know what you are, you're just a starry-eyed nymphomaniac from the sticks ready to fuck a thousand men, because you know you could never keep one man! No one man, once he knew you, could stick around for very long!"

"Except Adolfo Adoro," I said quietly and with absolute dignity. I had her. Glorianna could not deny my fabulous six-month marriage to one of the world's greatest lovers. Adolfo Adoro couldn't get enough of me. But she wouldn't quit.

"Except Adolfo Adoro, you say? Have you forgotten you brought so much stress into his life you killed him?"

"Run that one past me again," I said, hearing an accusation that in my heart of hearts I secretly feared was true.

"You killed one of the world's loveliest men," she said, her eyes flashing with fire, "because you're not a woman. There's no heart to you, no feeling. It's all fuck, fuck, fuck. All you know about men is fuck. Adolfo Adoro came to you with a lonely heart and all you cared about was his big Sicilian cock."

"But, Glorianna," I pleaded, terribly upset and in tears, "you don't understand—Adolfo loved what I did with his cock!"

"Diana," she said, cutting me off, "you're so cold and calculating you couldn't last a day as a common whore in this town; word of mouth would ruin you and you'd starve to death; you're nothing more than a fucking machine!"

Glorianna got me so upset that I decided to get dressed. My intention was to get out of that falling-down house as fast as I could. It was horrible. She stood there in her babyshit green caftan mocking my black satin hot-pants and my flesh-colored brassiere with the roses pinned on the points that just a few minutes ago had been hanging on Buck's big cock.

"You call that what a normal woman would wear?" she taunted. "Why, that's a costume, a costume for a fucking machine!"

I didn't answer her. I had enough trouble getting my high-heels back on my feet. I was so nervous it was like threading a needle in the dark. I didn't answer Glorianna. I didn't even turn around. I ran out into the streets of Trastevere blinded by hot, stinging tears. As I passed by, men in the alleyways made obscene sucking sounds and when I ran across the bridge over the Tiber at Castel Saint' Angelo, I almost caused a traffic accident because I had been too upset to hook my bra in back. I was confused and upset. What was the point of anything anymore? As great a time as I'd had with Buck Johnson, Glorianna had devastated me. I had lost my pride. I wandered back to the Hassler through the bustling Roman streets; some of the women in the doorways were laughing at me as I passed. Clearly, the only way to wear a flesh-colored bra with big silk roses on the tits is with a big sense of humor, which at the moment I didn't have.

At the front door of the Hassler, the doorman, whose name I found out was Carlo, and who reminded me of Franco Nero, my favorite movie star after Burt Reynolds, stopped me, saying, "No whores, please."

I said, "Carlo, it's me, Gertrude Makeme; this is the new look. Maybe." I stuck out my tits, just a little, to make sure he'd understand. I know that sounds cheap, but let's face it, men notice what they notice. Carlo definitely noticed. He removed his jacket immediately and covered me like I was a drowning victim, which in a sense I was. His hand brushed against my tit as he was helping me; I knew that on some level he cared for me. I burst into tears and fell into his arms. I couldn't help myself. "Carlo, tell me," I sobbed, "am I a real woman?"

Carlo could not believe my behavior. Who could blame him? The day before, I had arrived at the Hassler in a baggy tweed suit looking like an English nanny, and now, here I was in his arms, in black satin hot-pants with roses on my tits.

"Signora Makeme, you are ill," was his response. Of course. What else would a Roman doorman say? His jaw was so square, his black eyebrows so thick, his hooded eyes so blue, his perennial five o'clock shadow so faintly menacing that I knew instinctively that if I let him, he'd fuck me right then and there. They all would. That's all I was good for, wasn't it? A piece of ass. When I thanked Carlo, I discovered I was running my hand up and down his biceps, feeling the hard authority of his muscle under his shirt. I couldn't believe my own behavior; maybe Glorianna was right after all. I turned and ran into the lobby with its forest of square marble pillars and its lovely gilded ceilings. The clientele there is so smart-looking; all sorts of discarded royalty who knew where to invest their money when they had it. They sit in the lobby in those shimmery blue-velvet chairs on acres of Oriental carpets looking at the freshly cut flowers. Just idyllic. Too bad a crass working-class girl like me had to ruin the effect by marching into their midst with all my sexual juices flowing, but I had no choice; I had to check in at the front desk.

When I got my messages, I was more depressed than ever. Maxey was still in Zurich straightening out the details of our loan. He wouldn't be back for another day or two. Upset, I went straight up to my room, informed

114

the switchboard I would take no calls that day, returned Carlo's jacket with ten dollars and a "thank you" note, and hung the "Do Not Disturb" sign in four languages on my door. I spent the rest of the day in bed feeling sorry for myself. About four o'clock in the afternoon I fell asleep and had the most peculiar dream, which I will now describe.

I was in Italy in another century before the time of Christ. I was in the south, somewhere around Naples. The sky was an intense cloudless blue, the mountains in the background deep purple, the soil under my feet deep red. I saw myself coming out of a villa in the countryside, a simple stone house built around an inner courtyard with a square reflecting pool in which a couple of large goldfish were swimming. The outside of the house had four stone pillars cut from rough, unpolished marble. The sun that day seemed unbearably hot. I was wearing a white toga, made out of a very simple pleated fabric like cotton or linen. Everything about this farm, for that matter, seemed stark and uncomplicated. There were no decorations anywhere, no landscape architecture, no soft furniture, no vases of flowers, nobody singing or telling jokes. I remember seeing myself walking down a rocky slope to the vineyards carrying two jugs in my arms. The vineyards grew large purple grapes like our Concord grapes; they seemed to stretch for about fifty acres in all directions down rocky slopes in front of my house.

There were men working in the vineyard, dark men with black curly beards and bronzed skin. They wore sweatbands around their brows to keep their dark curly ringlets and the sweat out of their faces as they harvested grapes, piling them into wicker baskets. These men wore nothing else. They were completely naked. I can't say I was shocked; it all seemed completely natural. Their bodies were young, strong, supple, and splendid to look at. Men of southern Italian stock invariably have magnificently muscled torsos, chests, and upper arms, which taper down to small waists and asses. This type also seems to boast huge uncircumsized cocks which hang off the front of them like big, juicy slugs.

I don't know who I was supposed to be in the dream, except that as soon as I got near the men—there were six of them—I unclasped my robe and let it fall to the ground. I stood there, facing them, holding my jugs. At the sight of me, their cocks began to twitch and stiffen. I have to mention that I had a different body than my own in this dream. My breasts were not as globular. Clothed, I seemed almost flat-chested, but naked, with a delicious peaches-and-cream complexion and nipples as pink as bubble gum, I guess I was pretty spectacular in a Neapolitan vineyard. In fact, I remember being so turned on by my own body that I began to stroke myself in front of the men. By now, they were all pretty erect and had stopped picking grapes. They stood there waiting. What happened was like a ritual. I had done it before and I would do it again. I took one of my jugs and gave it to the first man, who drank from it and then passed it on to the others. It was filled with a strong red wine; rivulets of ruby liquid ran down the corners of their mouths, staining their chests, trickling into their pubic hair.

I knelt before the first man in this row of splendid specimens; he looked like a discus thrower of about thirty. From the second jug I poured thick honey on his cock, coating the glans and then the shaft with layers of thick golden nectar. Then I took my afternoon meal, kneeling before him, wrapping my arms around his robust thighs, stroking his hard ass, then plunging my moist lips over the shimmering head of his big cock, licking and sucking off every last drop of sweet nourishment.I fondled his testicles, too, and licked them where honey had dribbled on them. My Hercules came without too much effort; he shot a load of thick clotted cream that blended with the honey in my mouth to produce an intoxicating appetizer. Then, with the same sense of ritual, I went down the row and took the other five in the same way,

116

one by one. Some of the cocks were thicker, some longer, some were redder, some balls were twice the size of the others; the size actually didn't matter to me because every man was sexy in his own way. Like I always say, the most important sex organ is between the ears—and these were six very sexy men! I was sexy, too, in a way I have never before experienced myself in my present life of consciousness; I was calmer, more deliberate, more sure of myself. My body was less dramatic than in real life, but it seemed stronger. In a strange way, the dream itself was giving me strength.

I woke up from my long afternoon sleep as the Roman sun was setting. The Tiber ran red and gold. At first I was startled; I was just getting used to the Neapolitan vineyards and my new calmer self, but it was time to come back to harsh reality.

My suite was dark. There were little red lights flashing on my phone telling me I had messages waiting at the front desk. Probably Maxey from Zurich. I did not pick up the phone. I stood at my Renaissance window instead and watched the sun set over Rome. Then, unwittingly, I remembered Glorianna and her accusations. I remembered my dream, me in the vineyards, that other, deeper, calmer self, and a chill passed through me. It was a terrible moment. I felt wounded and alone. Maybe it was time for a change, I thought. Maybe I should go out into the streets of Rome disguised as a poor working girl and discover whether any ordinary man could respond to me as an ordinary woman. If such a thing were only possible! In the short time since Adolfo's death, had I really lost my roots and my self-respect? Apparently.

Chapter Seven

I stumbled down the Hassler back stairs and left by a side door. I didn't want Carlo the doorman to see me. I still hadn't changed my black satin pants. They were stained with come, mine and Buck Johnson's. And they smelled of sex. All things considered, I figured they'd give off a seductive shine in the black Roman night. The come stains didn't matter; come doesn't show after dark. In addition, I'd made a couple of adjustments to my outfit. Instead of my flesh-colored brassiere, I wore a lavender angora sweater cut down to my nipples. After all, it was night; in some corner of my troubled being I felt I was still a woman. For makeup I took my reddest lipstick and smeared it across my lips with my index finger, deliberately going beyond my natural lip line. I don't know why; I just felt like it. Have feelings gone out of style or something? For eyeshadow I took that same index finger and smeared dark gray mascara both above and below my eyes. As for my hair, I messed it up as much as I could. That was that. My Roman street-walker's look. Who cared?

The kid from Beavertown was going to mingle in the maddening crowd, or as we say in New York, "get down." Why not? What did I know about life? I was just a dumb twenty-three-year-old widow who liked to fuck. So who didn't? Glorianna was right. What did I know about life? What did I know about men? Just like she said, it was all "fuck, fuck, fuck." But, Christ, I know that every time I fucked a man, I learned a little bit more about all men, and every now and then I met some man I wanted to settle down with. I wasn't just fucking men for the sake of fucking them, like Glorianna said. It's true, I may have been fucking my beloved Adolfo just for the sake of fucking him, but that's how we got to know each other—in between the fucks—and eventually, after a few weeks, we got married. What's wrong with that? I had to be doing something right. My fucking had gotten me a wonderful husband and an international business empire and a new career in designing, and the wonderful thing was, I never once tried to sleep my way to the top. I just happen to like exceptionally virile and aggressive men and a lot of them, well, are rich and famous and love beautiful women like me. I can't help it if I look like someone a virile man wants to fuck in the hayloft. Maybe my problem was I didn't make myself available enough to ordinary men, men in the streets. Maybe I lacked the common touch. Maybe that's what bothered Glorianna. I decided that I'd try the streets first, see what the men were like there, see if I could make the ordinary Joe a little bit happier; and then, if that didn't work out, I'd consider working in a whore-house for a while, to really make myself available to the ordinary sexual needs of the ordinary sexual man. I just knew I'd find the way. After all, this problem bore on the heart of my identity as a human being and as a woman. If I couldn't be a complete woman, then what was the point of designing clothes for women who were?

Glorianna was right; if I didn't come down to earth and make myself available to regular people, I'd end up as some kind of airy-fairy princess. At least, I think that's what she was trying to tell me.

I decided to walk from the Hassler to the Colosseum; on the map it looked to be about thirty irregular blocks. If it took me an hour and a half to walk it, that was fine. Besides, a lot of things can happen to a girl like me in the space of an hour and a half. In any case, by design, no one would recognize me as Diana Adoro, the head of a growing fashion empire. To the average man passing me by I would be just a nobody with a terrific pair of tits. You have to realize I wasn't a complete innocent. I knew perfectly well that the area around the Colosseum was a pickup spot at night. I guess that Glorianna had so depressed and confused me that I temporarily lost my sense of self-worth, or something.

I was barely a block from the Hassler when a little Alfa-Romeo screeched to a halt beside me. The driver was a small man, about thirty-five, in no way conventionally handsome. He looked like a desperate professor. He spoke to me in loud Italian. I had no idea what he was saying, as I don't understand Italian. He kept getting louder and louder. Finally, I said, "I don't speak Italian." Well, he didn't speak English.

Eventually, a Roman policeman on a motorcycle stopped by and, in Italian, demanded to know what was going on. The driver produced identification and registration papers, then turned to me and said in perfect Oxford English, "I told him you were my wife and we were having a fight about the way you're dressed. He thinks you're a prostitute. If I were you, I'd get in my car and sit with your arms crossed over your chest, unless you want to get arrested and taken down to the police station."

Since my last visit to a police station, which I described in detail in *Diana's Desire,* had resulted in my being gangbanged by half of "New York's finest," I really didn't think I had the energy for another go-round with the law

121

in Rome, the ancestral home of satyrs and temple prostitutes, where even the gods had genitals. I got into the car as directed and crossed my arms over my almost exposed breasts. The policeman seemed satisfied. In Rome, it seems, the authorities prefer the hookers to be registered and working in regularly inspected houses of prostitution, not out on the streets free-lancing. The policeman climbed back onto his motorcycle and sped off into the pitch-black night.

The man next to me said, "I'm a psychiatrist. I can help you."

"Help me with what?" I said.

"Your depression is evident a block away," he replied. "You have such a sad look on your face."

"If you're such an expert on mental health," I retorted, "how come you pretended you can't speak English?"

"I was just playing games," he replied. "Game playing is the mark of a healthy mind, you know." He put his key in the ignition, started the car, and took off down the Via due Macelli. "Where do you want to go?" he asked.

"The Colosseum," I replied, anxious to see it in the moonlight, since my fashion show was going to be at night. The driver repeated his offer to help me, adding that he could help me "find happiness in Rome."

"Look, Doctor," I said. "you're right; I'm very unhappy right now, but I have no idea why."

"Maybe you need love in your life," he suggested.

"Look, Doctor," I said, "I get laid two or three times a day, I have orgasms till they're coming out of my ears. I'm rich, young and beautiful, and I take lots of healthy, challenging risks."

"Maybe you're afraid of commitment" was his choice reply.

"Doctor, I'm a twenty-three-year-old widow" was mine. There was a dead silence and I do mean dead. Eventually, I continued. "My problem, Doctor, is not love, at least, not receiving love. It's just that a woman who works for me has accused me of being a sex machine. She says I have no heart, that I take love but I can't return it, that men get their rocks off with me, but that I don't really let anyone love me, I don't let anyone touch my heart. Well, that's what she said."

"Is she correct?" was his next question.

"I don't know," I said." I really like the guys I fuck. I tell them I like them. I don't know what else to do. She says I'm a poor excuse for a woman."

"Well, then, you're going to have to decide whether or not you believe her, aren't you?" announced the doctor.

"It's that simple?" I said. And then I saw it. There it was. His stiff white cock, standing straight up in his lap. It was the biggest cock I'd ever seen. It was dead white with a lavender glans. That's when I realized what Glorianna was talking about; these men weren't in love with me; they only lusted for me. At best, I was only accommodating myself to their appetites. They never saw beyond the big boobs and the sensational ass and the legs that didn't stop. I was absolutely shocked.

Doctor, stop this car immediately!" I ordered.

"I can't stop this car!" was his reply. "I've got to help you! You have serious neurotic problems!"

"Doctor," I said, "Why is your penis sticking out like that?"

"That's right," he replied, "It's called a penis. Every man has one. My erection is perfectly normal. The real question is, why does normal male behavior make you so upset."

"Doctor, you don't want to help me!" I screamed. "You're just turned on by my ass!"

"I've got to help you," he repeated.

"Doctor," I screamed, "if you don't stop this car and let me out, I'll make sure you go to jail!"

The pitch of my scream must have gotten to him. "Here, here's my card," he said, producing his business card. "If you change your mind about me, come and see

123

me at eight o'clock tomorrow morning. I can assure you, you have nothing to worry about. I'm a Harvard graduate."

I looked at his card; it said "Enrico Goldberg, M.D., PhD. 'The shrink who thinks.'" His address was the Via della Croce, near the Hassler. That's when I handed him one of my cards, which I always kept in my purse.

"I'm Diana Adoro, head of Adoro International. We grossed a hundred million dollars last year," I said. "I see you're wearing one of my shirts from our small but growing men's line. My introduction jolted through him like a bolt of electricity; his mighty erection began to sag almost immediately. I must have confused his categories. His car screeched to a halt right in front of the Colosseum, which loomed in front of us like a ghost ship in the night. As soon as I got out of Dr. Goldberg's car, he sped off without even saying good-bye, no doubt to look for an authentic hooker who needed the money and who would accommodate his throbbing gearshift.

I was devastated. I felt completely fucked up. I didn't know what to do or where to go. Where was the man who could touch my heart? Glorianna had a point. I didn't want to be the perfect fuck any longer. I wanted to be the perfect woman.

That's when I ran into Remi and Baddi, two self-style Roman "orphans," eighteen and nineteen, who were leaning against the outer walls of the Colosseum sharing the last inch of a cigarette. I decided to give them the rest of my pack of Marlboros. Why not? It's a terrible thing to be low on cigarettes.

"Here," I said, "take mine." That's when Remi looked at my crotch and Baddi looked at my tits. Somewhere in their background, they must have come from the upper classes because they spoke better English than the average American teen-ager. They were both tall and well developed. Baddi was very Nordic-looking, a common enough feature of the northern Italian industrial classes.

124

Furthermore, their ragged hair looked almost styled and their three-day-old beards just happened to be the rage of the European intellectuals who used special safety razors that cut exactly at the three-day length. Remi was my dark pirate, I decided. He had a Greek look; as I later found out, his father was an Athenian shipping tycoon, his mother an Italian princess.

"Are you for sale?" he asked me.

I was caught off-guard in a moment of rare vulnerability. "I'm not for anything," I said. "I'm not even sure I'm a woman."

The boys thought that was very funny. "We think you're a woman," said Remi, "and we even think you're for sale." These "boys" both had square-cut jaws and cleft chins, and Baddi was dimpled. Their teeth were perfect, although I could see gold glinting from the back of Baddi's mouth. In New York they would properly be labeled "hunks."

"Ah, I see," I said, "a couple of capitalists out slumming, is that it?" I must have unnerved them with my jargon; they probably never met a prostitute who read the daily papers.

"No, we're actually Marxists," Remi said.

"I can understand," I said. "I'm a Marxist myself— a Groucho Marxist!"

There was a silence; they didn't get my joke. But I decided to push it. Why not? Maybe I'd get lucky. Maybe they'd murder me and I could move on to the spirit world, whatever it was, and see my beloved Adolfo again. Then I wouldn't have to dwell on what Glorianna had said to me. I wouldn't have to wonder if I was a real woman, if I could receive love from a real man.

"My name's Diana," I said, throwing caution to the winds. "What's yours?" They introduced themselves as Remi "Scarlatti" and Baddi "Lenini" (I never found out what their real names were), "out-of-work actors." Every time they said the word "actor," I heard "hustler."

They asked me what I did, with twin leers on their faces. I told them I was a clothes designer, which they thought was funny.

"What kind of women do you design for?" Remi wanted to know. I decided to play their game.

"I design for prostitutes and Marxist revolutionaries," I said. "What else is there?" That seemed to please them. "What do you gentlemen do when you're not acting?" I asked.

Remi, with his tousled black hair, couldn't wait to answer that one. "We're prostitutes and Marxist revolutionaries; what else is there?" We were definitely into a new generation's humor.

I was beginning to notice them in greater detail. They were wearing T-shirts with the sleeves cut off to display their strongly muscled arms—high-school athletes turned weightlifters, no doubt. They were at pains to show off their nicely bulging crotches and well-shaped rumps. They would have been right at home on any American street.

"Do you sleep with men or women?" I asked.

"We sleep with whatever pays," they told me. "How about you? Do you want us for the night? We have a going rate for anything you want."

"Oh, boys," I said, "I never pay for sex and even if I did, I wouldn't because I'm beyond love; at least that's what they tell me."

"What do you mean?" Baddi asked, suddenly curious; "*beyond love*?" That really stopped him. I decided, what the hell, I'd let it all hang out.

"Gentlemen, you're looking at a woman who's been accused of being a cold bitch. They say I can take a man's lust, but I can't open up to his love."

Remi, the swarthy one, looked at me with his melting brown eyes. "Maybe it's true," he said, "maybe you are cursed, but I don't think so. I think we can help you." With that, he unzipped his fly; out popped a half-erect cock, which bobbed proudly in front of him. I knew

126

instinctively that he and I would fit together perfectly, but I didn't dare open my mouth to speak, I mean.

"You don't want to make love, do you?" I asked.

"Come inside the Colosseum," Remi suggested. Baddi nodded in agreement. Deep in my brain I had an image of my own murder. I could see myself splashed and splattered on the Colosseum floor, but I no longer cared. I decided to live dangerously. I reached inside my purse and threw them my wallet.

"Here, boys, if you want my money, take it, it's yours."

"We don't want your money," they responded, "we just want you!"

By the time we were fully inside the Colosseum, the only light came from the full moon. It was more than enough. By now, Baddi was stark naked; he had one of those knitted bodies that only young men of Nordic stock seem to have and the familiar fat cock to go with it. Remi didn't waste much time in getting his clothes off either. In contrast to Baddi, he was the Greek god. Little did I suspect then that in the weeks ahead, before I left Rome, I would be involved in a life-and-death struggle with these two beautiful young men in a relationship that was one surprise after another, at every turn the opposite of what I expected. I was already in the middle of my first surprise right there in the Colosseum. There they were, stark naked, and they didn't want my money.

"What do you want from me?" I begged.

"We want to help you be a woman," was their unexpected reply. "We are both a little in love with you because you tell the truth."

"I tell the truth?" I replied.

"Yes, most women who meet us try to buy us immediately, if they haven't first dragged us into the back seats of their limousines to feel us up, sometimes at gunpoint. You, you're not sure what you want and you don't mind saying so."

"But I don't feel anything, so I don't know what I want," I said, half-lying.

"May we please take off your clothes?" Baddi asked.

"Go ahead. Sure. Why not?" was my answer. I really did not care. What difference did it make? So Baddi stripped me, which wasn't hard, considering I was barely dressed to begin with. I could hear an audible gasp. They were muttering in Italian in low voices. Right in front of me, their cocks grew red and full and Rami began jerking himself off, as slowly as he could, first by working the flesh up and down on the base of his cock, just the base. He didn't want to come immediately. He might miss something. Like me, for instant.

Baddi was accidentally on purpose rubbing up against me as he thought out loud. "We want to fuck you, Diana," he announced.

"I know," I replied, a little disappointed, "but it's just your lust, it's not really you. It has nothing to do with love and, if it did, I wouldn't know how to receive it, so what's the point of anything?"

Baddi didn't wait for an answer. He reached behind me and took each cheek of my ass in either hand and, pressing his knees forward on my thighs in a kneeling position, he pulled me down about six inches, throwing me completely off balance. Before I realized what was happening, he had entered me with his great primed tool.

"I don't feel a thing," I said.

"How come you're so wet?" was his reply.

"It's an automatic reaction," I said. "It has nothing to do with anything I feel. It's just more lust. It means nothing but animal lust."

Remi apparently carried his own tube of Ky2 jelly, because he grabbed me from behind, kissing me on the back of my neck and shoulders. Then, before I knew what was happening, I felt a greased cylinder of hard cock-flesh working its way up my anal track. The two of them pressed their cocks toward each other. They clearly loved the sense of shared company they got. There was a thin wall of my inner flesh between those cocks, a membrane, really.

"Do you feel anything yet?" asked Baddi.

"I feel something," I said, "but I can't say what exactly."

"Is it physical or emotional?" Remi asked.

"I feel trapped between two big cocks," I answered.

Baddi was fucking me—"Thud. Thud. Thud. Thud." This cock was a big plank hinged to the space between his legs. It meant nothing to me. "Diana," Baddi whispered, "please don't hurt our feelings."

"What feelings?" I said. "I don't feel any feelings in you. All you want is a good fuck."

By now, Baddi was straining. His thrusts were deeper and harder. "Diana, we love you! Why are you doing this to us?"

"I don't know," I answered.

"Maybe if you stopped worrying about your self and concentrated more on us, you'd feel better," said Remi, who was behind me, clearly getting off on my ass. He was sweating profusely. I could feel his balls slapping against the bottom of my cheeks. He was kissing the back of my neck with slurping sounds. How many women, even men, had these boys fucked in the previous twenty-four hours? Why were they hungry for me?

"You have the most beautiful body I have ever seen," Remi, "and I'm not telling you this so I can make love to you, because I'm already making love to you, so why would I flatter you?" "But tell me, what are your needs?" I asked desperately.

"We have no needs at the moment which are not being met," whispered Remi, nibbling my ear.

"No," I cried, "what are your personal, human 'love' needs as opposed to your 'lust' needs, if you know what I mean."

"We don't know what you mean," said Baddi. "You are giving us exactly what we want." They were both heading toward orgasm and I wasn't. Imagine, here were these two deeply caring, intelligent, well-brought-up, well-hung men that most women I know would pay a week's salary apiece for, who were sandwich-fucking me out of the goodness of their hearts in the Roman Colosseum and they meant nothing to me. It was an absolute tragedy. Why just that morning I had thoroughly enjoyed Mr. Buck Johnson's black magic. Now my life was in ashes.

Remi and Baddi came as young men come, their bodies shaking, moaning, gasping for breath, their rivers of sperm gushing deep within me. My own orgasm was a little shiver; that's all. I told them they were terrific, but I didn't fake a fantastic orgasm like so many women do. I was too upset. My life was over. I was only twenty-three.

I put my clothes back on, including the cover-up raincoat I had brought along in case I ran into rain, a religious procession, or one of my aunts from Beavertown. Then I kissed the boys good-bye. Their eyes looked dark and sad and haunted, I had failed them. Of course.

By the following week, after a series of catastrophic events, which I shall describe at the proper time, I came to realize that I had overlooked the anger in those two boys' eyes, a smoldering ember that would burst into the flame of revenge and almost destroy me.

I went back to the Hassler in my raincoat and made a series of calls to Max in Zurich and to Lulu Touché in New York. I had come to a decision. There was a certain English speaking psychiatrist in Rome I had to see at eight o'clock the following morning.

Eight A.M. Dr. Enrico Goldberg's office. A jewel of a room. Parquet floors. Antique Oriental carpets. Cut-crystal doors. Eighteenth-century furniture from Versailles. An Empire sofa for nut cases like me, upholstered in the skin of unborn lamb. Framed diplomas from Oxford, Harvard Medical, and leading hospitals in New York, London, and Zurich. Up close, in the day, it turned out Dr. Enrico had contacts over his watery brown eyes which caused him to blink constantly. As I found out later, he'd been raised an Italian Catholic by his opera singer mother and a Jew by his American industrialist father. This upbringing gave him a brilliant perspective on human nature and a deep division in his personality. The man was a genius, absolutely fascinating and totally fucked up. He told me he knew I'd show up; I had deep personal problems. He could tell from my haunted blue eyes; they reminded him of storms at sea. He looked pretty haggard himself. I doubted that he'd gotten lucky the night before. I told him he had one hour to cure me before I faced the wicked world and my friend Glorianna again. Yes, preproduction meetings were about to begin at Adoro International, and I did not intend to be carted off in a basket because of some dumb employee's remark.

"Dr. Goldberg," I began, "until yesterday morning, I thought I was, well, rich, young, and pretty ... and a pretty good lay. Then, by accident, an employee of mine, who's not as attractive as I am, found me fucking her boyfriend—a man I had not known was her boyfriend—and she said things to me which I know must be truth, because I've been completely depressed ever since. I can't eat or sleep or even have an orgasm worth talking about."

"What did this woman say to you, Diana?" asked Dr. Goldberg.

"She said that I can dish out my brand of love, but it's really lust; it has nothing to do with love. I'm not capable of love because I can't open myself up to the naked heart of an ordinary man. She said all I do is encourage these super-studs to fuck me."

"Is this true?" he asked.

"Is what true, Doctor?"

"Have you ever opened your heart to the heart of an ordinary man?"

I must say I did not like either his question or the tone of his voice.

"Doctor," I began, "I can't help who I'm attracted to. I like stud types and they like me."

131

"But you think this woman employee of yours must be telling you the truth; otherwise, you wouldn't have taken her so seriously."

"Yes."

"All right, please take off your clothes and lie down on my couch."

"Take off my clothes?" I said, aghast.

"I'm a graduate of Harvard Medical School," he replied. "Trust me."

"Why do I have to take off my clothes?" I said.

"I have to know how much of your fantasy about yourself is based on truth," he replied.

"Fantasy about myself?" I repeated.

"Just do as I ask you, Mrs. Adoro, or I can't help you."

I did as he requested. After all, he was the doctor and I was the patient. I was dressed in a white, long-sleeved ribbed-knit tunic dress with a shawl collar. My charm bracelets jingled as I took off my dress and then my underwear. I had a bra I designed myself with panels cut out for the nipples to breathe freely. When I was fully undressed, I looked up at Dr. Goldberg, whose mouth was hanging open.

"Please lie down," he said. "Yes, lie down."

I did as he requested. I could swear from the sounds behind my right ear that he was also getting undressed, but I decided that was my overactive imagination. I thought I heard two shoes fall to the floor. Clunk. Clunk.

"Doctor, can you help me?" I pleaded.

"Tell me the truth," he said. "Do you think you're capable of loving an ordinary man."

"Well, Doctor," I began, "the truth is that because of the way I look, I don't meet many ordinary men. The extraordinary ones get there first."

"What do you mean, the extraordinary ones?" he asked.

"I mean, the men who really like to fuck their brains out. They're mostly super self-confident super-studs.

"How do you think you'd feel if you met an ordinary

132

man—sexually speaking, I mean—who fell in love with you and wanted to make you happy?" he asked.

"I don't know, Doctor," I said. "Like I keep telling you, I don't know any ordinary men."

"Don't you think I'm an ordinary man?" he asked.

"You are?" I replied.

"Yes," he said. And then, suddenly, without warning, there he was in front of me, standing by the side of the couch, facing me, all five feet three of him. The man was built like a brick shithouse; his bulky look came from overdeveloped muscles and baggy clothes. And there was that cock again, which flaccid must have been eight inches long. How could I tell him I had finally met an ordinary man?

"Doctor, you're not really what I'd call an ordinary man," I replied, as his humongous cock began to grow in front of my eyes.

"Tell me the truth," he begged, kneeling by my bed.

"You're very handsome, Doctor," I said. "I can see why you're successful."

"How can you tell me I'm handsome?" he asked. "I'm a freak. No woman wants me. They tell me I'm too big. They tell me I overwhelm them. They say I'm too smart and too hung. They don't want to be impaled on a computer. Help me, Diana. I know you can do it." Before I could properly analyze the turn in events, he sunk his ravenous mouth into my cooze, which was dry from fright, just as his expanding ramrod reached the twelve-inch stage. It seemed about two and half inches across. "Help me, Diana," he implored, as he took a breather. "Tell me I'm not a monster."

"Doctor," I said, "I came here for you to help me. I'm the one who needs help. Why do I have to help you?" He was dry-humping me now, the ridge of his undershaft coursing through my dark honey fur, his finely trained hands stroking my inner thighs, then grabbing my tits.

"I've never seen a body like yours. Never!" he cried.

133

"And I used to be a gynecologist. I've examined thousands of women. Please, please, just let me look at you. I won't touch you. Oh, but I did touch you, didn't I? Diana, I mean, Mrs. Adoro, please trust me, I went to Harvard Medical School, no, no, what I mean to say is, I know I'm deformed, I know I'm a freak; pussies weren't made for cocks like mine, but you, Jesus, if women really looked like you, I'd go back to being a gynecologist. Diana, you don't need a gynecologist, do you?"

"Shut up!!!!" I screamed. "Doctor, I've had enough of this!"

That's when the miracle happened. My intense anger had somehow cleared the air. "Doctor, I feel something!" I shouted. "You must be helping me. I feel something. Do you think if you fucked me, I'd feel anything? Would I still be depressed when it was over?"

Mrs. Adoro, I promise you," he said, "if you let me fuck you, I promise you, you won't be depressed when we're finished." With that, his mouth and his hands were all over my breasts. Yes, something was definitely happening. Yes, I really did feel a little bit of sensation in my nipples. I decided to try a little more anger.

"Doctor, may I have your permission to scream at you?" I asked. He didn't hear me. His tongue was encircling my nipples, first one and then the other. "You pig!" I shouted. "You overhung pig! You ugly beast! Fuck meeee!"

It worked! I felt wonderful! I was ready to feel some more.

"You've got to help me get it in!" he said.

"Get what in?" I asked.

"My cock!" he replied. So, with me pushing up against him, holding onto his cock with both hands, we managed to get his glans past my tight rose-red labia. Thank God I was able to lubricate a little, enough to accommodate him, enough to feel a relaxed little shiver of sexual thrill as he split into me. I just knew that if I could get past my block, I would make Dr. Goldberg my permanent psychiatrist. I could even fly him to New York if the need arose.

"Mrs. Adoro," he cried, "I think I'll cancel all my appointments today. I want to fuck and fuck and fuck you all day. Wait, it's going in!" And so it did. I took eight inches at first.

"Oh, thank you! Thank you!" he cried. "I told you you'd like it. You like it, don't you? Don't you?"

"Oh, Dr. Goldberg," I cried, "I feel better than I've felt all day, but I'm still not cured and I've got a ten o'clock appointment"

"That's good," he said. "You can come back this afternoon and then again tomorrow. This cure may take a month, but you've got to have patience. I know we can do it. But first, please, let me come. Come show me a little love, Mrs. Adoro, that's what you're here for, isn't it— to discover how much you can love."

"Oh fuck!" I thought. "I don't know where I am, but he seems to be helping me, so I better let him have his way."

"Mrs. Adoro, your pussy is so thrilling, so thrilling. You're magic, Mrs. Adoro. Now just take four more inches, please."

"All right, Doctor," I heard myself saying, "I'll try; I'll try."

I tried. Muscles I didn't know were there, and what must have been my cervix opened up, gave way, and an insistent column of hot flesh entered dark areas of mystery deep within me. I felt sensations I did not know I had. I felt glands deep within me begin to function. I was awash with warm juices. I felt touched. I felt cared for. The man was jubilant.

"Mrs. Adoro, I don't feel like a freak anymore! Mrs. Adoro, I don't have to be deformed if you don't want me to be!" His hands were tweaking my nipples, and his mouth on my mouth was out of control as he began to come. He shuddered like a volcano about to erupt. "Aaagh!"

At the crucial moment he withdrew from me and splattered his come between my breasts, a white river from my collar bone to my diaphragm.

"Mrs. Adoro," he cooed afterward, "there's more love in you than you can ever begin to realize; you are a sensational lover; I've never had a lover like you."

"But Dr. Goldberg," I began.

"No 'buts,' " he insisted. "You gave love. That's what you wanted to know, isn't it; whether you can give love?"

"But, Dr. Goldberg . . ." I started to continue.

He cut me off again. "I know, I know," he responded, "You're still blocked. You didn't get that much out of it, did you, but that's why you're here, that's why I went to Harvard and Oxford and Columbia Presbyterian and the Jung Institute. Psychic growth takes time, a lot of time. Just think, Mrs. Adoro, in twenty minutes you've restored my confidence as a man. I've never had a better fuck. In fact, you're so terrific, I'm only going to charge you a hundred dollars a session. How does that sound?"

"Thank you, Doctor," I said, putting my clothes back on. "I do feel a little better and don't worry about your lovelife, I know plenty of women who would do anything to accommodate that cock of yours."

I left Dr. Goldberg thinking that although I did feel a little better, I still didn't know what was wrong with me. I promised to see him again at two that afternoon.

Part of my morning meeting in the Hassler's small conference rooms was to interview the local Roman models, particularly the young men who had been hired in advance by a local modeling agency for my fashion show. One of my big ideas was to use some local Adonises, about twenty of them, dress them as gladiators with shields, helmets, and leather jock straps, and have them stand around like living statues inside the Colosseum. I planned to plant the two or three best-looking on the stage itself. All of this male semi-nudity was designed to be a turn-on for women and gays, who together comprised about ninety percent of our audience. I also wanted some Roman women, "local types" was how I described them over the phone to the agency. I had a fantasy of big-bosomed, sad-eyed creatures with wild hair who looked about five months pregnant. Where I got that idea I don't know; must have been from Cecil B. DeMille in the fourth grade. The girls were my first stop. Conference Room A. Alas and alack, as my great-grandmother used to say, the agency sent me more blue-eyed blondes, Eurasians, and American blacks, all constructed like human gazelles. I instructed my Roman assistant Eduardo to pay the girls a day's wages and dismiss them.

In the next room, Conference Room B, were the young men. They were supposed to be stripped down to jock straps so I could see what I was paying for. This time the agency knew what it was doing. These macho studs were not only muscle-bound, they were straight arrows. At the sight of me with my tits bouncing under my bra-less tunic, more than one jock strap began to bulge. "It's too bad I'm so depressed," I thought to myself. "It's too bad I'm not a real woman. Otherwise, I might be in the mood for a gang bang."

I had to stop myself; I was revealing in sick, impersonal sexual fantasies. Thank God I was now in therapy; there was a chance I might be cured. The male models were making me dizzy. I was depressed; I had sick fantasies, and right in front of me was a roomful of everything I had always wanted but didn't know what to do with anyway, so what difference did it make? Now I knew why my Aunt Alice became an alcoholic; my mother always said we were just alike. I had to force myself to attend to the point of the conference room assembly: work, business, dollars and cents. Yes, another business idea was forming in my mind. At the end of the fashion show, right after the girls had taken their bows, I would have the "gladiators" strip off their leather belts and hold them above their heads, along with their swords and shields, utterly stark naked; in that way, with one startling image, I could make a symbolic statement about the marriage of Roman gentility and barbarian wildness. That was how I wanted my clothes to look and my women to feel—like they were half-empress, half-wild. Lena, my assistant, seemed concerned. She kept counting cocks, I mean men.

"What's wrong?" I asked. "Why do you keep counting these boys?"

"We asked for twenty," she said. "There are only eighteen here." When she questioned some of the men, most of whom were staring at me as she talked with strange smiles on their faces, she learned that Conference B had an inner room, a dressing room, where the two other male models and "the tall American woman" had gone to discuss international politics, or so they said. With this last remark, I could see that leer again; it was widespread.

The door to the dressing room was locked from the inside, but Lena had the key to every door we had rented. We opened the door. I couldn't believe my eyes! The great Glorianna, the cause of all my recent emotional problems was on her knees stripped to the waist, tit-fucking Remi Scarlatti, his never-ending Italian sausage looking as big in the light as it had felt in the dark of the Colosseum the night before! Glorianna, smiling, kept her eyes closed as she savored the feel of his ripe glans, wet with its own lubricant, coursing up and down the channel of flesh between the fullness of her breasts, which were altogether riper and more gorgeous than I cared to know. If I hadn't disliked Glorianna so intensely I might have been attracted to her on the basis of her tits alone. Her nipples reminded me of dark caramels they stuck out so darkly. Clearly, along with her so-called Cherokee ancestry, there was African blood in her lineage; dark nipples are proof of that. Many aristocratic European women, especially upper-class Italians, have, I have noticed (from watching them try on my designer gowns, of course), the oversized dusky aureoles of Egypt and Zanzibar. It seems that during the Renaissance, the European courts prided themselves on their blue-black boys who looked so splendid in

138

their bright brocaded uniforms. It seems that the women at court decided they looked even better buck-naked in bed after too many unsuccessful tries with the inbred bodies of effeminate courtiers. And so, it seems, according to legend, during the nights of the Renaissance, the majesty of Africa entered into the bloodlines of Europe in a big way.

Looking at Glorianna, that arrogant Midwestern snob, who probably didn't even know about her fantastic ancestors and her heritage of unbridled lust, I got so angry I found it difficult to breathe. If I hadn't hated her so much, I would have been merely jealous. As it was, I was merely consumed with rage. Something in me snapped. First, this cunt turns out to be the live-in girlfriend of my first great passion, Angelo O'Shaughnessy (cf. *Diana's Desire*). Then, she just happens to be the top model and ongoing lover for my beloved husband, Adolfo. Then, she just happens to be upstairs in the house of the black stud documentary filmmaker Buck Johnson, when I'm downstairs fucking him on his living room couch, which apparently gave her the right to try and destroy my spirit. As if all that wasn't enough, she now steals my pickup from the streets, Remi Scarlatti!

Even this I could have forgiven her, if I had thought that she was flat-chested, if I had thought that, at root, she was no competition for the likes of me. I could have indulged her. I could have kept her on staff with a quiet smile on my lips, imagining how desperate she was, how disappointed her lovers must have been with that cold ironing board of a body. Now, all that had changed. Rage? I felt a column of fire start at the base of my spine and travel right up through the top of my head. Everything had changed. Glorianna was now my arch-rival, an object of extreme hatred. Now, I finally understood why men found her so irresistible. Dressed, she was a streamlined machine, a robot, a greyhound, a mannequin. Undressed, her naked body screamed of longing and desire. It spoke of raw sex and unfulfilled appetite. Her breasts hung just enough to suggest experience. Her rib cage protruded just enough to intimate that she needed to be held and protected. Then, there were those dark exotic nipples, rampantly erect, begging to be sucked and fondled, and a thick black bush which framed more than a mouthful of exposed labia. The prepuce on her clitoris alone looked like an overripe fig that had burst open in the Roman sun, its delicious flesh waiting to be sucked clean of its incomparable nectar. There had always been rumors that her cunt hole could hold any cock and suck it like a python devouring its prey. Yes, Glorianna had a reputation; obviously, it was based on fact. If I hadn't hated her so much, I would have lain down on the floor under her cunt and made her sit on my face. Not that I was particularly attracted to her as a person; there was just no way I could separate her person from her cunt. Remi was not even aware that I was in the room. He kept pumping away in between her tits, each pump becomming breathier, evoking animal sounds from him. His cock became so red and thick I thought it was going to burst; his glans was purple from blood and desire.

I could contain myself no longer. I have never been a voyeur and nobody is ever going to call me one. I leapt on Remi, forcefully pulled him off Glorianna, and dove for his glistening lead pipe of a cock. At that very moment, he exploded, right into my mouth. That's when Glorianna opened her eyes.

"What are you doing in here?" she shrieked. "Get out! Get out!"

I was enjoying my little victory (and my midday snack) so much I couldn't stop smiling. "Glorianna, dear," I purred, "this happens to be the men's dressing room, a room I'm paying the rent on; and in case you've forgotten the facts of life, you working girl, I'm also paying the rent on you! Give me any more trouble, shove your glistening cunt in any more of my men's faces, and you can go back to selling toilet paper in the five-and-dime!"

Her response was more than I could take. "You'll never be a real woman, Diana; you're just a ruthless competitor. You just want to win at any cost!"

"Glorianna, you pig!" I screamed." Get out of here! I've had it! You're fired!"

"You can't fire me!" she shrieked. "I own five percent!"

"You'll get your checks in the mail!" I shouted back. "Just don't show your fucking face in here again!"

With that, I marched into the powder room off the dressing room to wash out my mouth. I was shaking. Glorianna wouldn't quit.

She called after me. "You can't talk to me that way, you little whore! That's right! This, this whore slept her way to the top. She fucked every man in New York to get where she got!"

"And I enjoyed every fucking minute of every fuck!" I shouted back. I was triumphant. I felt terrific. I felt great. I never felt better in my life. As a matter of fact, my head was cleared! I couldn't wait to tell Dr. Goldberg! I was cured! Still, there was Glorianna to deal with. Her rage was mounting.

"But the men never come back to her. They fuck her once and that's it!" She cried.

That remark got me out of the bathroom. "Oh, yes, they come back to me!" I shouted. "Maxey comes back to me and so did my Adolfo. And so did plenty of others I can't talk about without getting them and me in trouble!"

"Aren't you tough!" she cried.

"Yeah, tough titties!" I said and I slugged her just like that. I couldn't help it. I gave it to her right in the jaw. Glorianna looked dazed. I let her have it in the solar plexus. She couldn't breathe. She doubled over. She thought she was going to die. Remi ran to her side.

"She'll live," I remarked as casually as I could and went back to the powder room to wash my hands.

That's when Baddi entered the dressing room with his loaves of bread and bottles of wine for what was clearly

141

food for the "three-way" with Remi and Glorianna. He obviously thought he was alone with them. Too alone. His first line drove a stake into my heart.

"Somebody should tell that cunt Diana Adoro we don't take no orders from whores! Hey, Remi, you know that whore we fucked last night at the Colosseum; that's Diana Adoro who's in charge of this fashion show. I saw her publicity pictures. You know, we could fuck up her whole show if we wanted to; we could take it away from her."

There was a whispering sound, followed by a painful silence. I walked out of the powder room with tears in my eyes. "Remi, you're fired. Baddi. Glorianna. All fired. Get out."

The boys were ashen. Glorianna was livid. "You can't fire me. I own five percent!"

"You're fired," I said.

Baddi had a few things to say. "If you fire us," he fumed, "we'll fire you. Your fashion show will go up in flames!"

"What did I do to you?" I asked.

"No *putana* gives orders to Remi and Baddi."

"Is that what I am, a *putana*?" I asked.

"You're worse; you're a *putana* who does it for *nada*, for nothing."

"I expect respect from my employees," I said, furious.

"See! See!" said Glorianna, "that's what she thinks of us—employees. We're not even persons. We're not even fashion models. We're just employees. She wouldn't know what a person was if her life depended on it. She's a cold-hearted New York bitch who's fucked her way to the top. Go out and spread the news! Tell everyone in Rome! Diana Adoro the most successful hooker who ever lived!"

"What's a hooker?" asked Baddi, snickering. The three of them were giggling. I prayed for them to choke on their laughter. Remi, who had been observing our wrangling as his flagpole of a cock relaxed, dripping its last drops of come, turned on me. His face was an ugly shade of red. He was so angry he spat when he spoke.

"You whore! You American whore! Everything is money to you! Capitalistic swine!" He was so angry, I was having trouble following his thought. How could I be a whore? Did I charge money for sex? He was the whore, wasn't he?"

"Get out," I ordered. "Get out this instant before I call the police, and take your fuckin' cocks with you."

The two boys left guffawing. Glorianna grabbed her robe and burst into tears. She fled the room half naked with her bountiful tits bouncing in front of her.

I felt terrific. I couldn't wait for two o'clock to tell Dr. Goldberg I'd been cured, that I'd faced up to the Voice of Guilt, that I'd talked back to Glorianna. I was ecstatic. I felt freer than I had since the day I first got off the bus from Beavertown. Now, I could return love. I just knew I could. I could even love Dr. Goldberg. I could thank him in my special way.

Chapter Eight

By 2:05 P.M. Dr. Goldberg and I were back on his lambskin couch. I was waiting for the right moment to tell him. I couldn't wait to take his entire filet mignon of prime cock into me. I knew I would have the biggest orgasm of my life. At the sight of it, I began to lubricate. Yes, as soon as we saw each other, we tore off each other's clothes. My heart went out to this dear, overeducated, fucked-up Harvard psychiatrist who hadn't a clue as to who he was. Not a clue. The money he was getting was, apparently, supposed to tell him something about himself, but if money talks, it had nothing to say to Dr. Goldberg. His body looked different to me this time. It seemed much more attractive. He was stocky and his skin was unmarked except for pale freckles. His thinning hair had a red wash and gold highlights in the afternoon sun. Even his eyes looked clearer and calmer and infinitely sexier. He must have removed his contact lenses. Dr. Goldberg had wonderful stomach muscles, too.

145

Suddenly, I loved this man. He was trying so hard to help me even if he didn't know what he was doing

"Mrs. Adoro, you're so beautiful, I can't stand it," he began.

"Please call me Diana," I said.

"Oh, no, no, that wouldn't do," he replied, drawing circles around my nipples with his fingertips, causing me excruciating delight.

"You can't call me Diana?" I said. "Why not?"

No. no, my dear Mrs. Adoro, we must preserve our lines of authority, musn't we?"

"Oh yes, Doctor," I said, "whatever you say; please fuck me." It just came out like that.

"Mrs. Adoro," he began, "I've had three patients since I saw you this morning, including two suicide attempts and someone who's dying of a dread disease. And all I could think about was your ass and your muff with that precious flower of a cunt. Please let me put it in an inch, just an inch."

"But I want all of you, Dr. Goldberg," I replied. "I know I can make you happy because I'm happy."

"You're happy?" he said, surprised. "Do you want to talk about it?" As he was talking, he was pushing his huge glans into me. I wondered if I'd be able to accommodate him again. Finally, finally, his third leg was one inch inside me. I began to rotate on it, pulling it into me with both hands.

"I know you think you're cured, Mrs Adoro," Dr. Goldberg said. My patients always think they're cured; that is, until they slip back—that's why we have to keep meeting twice a day, every day. Ooooh, Mrs. Adoro, oooh Jesus, that feels good. Oh, you're so wonderful."

"I know, Doctor, I know. I love you. You're so dear. You're so sweet," I cried.

"We can discuss this," he said. "In psychological terms it's called transference. It means the therapy is working and working fast. Oooooh! Ooooh! I can't stand it. You're

146

so delicious. You're so wonderful. Hold me. Just hold me."

I could barely talk. That locomotive cock of his was almost completely inside me. Every inch of my flesh was screaming with pleasure. Every nerve ending was on fire; I felt an incandescent glow. This man, this terrible, wonderful man was responsible for my happiness. "Doctor, Doctor," I called out, hoping to explain to him what had happened to me before my orgasm, which was imminent, overwhelmed me. I could feel it coming.

"Doctor, I got angry at the cunt who made me depressed. I found her fucking two more men who, strictly speaking, belonged to me, sort of, and I lost my temper. Not only that, I decked her! Dr. Goldberg, I feel wonderful! I don't feel depressed anymore!"

We began to shudder together, our mutual orgasm came in such violent spasms I thought his rumbling cock would rip my insides out. I could feel my blood in tidal waves, my nervous system spewing out of every pore. But through it all, my labia held onto their man.

He kept repeating, "Oh, Mrs. Adoro, Mrs. Adoro, please marry me! No, I know it's just lust but I've got to have you; I've been so deprived of lust, I've got to have lust, to hell with sensitivity. No, no, I didn't really mean that. We're here to talk about sensitivity. Ooooh! Ooooh! Aaagh!"

Then there was silence; He fell into a light sleep. During that five minutes I managed, somehow, to slip out from around the fire hose inside me, wipe myself off with the Kleenex on his desk that he normally reserved for tear jags, and get myself dressed.

When, after five minutes, he opened one eye and saw me dressed, he remarked "Is your time up?"

No, Doctor," I replied. "I 've got ten minutes. I wanted to talk to you."

"Please marry me," he repeated. "We can have therapy three times a day and I won't charge you a thing. You'll see how much better you feel."

I appreciated his lovely offer, but I knew what I had to do. "Doctor," I announced, "I'm cured."

He snapped to attention. Mrs. Adoro, I have to warn you again that thinking you're cured is a common misconception of patients who have just begun analysis. We have to discuss your childhood, your father, your mother, how many times you had sexual intercourse with them . . ."

"Dr. Goldberg," I continued, "today, I took care of my problem, one that has haunted me almost since the day I arrived in New York. Her name is Glorianna. When I blew up at her today, I kept getting flashes of my mother and grandmother and older sister and Mrs. Pilgrim, my high school principal, and all the women I've known who have made nasty remarks to me suggesting I'm a slut because I love a good fuck."

"But, Mrs. Adoro," Dr. Goldberg went on, "loving a good fuck is not the same thing as loving an individual man. True happiness can only come when . . ."

"Doctor," I interrupted, "I felt a wall of fire go up my back and out the top of my head when I blew up at that witch. I tell you I am cured. For the first time in my life I feel guilt-free about sex. So, now I'm going to get some experience."

"What do you mean, 'experience'?" he asked. "You're not ready for experience, Mrs. Adoro; you need at least a year of intensive therapy."

"Dr. Goldberg," I announced, "I plan to enjoy my womanhood for the first time in my life. I plan to share it with the world. The operative word is Love!"

"Love? What are you talking about?" he said, wiping the come off the end of his big, white, python cock.

I was so happy I must have seemed a little odd to him. Dr. Goldberg," I announced, "I have three whole days to kill before I have to start rehearsals and I'm going to fulfill my oldest fantasy, because I'm in the perfect city to do it; the Eternal City of Eternal Love—Roma!"

"You're going to become a nun?" he asked, with eyebrows raised and eyes wide open. "Don't do it, Mrs. Adoro—even for three days!"

"Doctor!" I shouted, "I'm going to become a whore!" He knew he'd heard wrong. "Yes, but of course, Mrs. Adoro—what did you say? I must be hearing my own subconscious. I thought you said . . ."

"I did! Doctor, I'm going to become a whore! For three whole days, I'm going to return love to all the poor, lonely men who come to me, whoever they are. Yes, Dr. Goldberg, I will love them. I will enjoy them. I will enjoy my womanhood at last! Fuck Glorianna! Fuck my mother! Fuck Mrs. Pilgrim! I'm free at last!"

Dr. Goldberg was absolutely dumbstruck. "Mrs. Adoro, you're obviously still so angry you can't possibly be doing this for the right reasons. You're going to allow all sorts of strange men, some of whom may subconsciously actually hate women . . ."

"Actually, subconsciously, Dr. Goldberg, I'm confident I can handle myself."

"I'm not sure that's true, Mrs. Adoro."

"I handled you, Dr. Goldberg. In my darkest hour, I handled you."

"But, Mrs. Adoro . . . what about our Judeo-Christian heritage . . . ?"

"Don't rain on my parade, Dr. Goldberg."

With that, I picked myself up and went out into the bustling city of Rome, grateful for the sun and happy to be alive. I couldn't wait to begin the next adventure of my life.

Chapter Nine

My only whoring experience, despite what some people have accused me of, had been strictly vicarious, One of my best girlfriends in Beavertown, Mary Beth O'Malley, had been a hooker on weekends in Youngstown, Ohio, which was about an hour away. Eventually, her "profession" did her in one Saturday night when she accidentally screwed her grandfather O'Malley. It wasn't really her fault. She hadn't seen him since she was about four when the family stopped speaking to him. They claimed he was a card-carrying Communist since he was militantly against the Americans defending Western Civilization in Vietnam. Mary Beth saw his name when he tried to pay her with his American Express card. She had no doubts. How many Aloysius O'Malleys can there be in that part of the world? Well, poor Mary Beth had a semi-nervous breakdown and had to spend everything she had earned as a hooker on a New York psychiatrist, who she was convinced was a flat-out queer, since at a time when she was really vulnerable and needed the affection of an understanding man he wouldn't go to bed with her. Instead, he kept telling her that women who fucked and sucked every passing cock, starting with milkman and ending with the psychiatrist, whether they did it for money or gave it away, were completely lacking in basic identity and would end up like Marilyn Monroe; that is, a dead movie star at thirty-six. Two weeks after he told her that, he blew his brains out. May he rest in peace.

The question: What was the best whorehouse in Rome? For the answer, I had Lena, my American assistant, ask Eduardo, my Roman assistant. I had Eduardo ask the bellhop. I had the bellhop ask the night manager. I had the night manager ask Carlo the doorman. Carlo wanted to know who wanted to know. So, I finally had to ask Carlo myself. What was the best whorehouse in Rome? There was only one answer: Mrs. Boothby's, three hundred yards from the Spanish Steps.

To be sure, there were call-girl services with Radcliffe graduates who looked like Charley's Angels and who could speak seven languages. These girls could accompany European princes, American statesmen, and Japanese businessmen to any restaurant in Rome. Sometimes they even stood by their sides when they shook hands with the Pope. There were sado-masochism clubs with dominatrixes in four-inch heels who would tie up a man and beat him with whips and chains until he got off. There was just about anything for just about any price. But when it came to whores, most guys wanted something basic—they just wanted to have a good time. According to Carlo, Mrs. Boothby's was the place I was looking for, Rome's most traditional whorehouse and one of its most expensive. Prices started, in American money, at a hundred and fifty dollars an hour. Also, it was convenient. Mrs. Boothby's was less than three hundred yards from the bottom of the Spanish Steps, which made it a stone's throw from the Hassler. Carlo claimed he could "make arrangements" for any customer I had in mind. When I told him

152

what I had in mind, and could he please help me, the man did not bat an eyelash; for a hundred dollars, no questions asked, he wrote me a letter of recommendation. Like I say, no questions asked, but the man looked at me with desire; I wanted to ask him up to my room, but I decided if he really wanted me, he could come to Mrs. Boothby's. Why not?

I left the Hassler for Mrs. Boothby's wearing a long-sleeved see-through black blouse that showed off my size 36C tits to perfection. I should know; I designed it myself. I had two tiny eyelets embroidered on the front for my nipples to stick through. Not the aureoles, just the nipples. There is still such a thing as good taste. Most people seeing me on the street naturally assumed I had two pink polka dots on the front of my black blouse. But any man standing close enough to smell me knew without a shadow of a doubt. Pink buds, semi-erect, begging to be favored with his kiss. Am I being sentimental? Good. The rest of me did the nipples one better. I'm surprised I didn't get arrested in the Hassler lobby. Red silk hot-pants and black patent-leather high-heeled boots. The hot-pants were see-through, too. You could see my bush right through them. It looked like a dark shadow. No, let's face it, it looked like a bush. And that wasn't all. My hot-pants were so tight, the slit in my vulva was visible from across the street!

The Spanish Steps; what can I say? The world's most desperate pickups of all sexes wait there for hours hoping some dark and attractive stranger, preferably male, and hopefully rich, will take them home for the night. The boys stand around provocatively in silk pants that are tighter than skin, their semi-erect genitals protruding, their asses as firm and ripe as perfect peaches ready to be sucked, eaten, devoured. Maybe that's why in Beavertown, we called these boys "fruits." But here, they'd just as soon make it with a woman if she's rich enough to afford them and bold enough to ask their price, which averages around fifty dollars for the night. It usually takes a rich American

153

widow, a woman who's somewhere between her first face-lift and her first stroke, who's hungry for the kind of male body she can't beg, borrow, or steal at her local country club without causing a scandal.

When I began my descent down the Spanish Steps I was pursued by these male prostitutes with their over-stuffed crotches and too-tight pants that sudden growth had split up their backside and across their rippling thighs, young muscles covered with coarse hair and sweat. I thank the gods every day for giving me such a fantastic ass. I really love to be paid attention to. Money and business success mean nothing if people don't think you are sexy. After all, according to my favorite psychic, originally a Presbyterian, "the only reason God put us on this earth is so we can fuck our brains out! What else is there?" The boys with the crotches on the Spanish Steps taunted me in Italian, which I didn't understand, and English, which I did. "Hey, babee, let's fuck!" "How much you charge?" "Wowee! Wowee!"

As happy as I was to be noticed by so many attractive young gentlemen, I made it down the steps, across the Via due Macelli, and down the Via dei Condotti to Mrs. Boothby's, a sober-looking palace of dark gray cut granite, just as a tall young German lad, strictly S.S., put his aggressive hand between my legs, sticking a stout index finger into my slit as he dry-humped me, his hard mound of an erection palpable against my ass; all this in the space of fifteen seconds. Luckily, I had already knocked on Mrs. Boothby's ancient bronze doors, which opened just in time. I was shocked to see a nun standing in front of me, a Sister of Charity, no less, with her enormous starched white headdress flaring out like doves in flight.

"Sister?" I said, staring in disbelief. The boy with the hard-on stopped. He must have seen her, too. How could he miss?

"Sister" was a German, too. I know because she said, "Vat ist dis?" as she pushed my left nipple like a doorbell. That's when I noticed her double row of false eyelashes. If this wasn't Mrs. Boothby's it was a reasonable facsimile thereof.

"I've come to work," I said. I've got a letter for Guido from Carlo at the Hassler!"

"Carlo?" She looked wide-eyed at me. Definite recognition. "Come vit me."

The S.S. guard with the erection was now kissing my neck, but he was no match for Mother Maybelline. She confronted him. "Ve charge von huntret dollars un hour. Pay me now if you vish to come in." Then she repeated herself in German and this time she sounded angry. So did he. He was clearly used to being paid for his services. Faster than a speeding bullet, he whipped his cock out of his pants—a long, beet-red cock framed by a thick golden halo—and began to whack off in her face. She slammed the ancient bronze doors in his face just as the first huge glop of sperm arced in the Roman twilight and landed on the back of her black skirt. Her shriek coincided with the sound of door clanging shut.

She looked at me and muttered, "Gottamn tourists!" Then she led me up a grand red-carpeted staircase into the bowels of life itself.

But first, some background on Mrs. Boothby's, my home for the next three days. Mrs. Charlotte Boothby was, according to the story, an enterprising Maine Yankee who went to Rome in 1923 because so many nouveau riche Americans thought it beat the Poconos for having a good time. The truth is, she'd been thrown out of Bar Harbor for running a whorehouse where one of the Rockefellers allegedly got the clap. She figured that since Rome appealed to so many well-heeled, high-rolling, big-spending "boys" she might as well take a crack at providing them with a house where someone spoke English and knew how to make change for a dollar. It worked. For three decades, until Mrs. Boothby's death from an aneurysm in the mid-Fifties, while allegedly giving a blow job to the ex-king of Rumania, Mrs. Boothby's was a whorehouse with live music, great food, free booze, an attendant nurse, and the happiest hookers since the invention of pay sex. The house, formerly a palace of the Orsini family, had ten girls and ten bedrooms. That was it. Each girl had to be between fifteen and thirty, between five feet and five-six, with thick hair, perfect teeth, perfect skin, full breasts between 34D and 40C, and a pussy so tight that each year every girl was required to pass a test where she had to pick up her five-hundred-dollar Christmas bonus with her pussy lips from the hand of Mrs. Boothby herself. If she couldn't manage, it was good-bye bonus, good-bye girl. The next step was the streets. Either that or find a husband quick. Such were the ways of the world. Mrs. Boothby's had girls of every race and nationality, but the overall effect was the same: ripe, young, and golden.

Mrs. Boothby made an irrevocable decision early on: if certain men were turned on by frigid, flat-chested, forty-year-old dominatrixes (what do you think it means?), or by ten-year-old girls, sorry, they'd have to go somewhere else. She knew the average man wanted tits and ass and a tight pussy wrapped up with a pretty face and a smile. She wasn't against sexual variety; she just wanted to be known for a certain time-tested product. After all, she had men dropping in from all over the world. After her death, her half-Italian niece, Titti Boothby, took over. Titti was four-eleven and from all reports a raging nymphomaniac. She was the "free dessert," as she liked to put it, and she loved the clergy best of all; she said they fucked like satyrs, purely from lust. In the Sixties, however, Mrs. Boothby's hit hard times. Titti, after twelve abortions, was seeing a shrink, and, let's face it, the Pill had turned the girl next door into Annie Available and Come-and-Get-It Connie. By the Seventies, Italy had recovered nicely from World War Two; there was an Italian jet set and the average Milanese industrialist had more cock than he knew what to do with. Titti Boothby's Italian husband and all-round stud, Guido ("The Guide" and in more ways than one), who spoke halting, broken

English, brought the place back. Titti, was now in her fifties; nobody had seen her for years. The story was that she locked herself on the top floor with her vibrator and her back issues of *Playgirl*; more reliable sources said she had simply run out of steam and had gone off to live in Arizona with a new husband.

In any case, Guido spent most of his day and night in his back bedroom on the second floor interviewing prospective employees. Guido was called "Guido Cavallo," which, roughly translated, means "Guido the horse"; this name was given to him shortly after puberty when it was obvious to every woman he bedded down that the combination of his genital equipment, his animal heat, and his physical appetite for sex would make him the erotic legend of his time. There were whispers among the Colosseum crew, from whom I got most of my information, that Guido, for a fee and sometimes for free, performed sodomy on both men and women clients alike. In the era of women's rights, they were encouraged to come and enjoy Mrs. Boothby's whores, too. If they made themselves available to the customers, presuming they looked the part, they could be considered temporary employees. Gradually, the entire setup got to be a little too dark and sometimes a little too raunchy for the likes of a Henry Ford II or the Rockefeller cousins. Sometimes, they still landed a Kennedy, although the Kennedys, when they came, had to pay double in advance, since they had a reputation for getting into fights and tearing the place apart. All in all, Madame Boothby's, in an age of so-called sexual liberation, under the expert direction of Horsecock Guido, became successful again. It was the ultimate in debauchery, the Palace of Sin. Dark, a little bit dirty, smelling of bodies and peopled with nymphomaniacs desperate to be fucked, it was all deliberate. The music was gone and so was the food. Hard liquor was available; so was cocaine; so was heroin. Guido took care of the local police. Like I say, it was all deliberate; it was all desired. Men in the Eighties were sick of women with

157

PhD's who couldn't stop talking politics, even in bed. Even the women were sick of that particular breed. Everyone, it seemed, was looking for peasant girls with tits and ass, for whom fucking was mankind's noblest achievement.

I knew that if I could make it at Mrs. Boothby's, I would never again have to worry about sexually competitive women like Glorianna. I knew that once these Gucci–Pucci girls heard I had worked at Mrs. Boothby's they would gag from jealousy; although they would pretend to disapprove on moral or religious grounds, it wouldn't do them any good. I would finally have the satisfaction of knowing that when push comes to shove, sexually speaking, of course, I could compete with the professionals. The sorry truth is, that even though I have always seemed sexually liberated, able to make it with any man who wanted me, at bottom I have always felt like a rank amateur, a girl from the country. I never thought that I was in the same league with European women, especially the French and Italians, who exude the wisdom and mystery of sex. I decided that if I could make it in a Roman whorehouse I would never again have to doubt my sexuality.

Well, I'd made it inside the front door and up the grand staircase. I couldn't wait to see what would happen next. Going up the stairs we passed a girl in a see-through harem outfit going down, leading what looked like an American used-car salesman in a light-blue seersucker suit and red plaid bow tie to the front door. Her tits were magnificent, better than mine. I found myself staring at those pointed globes, wondering how they kept their miraculous shape, pointing upward at their ends, bouncing gently as she descended each successive step. If I were not so passionately heterosexual I would have let go of my semen-stained "nun" and rushed that girl, right there on that staircase, with one continuous motion ripping off her harem costume and planting my hungry mouth on her golden skin, devouring her inch by inch, mouthful by mouthful, until I came. I would have dived for her vulva, which seemed almost as plump and juicy as her breasts. In that moment I cursed my nearsightedness and my rampant heterosexuality. I just knew that when I got close enough to smell her cunt-musk, close enough to taste the juices of her well-practiced fuck-flesh I would drown in the delicate orchid of her vagina, or was it my own passion that would do me in? It seemed in that moment that my mouth and her cunt were one continuous bond of flesh; the unseen become visible—but sanity prevailed. I realized with a start that I had no real driving appetite for girls; "*tant pis*," as we say in Beavertown. The great temptation passed, at least for the moment.

For five minutes the "nun" led me down dark corridors that smelled of marijuana and Southern Comfort and sex to a back room. The door was open. She pushed me in and then deserted me, closing the door behind me. The room was a bedroom paneled in dark mahogany; the ceiling panels were Victorian oil paintings: fat naked goddesses lying on clouds with their fat white legs wide apart, their cunts merely pink shadows at the southern end of their fat tummies. The double bed was mahogany, too. There was scant light in the room; heavy red-velvet draperies saw to that. Guido was lying on the bed, half-asleep, his hand on his half-erect cock. I could scarcely believe my eyes. He was pure animal! He was about forty, a swarthy man with olive skin and a bushy black beard, every muscle hard and prominent, not from lifting weights, but clearly from something in his glands, something decreed by nature. He was covered with black body hair and his bush rose like a black pyramid to his navel; a black column of hair, in turn, ascended from his navel to the black forest completely covering his massive chest. And the genitals! Unbelievable! His testicles hung like two large chicken eggs in their dark, downy sack; on such a body as I've described, how could his cock be anything less than massive? Even half-erect, that cock had a weight and a presence that dominated the rest of his body. I knew that once he caught sight of me he would rip my clothes off, so I decided to undress before he got the chance. The half-opened black eyes must have caught the blur of motion of me undressing. Suddenly, he was wide awake and, seeing me, gave out a yelp.

"Signor Guido," I began, speaking as quickly as possible. "My name is Diana Hunt [my maiden name]; I want to work for you; I'm a waitress, but all the waitresses here are waiters, so I need a job. Here is my letter of recommendation from Carlo at the Hassler." I was trying to sound as businesslike as possible.

Guido grabbed the letter and quickly read it, reaching out hungrily to feel me up, his free hand already kneading my ass, his cock already fully erect; I knew I would be accepted by him.

"I don't take drugs, not really; I've got an IUD in place; I've never been pregnant, and I've never had the clap!" I announced to him joyfully as he finished the letter, threw it aside, and looked up at me like the most devout Italian priest looking up at a vision of the Virgin Mary.

"Mama mia!" he said. Then, like a king cobra who has just struck without warning, his mouth was exploring my breasts. I could feel my nipples so aroused I thought they were going to burst their flesh. His tongue drew deep circles around and around each inflamed nipple as his mammoth cock, with a mind and a will of its own, rose up to its full height and met my shaggy mound. For a moment he wouldn't let me descend onto him. He wouldn't let me grasp the huge head of his cock with my practiced labia. Oh, how I wanted to impale myself on him! I wanted him to think of me as his best little girl. But no, he wanted me to suffer first. He ground his hairy torso against my breast, the black wires of his chest hair were like live wires touching every nerve ending in my breasts. *"Mama mia! Mama mia!"* he kept repeating.

"Are they all right, Guido?" I asked, playing dumb, knowing full well my tits were mounds of molten honey, irresistible to all, even to fags. Guido responded to my question with a hot kiss, his mouth burying itself in mine, his animal lust filling me with desire.

"Oooooh!" he squealed as he pulled me down, finally impaling me on his battering ram. I was ecstatic! Maybe Glorianna was right; maybe I had forgotten the raw power of the opposite sex. If so, Guido was guiding me back home again. My cunt-lips parted to admit his bulkhead. They had no choice. He was ravishing me; my flesh opened before his animal force. His thrusts rose up and down from his torso with the power of a hydraulic piston driving deeper and deeper into me as we writhed together on the bed, standing, kneeling, rolling, our fists grabbing onto each other's bodies as we sucked, first flesh, then air, moaning, making death rattle sounds, whining, whispering over and over, "I love you! I love you!" *"Te adoro, Guido." "Te adoro Deean."* His rhythm gathered in its intensity and we made horrendous sucking sounds.

At that moment I was in love with that absolute stranger, this imperial animal, this Roman pimp who had probably fucked every woman who had ever entered his room. I was bitterly ashamed, but, in truth, I was more proud of my degradation than I was of my reputation in the business world. I came in a succession of overlapping orgasms so layered in their complexity I could not tell where one ended and the other began. I was half-unconscious, overcome by the power of orgasm. My insides shook with release, again and again. When Guido came, with a tremendous spasm, I felt the barrage of his sperm—white bullets firing into me. The ammunition melted inside my furnace and began to ooze down my legs, glistening wet in the glare of the bedside light. Guido withdrew his broad-beamed tool, still formidable, still half-erect.

Finally, after gazing at me with furious intensity for some time, he spoke in his glorious broken English: "You are she tiger," he said, and "Promise me you never you leave the room; I keep you in jail."

"I want to work for you, Guido, "I announced, again

nibbling on his lower lip, barely grazing his skin.

"Work?" he queried, amazed. "Why you work? You be my lover, no?"

"Guido, my darling," I explained as best I could in my simplest English as I licked the shimmering lacquer off his cock. "Guido, I don't expect you to understand what I have to tell you, but, my darling, it is important for me, for my self-confidence, my self-respect, that I know I am not a middle-class American girl who's become promiscuous; what we call an 'easy lay.' I have to know I'm a woman that men will pay a small fortune to be with, if they have to. I have to know I can satisfy men who are willing to pay for something better than a roll in the hay with a hatcheck girl."

Guido looked straight through me with his intense black eyes. *"Carissima, you want to be whore?"*

Well, that word threw me; it's so, so patriarchal, or something. "Whore?" I said, taken aback.

"Sí, you want to be whore?"

I realized Guido could understand what I was saying only on his own terms. What was the point of arguing subtleties? Of course, I didn't want to be a whore, as such. I didn't have to be a whore, as such. I didn't need the money and I didn't need the sex. I could have all the sex I wanted—for nothing. My whole intention of being hired at Mrs. Boothby's was to prove to myself that I was better than the best whore in the business; that's all. Besides, I intended to stay only three days, a week at most. Maxey and Adoro International were having unforeseen logistical problems in obtaining the permit necessary to install a temporary floor of three-inch-thick Lucite in the Colosseum. We couldn't do the show without it, most of our lighting was to be installed underneath the floor, which, when completed, would look like a huge sea of shimmering glass. I figured that sooner or later, certainly by the end of the week, Maxey would find out who to bribe and we'd get our permit. By the time the Lucite floor was installed, with, needless to say, maximum publicity, my

New York assistant would have finished rehearsing the models in Manhattan, our three separate orchestras—classical, rock, and country club—would be arriving, and I would have regained enough self-confidence to run my own show. I was taking a terrible chance, considering all the last-minute details, but Lulu Touché, my workroom boss, knew more about details than anyone in the fashion business, so why worry?

Guido agreed. He had no choice. I threatened to walk out on him forever if he didn't. Besides, as much as he wanted me all to himself, there were two other considerations. One, he couldn't take long-term one-to-one relationships. Two, he was in it for the money, and in this era of sexual liberation, he couldn't afford to waste a blonde bombshell with eyes the color of star sapphires and perfect skin that shone like 24-carat gold. Did I mention my abundant no-sag tits with the caramel nipples and my high-riding ass that would suggest to an interested party that I possess a dose of African blood, all in the right places. I guess I'm basically insecure; I am always reminding myself of my good points, no pun intended. It's called the Power of Positive Thinking; it's something a smart girl needs to make a habit of. And my pussy! Don't let me forget that! I keep my bush trimmed; it's naturally thick and luxuriant, a real muff if there ever was one. My cunt is so plump and juicy to look at, I get excited just thinking about it. My labia seem to hang out of me; it drives some men so wild I have to be careful not to stand naked in front of strangers.

Guido pushed a buzzer, then grabbing my buttocks, kissed me tenderly on the choice prepuce enveloping my clitoris, which was still swimming in the juices of my desire for this unkempt beast. Just as he pushed his thick, garlic-smelling tongue into my slit the door opened and my friend, the "nun" with the false eyelashes, was standing there smiling, a ring of keys in her hand like St. Peter at the Pearly Gates. In Italian he told her to bring me upstairs. As I was still naked I reached for my clothes.

Guido had other ideas. "No, no, I no want you in no clothes. All the girls upstairs, they wear clothes. I want you the naked girl. You wear shoes; shoes enough."

So, in my black patent-leather knee-high boots and nothing else, I followed my strange religious friend with the come stain still on the back of her black dress up the grand staircase to the third-floor reception room at the top of the stairs. The room had once been elegant in a predictable way; gold brocaded walls with formal red satin draperies and a worn carpet that looked like a Renaissance tapestry with a scene of the mythical founding of Rome smack in the middle of it; Remus and Romulus sucking the teats of the she-wolf. The resident prostitutes were something else. About seven girls were sitting on red satin chaise lounges dressed in the expected "turn-on outfits" of harem girls, nurses, policemen, and can-can girls. I have to say that some of their bodies looked pretty spectacular, but at first I was very defensive. I decided their eyes looked sooty from too much makeup; their lips were too wet; their cheeks were too red. Steady, Diana. When I walked into that reception room looking as fresh as a Minnesota farmgirl who'd just been laid in the hayloft, which wasn't far from the truth, I thought I heard several gasps, and I overreacted. If these were the "real women" Gloriana thought so highly of, I decided that they were as inhibited as my mother's bridge club back in Beavertown. Were they jealous of my God-given attributes or were they shocked at my nudity? Either way, it was familiar feminine behavior. How good could they be in bed? From that moment, the competition didn't bother me; I wasn't planning to speak to any of them. Later, when I got to know these "girls," I let down my defenses; I was willing to admit just how voluptuous and delicious they really were. I was willing to hear that when I had first walked naked into their reception room, their "gasps" had been noises of arousal and extreme delight. More about my co-workers later. Before I left Rome we were destined to put each other on the map.

In the next three days, which was as long as I could take it as a whore, I must have fucked a hundred men. The first night I worked only six hours, but it seems there is a grapevine in Rome, a word-of-mouth campaign. By the end of the third day, men were paying for me sight unseen. In other words, this little girl had a "reputation."

Several of my sexual encounters at Mrs. Boothby's are worth relating because of their unique character. I have to say, however, that in my entire life, so far, I have never had a bad fuck. Maybe that's why men like me; they can sense my carte-blanche approval. The fact is, I find something to enjoy with every man I'm with. With some men it's their magnificent bodies, with others it's their personality, their warmth, their sense of humor; with others it's the depth of their feelings, their vulnerability. I suppose that, given a choice, I would prefer the more animal types, but only because, as I've explained before, nothing turns me on like desire and it seems to be the animals where desire is most alive.

My first fuck at Mrs. Boothby's was one of the best. He was a fourteen-year-old red-headed schoolboy, who told me he had come to Rome from Lexington, Kentucky, on a business trip with his industrialist father. It seems the boy was being raised Baptist by his gorgeous but puritanical mother, who had herself come from one of those politically prominent and super-rich Baptist clans that abound in New England and especially in Boston, and whose devout and pious members, the atheist Kentucky husband was soon to discover, are burdened down with sexual repression and guilt for most of their tormented lives. The father's real reason for bringing the boy to Rome was not, as the mother was given to understand, an ecumenical one—namely, so that he could shake hands with the Pope and see the Sistine Chapel close up. The real reason was to get him laid at Mrs. Boothby's before it was too late to save him from a fate worse than death. As it turned out, "Red" was my biggest challenge and my greatest satisfaction of the whole three days.

I was lying in my big brass bed in my third-floor room eating Godiva chocolates and sipping Moët champagne, fantasizing about the Roman bulls who would soon be fucking me, hairy-chested Herculean he-men whom I could stroke and suck and whisper sweet nothings in their ears. In the middle of my erotic fantasies came a knock at the door.

"Come in," I cooed, hardly prepared for a slender, carrot-topped, freckle-faced boy in a Brooks Brothers gray flannel suit and white button-down Oxford cloth shirt with a navy-blue club tie. To complete his preppy look, he wore horn-rimmed glasses.

"You speak English?" he said in the cracked tones of puberty. With that, I spread my legs apart. The boy turned beet red. His jaw dropped about a foot; his glasses slid to the end of his nose. "Are you D-D-Diana?" he stuttered.

"All the way," I answered, not quite sure what he wanted. He kept staring in the general direction of my cunt. I couldn't detect a hard-on of any kind, not even a bulge. Was there a body underneath the suit? I decided to lay it on the line. "Listen, young man, you've never been laid and your father thought the time had come, right?

"Um. My f-f-father made me c-c-come here. I didn't want to c-c-come. The school psychiatrist, who's a m-m-inister, says fourteen-year-olds aren't psychologically m-m-mature enough to handle, um, you know, s-s-sex," he said as best he could.

"I think you're gorgeous," I said, lying through my teeth. "Nothing turns me on like young muscles and a long, lean body and skin like yours."

"S-s-skin like mine?" he said, smiling through adolescent blemishes. Clearly, I was going too fast.

"Yes, your skin is so white, it scares me," I continued, not sure what he needed to hear.

"S-s-scares you?" he replied.

"Yes," I said, "it's so beautiful. I'm afraid to touch it; I'm afraid I'll blemish it."

"M-m-me?" he asked, still beet red.

"Close the door, Red," I said, "and come to Diana. I have a secret I want to tell you."

"A s-s-secret?" he said, closing the door and locking it. "What kind of a s-s-secret?"

"Come and lie next to me," I said. "I don't want to strain my voice."

"S-s-should I take my shoes off?" he said, removing his black-and-white saddle shoes as he asked the question.

"Don't be nervous," I said. "I don't expect you to do anything, but I'd love to lie here and just get to know you. You have such handsome eyes and I'm so lonely." I lied again, I couldn't even see his eyes with those fucking prep-school horn-rimmed glasses.

"M-m-maybe I should take off my t-t-trousers so I don't wreck the crease."

"Yes, don't wreck the crease, whatever you do," I said, smiling wickedly. "Creases have to be handled carefully." My innuendoes went right over his head, but at least he got his pants off in record time and removed his shirt and tie without comment. I must say his body gave me quite a start. This kid had clearly come through puberty and was out the other side with the kind of clean, hard muscles that belong on a white marble statue. The whitest skin I've ever seen, with dark body hair, not red-gold as I expected. "What hath God wrought," I murmured to myself figuring that I better keep the subject of religion as far as possible from my schoolboy's mind.

"Would you like some champagne?" I asked him coyly.

"Oh," he replied with a downcast look, "I'm not allowed to d-d-drink."

"How about a piece of chocolate?" I said.

"My d-d-dermatologist says it's bad for my s-s-skin."

I decided to push harder with the Moët. "I think you should take a mouthful of champagne," I said. "I'll never tell."

"Will I get d-d-drunk?" he asked.

167

Lying again, I explained to him that he'd have to drink half a bottle of the stuff before he felt even slightly tipsy. "Here, let me pour you a glass," I said, not waiting for an answer.

Still lying down, I leaned to the bedside table at my left to pour from the heavy green bottle into delicate Venetian red-glass champagne glasses. Green and red. Christmas in July? From out of the corner of my eye I could see this boy was staring goggle-eyed at my breasts. "I think you better get into bed first," I said.

"Into the b-b-bed?" he repeated.

"Yes," I said, "otherwise, you'll spill it." You want me to drink ch-ch-champagne in b-b-bed?" he asked.

"You know what they say, stud," I retorted. "When in Rome, do as the Romans do."

"Oh?" he said, climbing onto the bed, so close I could smell him. The smell of sex. I wondered if he knew what he smelled like, or if he cared. "Christ!!" he suddenly screamed, clutching his head.

"What's wrong???" I shrieked, my imagination flooded with images of him being carried out half-naked on a stretcher dead from a cerebral hemorrhage at the age of fourteen, without having fucked me first.

I've got a m-m-migraine," he cried.

With that, I had had it. I decided that if his Baptist subconscious was working overtime, I hadn't come all the way from Beavertown to Rome to be defeated at the gates. I took a deep breath. "Don't worry, you red-headed god," I said, "I know how to cure a migraine."

"You do-d-do?" he said, reaching across me for the champagne bottle, the side of his hand just barely grazing my suddenly aroused breast.

"Take a sip of the champagne," I said, "and I'll massage the back of your neck." With that, I wrapped my arms all the way around his shoulders and began to stroke the back of his head as I snuggled up to him, making sure the smooth and rounded surface of my silky thighs stroked rhythmically against the insides of his own hard-muscled legs. "Am I invading your space?" I said. "I'm too close, aren't I? You feel so good, I can't help myself. The pain is probably in your back, too; headaches usually start at the base of the spine."

"They d-d-do?" he whispered as I stroked his back, making him shiver.

"Take off your underpants," I ordered. "They're constricting your spine."

"My sp-sp-spine?" he answered.

"Please do as I say, "I said. "I promise you, this has nothing to do with sex. I know you're not mature enough for sex, but I can't stand the thought of you with a migraine headache."

He did as I said without saying a word. His penis, as beautifully formed as he was, was perfectly flaccid. It lay there like a slug. No blood in it. No tumescence. Nothing. This boy was clearly blocked. I thought to myself, "Oh, boy, I can see it now; three hours of playing psychiatrist, telling him, 'Don't worry, it's all right,' three hours of sucking on a worm hoping it would get the message and turn into a python."

"Is your headache gone?" I asked.

His reply was no help. "It's worse than ev-ev-ever." Then something happened, as they say. We looked into each other's eyes and his were sea-green. As silly as it may sound, they reminded me of my first lover's swimming pool with its placid blue-green water lapping up against the aquamarine tiles where a horny dentist first made love to me under the steamy Pittsburgh sun. For a moment I was completely mesmerized. There are so many connections, seen and unseen, sometimes both, between two people, yes, even a self-styled hooker and her customer. My red-haired babe must have thought I was in love with him. Maybe I was. He was more naked than any man I had ever been with, because his soul was naked, too. For once, it was I who first felt desire. I did not have to respond to someone else's mood. For once, I was beyond ecstasy. For once, I was a mother with my child. With a shift in my hips, I positioned myself so that my vulva rubbed against his flaccid slug. My outer lips, those coral lips, richly charged with blood and lacquered with my body's own lubricant, embraced that sleeping penile sheath and planted a cunt-kiss on his glans, a passionate kiss to be sure, sucking it, smothering it. I could see a puzzled look in my little boy's eyes.

"What's g-g-going on?" he whispered. Instead of speaking, I took his hand and placed it on my cunt, running his fingers up and down my swollen, puffy, glistening labia. I began to breath hard. I was hot with desire. I stuck his fingers along with my own into my rosebud cunt whose petals were about to bloom. I had to be careful. I didn't want to frighten him. Already, I was hot and steamy. I was afraid I might go berserk with lust and begin to moan as I sucked that fragile snow-white skin of his from his inner thighs to his pink nipples lying before me, untouched, innocent, and ravishing.

But, as I have since learned, never underestimate the power of puberty. I could call this chapter, "Never Trust a Baptist." I should have seen the click in his eyes. I should have caught his pupils expand to twice their original, dilated size. Because, suddenly, without warning, it felt like there was a heavy lead pipe between me and my barefoot boy. A lead pipe leaning against my crotch. I barely had time to look at that broad beamed member, as straight as a baseball bat, coursing into me. What was I supposed to do at that point, cry "Rape!" or worse, "Hey, Red, you're supposed to be Mama's little boy! Why are you fucking me?"

There was no time to reflect. There was a full-grown stud lying on top of me, his hands full of my ass, with his longshoreman's muscles lifting me and releasing me as he drove home, bur ing his member to its hilt, the black wires of his bush electrifying the nerve endings of my clitoris, my inner muscles charged with blood and fully aroused, hanging on for dear life as he rammed me again and again. He was shouting, "Fuck my mother! Fuck my grandmother! Fuck the fucking Bostonians! This feels great!"

"My stud! My fucking stud!" I cried. "Hit me again! Hit me again! Harder! Harder!" thinking to myself I sorely missed the shy boy who had come to bed with me to drink champagne. My head began to thrash in orgasm. With Red I had no control. There was no delicacy, no whispered flattery, no nibbles on the back of my neck, no sweet sucking of my clitoris, no intimate foreplay. It was going to be "Slam bam, thank-you ma'am. That was okay with me.

I don't care what women's libbers say, I'll take my sex any way it comes. Fucking Red was like running an Olympic mile. It was full of spirit and youth. Unsubtle as new wine. He obviously enjoyed my body. He got off on me. He thought I was great. What the hell, he had sixty years to learn about the complexity of a woman's heart. For now, he was doing what his body told him to do.

"Christ, oh, Christ, this is great! You're great! Hot damn! Fuck! I really like this! Fuck!" Not a stutter in sight! He was cured! And he was great! In the case histories, boys seem to ejaculate within the space of a minute. Red rode me for ten minutes that first time. Every time he thrust into me I met him and I held onto him with warm, sucking flesh. What an event! His first time with a woman and I knew, somehow, no matter what Glorianna said, there was no one in Kentucky as good as me. I took his hands and put them on my nipples to teach him how to pleasure me there. Without elbows to support himself, he fell onto me, still fucking me royally I wrapped my legs around his ass, allowing him to drive even deeper. His shaft began to swell in anticipation of orgasm. I was not satisfied. I wanted him to kiss me; I wanted the warmth of his mouth to mingle with the warmth of mine. I wanted to be kissed. I can't help it. I'm an old-fashioned girl. I took his face and drew it

171

down to mine. Our mouths met with what seemed like an electrical charge.

"Oh, Red, you're a super-stud!" I cried, as the two of us came together, breathing hard, my head thrashing from side to side as release ran through me like lightning, opening every pore, relaxing every muscle. I clutched at the pillow. I clutched at Red. Finally, I could stand it no longer; I let go! Red exploded into me. I could feel the blast of sperm hitting my cervix. I tingled; I shivered. I ran hot and cold. All the while Red was grinning like the Cheshire Cat.

"My father paid for three hours," he announced jubilantly. "We have two more hours to go!" I was delighted; what such a short time ago had seemed like my good deed for the week, namely, Red, was now a pleasure beyond belief. And to think I owed it all to Mrs. Boothby's. Yes, my instincts were good. Very good. I reached down between my legs and wedged my hand between us to wet my fingers with some of Red's come.

"Sh-h-h, don't move," I said. "I want to keep you on top of me. In a few minues we can go again." And with that remark. I licked his sperm on my fingers and offered some to him to taste.

"What's that?" he asked.

"It's come," I responded. "It's delicious."

"Ugh!" he muttered when he tasted it.

"Wait till you taste me," I said.

"Will I like it?" he asked.

"Maybe not at first," I answered. "At first, the smell of cunt seems a little too strong. Some say cunt is an acquired taste. But so are oysters and caviar. Eventually, the smell and taste of women will invade your dreams and fantasies until they become your favorite food, and when your mother tells you you're not allowed cunt in between meals or before breakfast or before you go to bed, and when the psychiatrist, if God forbid you ever need one, says you must eat one kind of cunt your whole life long, they will have no more effect on you than if they told you you can't eat oysters or drink champagne three times a day. Somehow, Red, you will know in your heart they don't know what the hell they're talking about."

As I promised Red, we spent two more hours together. He fucked me three more times, and in between each fuck, he told me the story of his life. He never once mentioned his mother. I must say, I developed an inordinate respect for fourteen-year-old boys from my experience with Red. There is no reason to despair about the youth of our time; to the contrary, there is only reason to hope.

In my next account of my adventures in love, *Diana's Paradise*, I tell what happened to me when I went to Rio to check on my Brazilian textile factory and, unbeknownst to little ol' Wasp me, there was this thing called Carnival that wouldn't let me alone. I will tell how I ran into Red again. It was a whole year later; he was fifteen. This time I taught him how to go down on me. I met his former quarterback industrialist father, too, and the three of us made it big, a frankly shocking story of incest and lust that taught me how ordinary ecstasy does not begin to touch the edges of what only forbidden sex makes possible. But for now, as the fourteen-year-old Red dressed in his gray flannel suit and horn-rimmed glasses and then unlocked my bedroom door to leave me with a half-broken heart, I had such pure and simple emotions of love for him. After all, I had just spent three hours fucking the dearest, sweetest boy, who fully appreciated everything I was trying to do for him. What a treat!

By now I was ready for a big Italian meal and a night at the opera. I mean, how many hours a day can a girl spend fucking? I realized that two hours a day is about my limit; well, maybe three, but after four ... give me a break! Maybe I'm being stuffy, but for me, fucking more than four hours a day is like trying to live on ice cream. That's when I found out the true meaning of the word

173

"prostitute." I had only been working three hours. I had at least five more hours to go. In addition, it was even possible I'd have a companion by my side all night, a mystery guest I had not even met, maybe an eighty-year-old man, half-deaf and missing a leg. In any case, I was tired, not so much from fucking, but from all the energy expended on meeting a new friend, Red. And on top of that, I had had too much champagne. And too much chocolate. I was ready for a nap. After I kissed Red goodbye and let him go with a heavy heart, I sponged myself off and went back to bed for a snooze. But certain things were not meant to be.

There was a light rap on the door. It was Guido himself, wrapped in a gray silk bathrobe, escorting a middle-aged Italian gentleman, right out of a B-movie. He had the prerequisite patent-leather hair dyed jet-black, and a mustache that looked like he'd drawn it with an eyebrow pencil. He was wearing a black frock coat with a Chesterfield collar and a gray silk suit, perfectly pressed. He carried an ebony walking stick with an antique silver head and an alligator two-suiter, indicating he was about to take a trip somewhere. His hands were perfectly manicured with clear polish on the nails. His cologne was overpowering. He was what some people call a "gentleman of the old school." I don't mean to go on at length about every one of the hundred or so men (and women, as it turned out) I fucked during my three days at Mrs. Boothby's. It just so happened that my first and second fucks, Red and Signor De Gusti, as he was called, were among the most interesting. Guido introduced us at the door with the expected leer, telling me to do whatever Signor De Gusti wanted, and then he fled, not without first exposing himself to me behind Signor De Gusti's back, his full, white, uncircumcised penis hanging there in the dark shadows of his thighs in marked contrast to his jet-black bush; his cock hung there like a pagan god carved out of ivory glowing incandescently in the dark. Then, thank God,

Guido left; I say "thank God" because if he hadn't left I would have flung myself on him, a move which might have alienated my poor customer, who undoubtedly had come to Mrs. Boothby's and to me for special love and attention. How naive I was about the complexity of man! What followed was an educational experience, to say the least.

I stood facing Signor De Gusti, wondering what would happen next. This gentleman looked at me with disdain I wondered what he wanted.

"Take off my coat," he ordered in heavily accented Italian. I did as commanded, hanging it in the mammoth bleached pine wardrobe, which dominated the wall next to the bed. "My cane." We followed suit with cane, hat, and jacket. Cufflinks went on the bedside table. He did those himself; took them off, I mean. This was a ritual strip-tease, in case he didn't know it. Signor De Gusti acted like he was the Italian king in exile, condemned to live with servant girls. He had not finished issuing orders. "Draw the draperies and turn off the light; I need complete dark. Complete dark."

"Oh, one of those!" I thought. Strange, thirty years ago, fucking in the dark was normal sex; today it was absolutely kinky.

"I must be ashame of what I do," Signor De Gusti said. "What do you do?" I asked, adding quickly, "I am not into sado-masochism, Signor De Gusti."

"You may now turn on one light," he said, "the light next to the bed." I did as commanded. In the interval, while the room had been pitch-dark, he had opened his two-suiter and donned a T-shirt with an archery target painted on the front of it. To my amazement, I saw that the rest of his suitcase was filled with navel oranges, about a hundred of them. Signor De Gusti walked to the opposite corner of my bedroom and faced me. All I could see was the target. It glowed in the dark.

"Now!" he ordered.

175

"Now what?" I replied, absolutely baffled.

"You throw the oranges at me; you try to hit the bull's eye!"

"Did you say "bullshit?" I asked. I was trying to be funny. Ha, ha.

"Please," he implored. "Signor Guido tell me you are nice lady. You do what Signor De Gusti command, no?"

I threw the first orange. It hit him in the nose.

"Please try to hit the target," he cried. And so I continued, one orange at a time, as the man jerked himself off. I could just barely make out his activity in the dark. Every few oranges he would cry out, "Hit harder! Hit harder!" and I would throw harder, thus causing greater and greater sexual excitement. When I had finished throwing the hundred oranges, there was silence. I found him on the floor huffing and puffing. He had just come. I have to say he seemed much more relaxed than when he came in.

"That was wonderful; you beautiful girl," he exclaimed.

"Can I kiss you, Signor De Gusti?" I asked as sensitively as I knew how.

"No! No! Don't touch! Don't touch! That was wonderful; you beautiful girl. *Si*, I come back and see you again." I started to pick up the oranges and return them to his suitcase. "No, no, you keep oranges," he said. "Every week, I bring different oranges. You keep oranges. You beautiful girl. Now you please turn off the light." I did as ordered. Signor De Gusti dressed in the dark, snapped his suitcase shut and was gone. End of episode. Draw your own conclusions.

I do have to mention two more surprise customers, Dr. Enrico Goldberg, my psychiatrist, and Carlo, the doorman at the Hassler.

On the afternoon of the second day, I was propped up in bed reading *Italian Vogue;* I had just spent two hours, one after the other, hearing the life story of an old man who couldn't get it up anymore, an Irish-American vaudevillian named Mickey Money who told me I reminded him of a wonderful nun who used to work at the Vatican. He said we had the same kind of clitoris, and he was an expert at clitorises. I was dying to tell him about what a great fuck the Pope was, but I knew my "Poppa" would not appreciate my talking about his sexual technique with brothel customers. Mr. Money kissed me on my clitoris before he left. Well, actually, he did a little bit more than kiss it. He really was into clitorises. I kind of liked him. Pretty good for eighty-seven, I thought.

He had barely left when my favorite five-foot-three Harvard psychiatrist, Dr. Enrico Goldberg, came barreling in and shut the door and started taking off his clothes.

"Dr. Goldberg," I said, aghast, "I don't know how you found me here, but I didn't ask for an appointment and I am not mentally ill!" In a flash, he was on his knees in front of me.

"Please, Mrs. Adoro, I beg you. Hear me out! I know I told you you were kidding yourself, that what you were doing here was in violation of everything we define as humanistic and Judeo-Christian and mentally healthy, but please, Mrs. Adoro, don't roll your eyes, no, don't look away; I know I'm a boring, overeducated, fucked-up psychiatrist with a ridiculously oversized cock that only a faggot could know and love, but please, Mrs. Adoro, for two days I haven't slept, for two days while I sat and listened to nymphomaniac lesbians and suicidal lawyers and alcoholic dentists and even a pregnant nun, I was no good to anyone. All I could think about was you with those plump golden thighs of yours, and Christ!' those incredible boobs and you just lying here with your legs spread apart with that fucking piece of raw cunt between your legs. Jesus! Mrs. Adoro, I'm crazy about your cunt, pussy, pussy. Fuck, the image of you lying here all day available to any man who wants you is driving me fucking crazy. See, this time, I'm paying, you don't have to pay me. I'm paying, and for me, that's losing control. You're making me lose control, Mrs. Adoro. I can't help it. I want your pussy. Fuck. Give it to me! You don't have to love me; just let me fuck you, that's love enough. Please.

177

Just take my cock. Please. Please. You've got to let me fuck you, Mrs. Adoro. I don't want psychological understanding. I just want you to let me fuck you. Please, I'll pay double."

"What happened to your Harvard education, Dr. Goldberg?" I asked, smiling and spreading my legs as he stripped to reveal his fireplug body and firehose cock.

"Do you like my body?" he said.

"Like your body?" I said. "I love your body; I want your body; I want your brawny chest, those massive pectorals are making my juices flow."

"I'm too short, aren't I?" he said.

"No shorter than Napoleon," I replied, which made him smile for the first time since he'd entered the room. "Besides," I continued, "your cock is the biggest cock I've ever see."

"It's too big, isn't it?" he said. "It's a joke, isn't it? It's like a baby's arm, isn't it? Look at that."

Well, the truth is, a cock *can* be too big, and Dr. Goldberg's took a lot of work. Who wants to fuck an arm or a leg? Enough already. But I do have to say that trying to work that mother into me gave us our own private ritual, our own private accommodations, which is what it's really all about anyway.

"I do love you, Dr. Goldberg, for all your madnesses, all your exposed wounds," I remarked. "At least, with you, there's a person."

"You mean, there's more than a cock?" he asked.

"Believe me, Dr. Goldberg, there's a real live person attached to that humongous cock of yours."

He began to relax. "Mrs. Adoro," he suggested, "since I'm paying for this session, may I call you Diana?"

"Certainly," I replied. "Maybe I could call you 'Rico'?"

"Rico?" he said. "My name is Enrico. Some people call me Henry." Then, there was an expected pause. "Rico?" he mused. "I like that. It's because you're so sexy," he said.

Then we had to stop talking; his mouth was inside mine

178

—warm, exploring, relaxed. It had found its natural home. His skin pressed against mine; our nipples matched exactly, so we aroused ourselves, one nipple prodding the other, flesh buttons wired to our genitals, triggering sexual excitement up and down our torsos. When he finally fucked me, as he had so deeply desired, his swollen shaft, with steady, almost hydraulic action, drove me into an ecstasy I had never known. My whole body was one huge pussy wrapped around that driving piston. I came before he did; how much could it take to set me off? My vibrating flesh was the last stimulus he needed to detonate the warm come which splashed against my innards like the waves of a tropical sea. Every bit of his seminal mucus was something I treasured because it belonged to him; it had come from him.

Imagine, Dr. Rico Goldberg, my favorite fuck; how was that possible? A day before he had been the most anal-retentive, uptight shrink I had ever imagined, but you see what happens when an All-American girl has the courage to become a whore? The man came to me. He came begging. If I had been dependent on him, whining like an alleycat in heat, he would have put up with me and fucked me only when the biological need arose. I would have been kept literally at arm's (and cock's) length. Because I was willing to give love to any man who wanted me, the miracle happened. Rico Goldberg bowed to my power, the power of a whore, and discovered, finally, his own wonderful, warm, and most charming sexuality. Irresistible. The cock he had despised for being too big, in the warm cunt of the right woman, became a treasure for the two of them.

Rico Goldberg comes up again and again in the stories of my life. I mean, let's face it, a girl can always use a Harvard psychiatrist with a twelve-inch cock when she's down and out in Rome, or anywhere else for that matter. Because of me, Rico turned a corner in his own psycho-sexual development. Thereafter he referred many of his attractive young patients to Mrs. Boothby's. Many a

"Bloomingdale's Princess" became a woman while working as a part-time whore in that wonderful old house in Rome.

One more customer, this one the biggest surprise of all, and a man who, like the Pope, was to forever change my life before I left Rome.

On the third day, wearing a see-through lavender nightie, I opened the door to find Carlo, my Hassler doorman, still in his uniform.

"Carlo?" I said.

"Signora Adoro, I have spent my life savings to see you," he announced, head bowed.

"Nonsense," I responded. "For you, Carlo, I will pick up the tab myself; you've been so kind to me, so unselfish; come in, my love."

I was playing my new role to the hilt and I loved it. There was so much I could do for Carlo. It never occurred to me that Carlo could possibly love me in return or that he was far more brilliant than I gave him credit for, or that he and Remi Scarlatti, of all people, were dear old friends, that they were both passionately involved in plots to change the world. But I don't want to divulge the rest of the story before it happens. For the moment, I was overjoyed to see my Franco Nero look-alike. When I kissed him affectionately on his lower lip, he took my head in his two strong hands and drank from my mouth until I could no longer breathe. His pale blue eyes were white from desire. Carlo was a leopard in the night staring into this woman's fire.

"There should be no payment for you," he proclaimed.

Not understanding his meaning, I repeated my offer to pay for him. "Don't worry, Carlo, I'll take care of it."

"No," he replied. "If things were the way they should be in this capitalistic world, you would belong to the people."

"My goodness, Carlos!" I exclaimed, "if I provided my services free, how would I eat?"

"If things were as they should be," he responded, "the state would provide free food for everyone, whenever they needed it."

"Well, he sounded like a Communist, much too serious for me. I figured he's been working too many hours; he was much too tense. The best thing I could do for Carlo, I decided, was to cheer him up. But first, I went to my purse under the mattress; I reimbursed him for what he'd paid Guido, the equivalent in lire of two hundred dollars for an hour. My take from that sum was only twenty-five dollars, but, of course, I wasn't fucking for the money. I stuck the lire in Carlo's back pocket. Mind you, I had tipped this man till I was blue in the face, but what the heck, it was good p.r. for Adoro International and it made up for some of our employees staying at the Hassler, who probably didn't tip a dime. Little did I realize that my generosity to Carlo would save my life three days later. I thank God that I recovered my capacity to love just in the nick of time.

But first, the obligatory love scene. It's important to know what happened between me and Carlo in light of what happened later. When he took off his doorman's uniform, I was surprised to discover he had a working-man's, hard physique. He had clearly spent his youth lifting heavy weights.

"Carlo!" I exclaimed, "you have a beautiful body!"

My body is strong for the work that must be done," he replied. Since my only memories of him working were of his opening doors I couldn't imagine what he was talking about.

"You're much more handsome than I realized, Carlos."

His by now predictable response: "Certain things are necessary for leadership."

I realized then that the man had delusions of grandeur. A little bit "teched in the head," as we used to say. What was the point of arguing with him? Nuzzling him, I ran my right cheek up and down the hollow of his back. At

181

least, for all his coded language, he did have a crowbar erection. I had to struggle to help him work his boxer shorts over his rampant cock, which kept sticking through his front hole. Finally, I unbuttoned them—they were English boxer shorts—and pulled them off him along with his socks. He still refused to relax.

"I hear Adoro International is worth about thirty million in assets," he announced.

"Carlo, the truth is, we're only good for collateral against a two-million-dollar loan. I've got everything riding on our fashion show."

"Have you paid two million dollars in bills already?" was his next question.

"Carlo," I suggested, as tenderly as I knew how, "let's not talk about collateral and million-dollar loans; let's make love." I gently massaged his balls, which, like the rest of his body, seemed too intense, like small hard-boiled eggs tight up against the base of his cock. Then, I blew in his ear. That made him smile for the first time, so I did it again.

That's what brought him back to the real world. Suddenly, he was on top of me, tickling me. I fought back with the same weapon; I tickled him back. In no time, we were both roaring with laughter, having a wonderful time, spasmodically erupting into teen-age giggles. And once I got the man to laugh, it was evident that this hyper-serious doorman loved to fuck. He lunged at me from behind and entered me doggie-style.

"I love tits!" he proclaimed, laughing, grabbing my jugs in great handfuls, as he began to pump me with his red-hot tool. Did I forget to mention that I love to be fucked doggie-style, because that leaves me free to masturbate myself with one hand and fondle his balls in my other, while he's free to fondle my tits, something that drives me crazy with pleasure. His hairy chest rubbed against my back; he mouthed the sides and back of my neck, pressing the wet meat of his mouth down hard on me. Then, without any warning, he withdrew his cock, turned me around on my bed, and fucked me missionary style.

"Diana Adoro, I need you softness and your warmth. Hold me, please. You feel so wonderful." I stretched my long legs up over his shoulders and locked my ankles behind his neck to allow his deeper thrusts. The man felt sooo gooood!!! Then I squeezed his testicles from behind; they were hanging now in their soft sack, swinging easily for the first time all night.

"*Grazie, grazie,*" he kept saying over and over, which means "Thank you, thank you." I loved knowing I had relaxed him. I made him laugh. When he came, he came with a smile on his face. His body did not vibrate like a teen-age boy's. When he came he seemed to glow; a quiet warmth spread from one end of his body to the other.

"Signor Carlo, you are a wonderful lover; thank you for coming to me." He said nothing, but I could see from the expression in his eyes I had made him happier than he had been in a long, long time. He spent his last five minutes kissing me from head to toe. But, alas, when he got all snazzed up in his doorman's uniform again, he seemed to regain a certain formal attitude. He looked at his reflection in the mirror for a full minute.

"Mrs. Adoro [notice, no more "Diana"], as happy as you have made me, I have become a servant again, a servant of the rich. The only servant who can be happy is a servant of the poor. I hope no harm will ever come to you." With those mysterious and ominous words, he left me. The next time I would see Carlo would be under completely different circumstances.

First impressions can be wrong. Eventually I got to know "the girls" of Mrs. Boothby's during meals and on occasional breaks when I was able to take advantage of the reception room on the second floor. I say "occasional breaks"; there were three to be exact: one, during an earthquake scare (nothing happened), the second, during what Guido called "the worst lightning storm of the century" (it wasn't), and a third when the head of one of the two major political parties, no names mentioned, had a near-fatal heart attack jerking off while my great and good friend, the come-soaked Sister of Charity, was whipping him with a cane. Within five minutes of the gentleman's coronary, Mrs. Boothby's was filled with scores of policemen, CIA agents, medics, ambulance drivers, and priests hearing the confessions of at least four lapsed Catholic customers who had been roused from their sexual reveries by the sirens in the street.

During these brief times of chaos and interruption, I made it my habit to throw on a robe and run to the reception room to see the other whores. I mean, what choice did I have, right? I gradually came to understand that my fellow prostitutes were extremely gifted women, artists, really, with complex emotional patterns, almost ethereal sensitivity to beauty, an incredible capacity for giving and receiving love. Oh, sure, some people might call them "dirty whores," with no feeling for the men who came to them for easy release, but those sanctimonious fools could never begin to know the depth of feeling, from rage to hysteria, from crying jags to sudden outbursts of laughter that this difficult and important work engendered in the hearts and minds of Mrs. Boothby's whores. Who knows how many rotten marriages they saved? How many suicides they prevented? How many depressed businessmen whose spirits they raised, asking nothing for themselves but a hundred and fifty dollars an hour? I must dwell on these remarkable and often courageous women, pioneers in their time, who, later on in this saga, were responsible in large part for giving me my great success in Rome. I cannot at this time in my account tell exactly how they were responsible for my great fashion coup. I don't want to give away the story. But I do want to dwell on the women.

Anita was Rumanian and claimed to be twenty-nine.

She knew many phrases in most spoken languages. Mostly, she just played with her tits, which were the biggest in the house. Anita wore a special bra built like a harness, which revealed almost everything and kept her nipples pointed in the right direction. Otherwise, her most outstanding characteristic was that she had a fancy for gold; a gold lamé turban, gold rings on every finger, and gold ankle bracelets. Usually, she wore sheer black harem pants, which, when she sat down without crossing her legs, revealed that she'd forgotten to sew up the crotch. Of course, she hadn't forgotten. Anita was no fool. Like most of us, she had a carefully edited memory. Her clit was also the biggest in the house. It seemed to be at least two inches long. She never played with it in public, exactly. She'd just spread her legs and let it hang out and wait for one of her more generous-hearted friends, usually Ramona, to kneel in front of her and take a dive into her intoxicating muff. I was too inhibited to follow Ramona's example in public. I got my big chance to sample Anita before I left Mrs. Boothby's, though. I'll get to that later.

On to Ramona, half Italian, half American black, with an ass that had a mind of its own, a king-sized portion of sinfully rich chocolate mousse waiting for a dollop of any man's whipped cream to top it off. When she walked across a room with nothing on but her garter belt and bra (she was a real lady when it came to showing her tits in public), her ass rode to its own rhythm; if you were lucky enough to be lounging in an easy chair as she came toward you, you got a million-dollar view of her coral slash as she lifted each leg to walk. It was a vision of a king's ransom in rubies, gleaming in the dark of a Moorish citadel. A gleaming treasure of exotic, tropical fruit, ripe for the tongue's taste, created to be mouthed and sucked by lips, mouth-lips or cunt-lips, whichever you prefer. Sometimes, although I'm not a lesbian, I'd position myself in the lowest-slung chair in that reception room right where I know Ramona would walk, so I could catch a head-on glimpse of her juicy fruit. She knew I was looking at her.

"Honey, what you want?" she demanded to know with her black tease.

"I don't know," I said, terrified that she'd think I was a dyke and throw a fit.

But she wouldn't give up. "You know what you're looking at. You do know, honey."

I was feeling self-destructive. I had no confidence that my fashion show would ever get off the ground. I was a lonely young widow and suddenly I didn't care—about anything. Except I wanted to put my tongue in her ruby slit and wrap my hands around that warm black ass. "I want to put my tongue in your slit," I said, "and suck your pussy till . . ."

"Till what?" she asked.

"Till you come so hard you make the roof shake." Ramon began to laugh in that familiar, free, full-bottomed laugh that only blacks seem to have. I felt like a fool, at best, a twelve-year-old schoolgirl. The other prostitutes were not exactly sure what Ramona and I were talking about, as their English was rudimentary, but I noticed there was more than one ear cocked in our direction.

Suddenly, without warning, Ramona was sitting in my lap, an Afro-Mediterranean goddess, her eyes as green as emeralds in a golden sea, her hair as black as the African night. She wouldn't stop staring. "I want you," she said. Somebody giggled.

Ramona turned on them. "Whores! *Putani*! You ugly dogs! Diana's a choice piece of meat!" Ramona raged. "The only choice meat in this stinking honky dive!" Then, in a flash, she turned back to me with such tenderness and sweetness I was limp from the power of her charm. By this time, her firm arms were wrapped around me, her burnished flesh glowing in the late afternoon light, her eyes smoldering, looking straight into mine. She had no shame. In that moment, all time stood still. She shifted position and so did I. We crossed and uncrossed our legs, she sitting on my lap, until we were entangled in our own flesh. I found myself in some kind of hypnotic trance, oblivious to everything and everyone but Ramona's musky smell. Her physical presence was overpowering

Then it happened. It came like death. It was inevitable. Our cunts were suddenly sucking, kissing, touching, one swollen petal sliding into another, the nerve endings along the edges of our labia triggering jolts of pleasure through the flushed walls of my vagina, provoking perfumed sweat and marshaling blood.

"Eeeeh!" I squealed involuntarily in extreme pleasure.

"Welcome pleasure, welcome heat, welcome the lust of Ramona!" she whispered to me, breathing heavily into my ear.

"Black goddess, I am your slave!" I whispered, choking on tears of release and surrender.

"You, Diana, you are melted gold to me, "she said, the words strangling in her throat, tears coursing down her cheeks.

We rolled off the chair, fucking as women fuck, our cunt-lips sucking, kissing, pressing firm on our pleasure buds, stroking ourselves back and forth, aroused by the heat of our passion. In that single moment, I was consumed by my African goddess of love. I looked to her ebony soul for the key to my sexual deliverance. My sexual deliverance, you see, had to start in my soul. It was my lily-white suburban soul that had not yet walked through the dark mystery of Africa or for that matter, even the dark mysteries of Beavertown. So it was that it was Ramona who delivered me, Ramona who held me, Ramona who walked with me. There was no woman in those dog days in Rome more luscious, more tied to the earth, more sure of her body, more certain of her immortality. I swam in the melted chocolate of her thighs, coating myself in her sweet liquid. For a moment, I, too, was black. She awakened something dark in me. My orgasm began in that deep reservoir of mystery. It

187

began deep in my pussy, from signals sent by my clitoris, that irresistible pleasure bud which is wired to the million nerve endings that course through the flushed walls of my cunt. My orgasm began like a tidal wave far out to sea, imperceptible at first, gathering momentum, growing into a force, a force that knocks down everything in its path, then comes back for more, ten times over. I was held and released by the forces Ramona unleashed in me. We held each other for the better part of an hour until the customers came back.

Like I said, that was the day of the earthquake scare. The earthquake in question never hit Rome. No, honey, the earthquake hit me. After that first "interpersonal encounter," Ramona and I became the best friends and occasional lovers. Since, of course, neither one of us was a lesbian, we decided that the meaning of our relationship was basically that of a spiritual thrust, a humble attempt at interracial harmony. You dig?

Gerda was unbelievable. Gerda was a Russian defector, twenty-seven, who refused to wear a bra. Ever. Even when Guido said she looked obscene. Her tits were like Dolly Parton's, definitely too big to wear without a support bra. She said a man's mouth was enough support. Those fabulous globes had the consistency of vanilla custard. Her nipples were like globs of clotted cream, barely darker than the rest of her. Her ass had the same consistency; pure and unblemished, neither solid nor liquid, like jelled whipping cream. When Gerda walked about, half-naked, tits hanging out, her flesh had its own language and its own messages. Gerda's basic philosophy was "Fuck me! Fuck me!" Considering her professional status in life, her basic message seemed pretty sound.

Did I mention Valerie, the English slut with the glass eye? She conned Guido into thinking that the glass eye was paralyzed. He was dumb enough to believe her, or else Valerie was one of his better fucks. In any case, the glass eye gave Valerie a "sorry victim" look, which made many gentlemen, probably insecure but who cares, make a beeline for this seemingly shy Victorian lass with the brick-red hair, the snub nose, and the freckles. They wanted to "take care" of her, figuring she'd be more appreciative than most. Apparently she was. Valerie, you have to realize, went to great lengths to appear like a visiting member of some London literary set. She lounged in the reception room fully dressed in a jet-black taffeta dress with a high collar, long sleeves, and a crucifix around her neck. Under the dress were black stockings and high black boots. "The great lady guardian of high culture and art act," I called it.

At first, I felt sorry for Valerie. Then I found out through reception room gossip that Valerie had a bush that was more like a forest and a cunt that practically reached out and grabbed the guy's cock and sucked it with all the force of a vacuum cleaner, while she screamed, "It's too big! It's too big!" and afterward, "Oh, God, it's a miracle—my first orgasm! I'm not frigid anymore!" And Valerie made sure that before the guy ejaculated she'd deep-throated him, then taken the full length of his magnificent, never-to-be-equaled cock up her well-lubricated, never-to-be-equaled ass, telling him she'd never done that before, either, but she was so turned on by him she wanted him in every opening she had.

Once Ramona told me that Valerie had confided to her that she felt she had to develop the best technique in town to compensate for her glass eye and for the fact that her breasts weren't big enough to tit-fuck a man, so she learned to tell every male customer what he wanted to hear—that his cock was incomparable and he was the first man to make her feel like a woman. When I got to know Valerie, she once confided to me that, in truth, when she was with a customer she forgot every other man she'd been with, and did, in fact, feel like she was in the middle of a miracle. She suspected she was emotionally unbalanced and found it easier to pretend she was lying.

The year after my debut in Rome, Valerie opened

her own house, an intended haven for Japanese business-men of breeding and scholarship. She developed a new whorehouse technique that made her a fortune. Her technique is this: when the customer arrives, he is given a list of house rules and regulations in his own language, then taken to a separate apartment where he strips and is given a silk robe to wear while he reviews the available girls on a movie screen. In the middle of this media blitz, Valerie the slut (Christ, I'm so competitive; I hope it's part of my basic appeal) enters and says that, in the opinion of the management, the customer is so charming that they are going to let him break any rule he wants. He may have two girls for the price of one. He may have free marijuana, and drinks at half price. *And* they are giving him the "special girls" (who are, in fact, anybody who's available). Every girl, however, has been trained in Valerie's technique. They are, in effect, to act as love slaves. Unbeknownst to them, they are secretly monitored. To this end, every room is bugged and any whore who does not follow the Valerie technique is fired. No fresh remarks or wounded expressions are allowed. One of her girls got converted to Woman's Liberation and Gestalt psychology and started telling the customers the naked truth about their so-called male chauvinism and got her-self fired. She tried to take Valerie to court. But Valerie, it seems, had friends in the right places. The girl in ques-tion was roughed up and told to get out of town. She left, screaming to the press that Valerie was a traitor to womankind. Valerie's business doubled.

Back to my career in sex. First of all, you have to understand that, unbeknownst to me, within twelve hours of my arrival, word of mouth about me spread like wildfire around Rome. Guido and his "nun" had men in lines five deep waiting to fuck me. Why men prefer me to other sexy beautiful women, I have no idea; I guess I remind them of their sisters or their mothers. I'm not exotic; I'm not particularly glamorous, even in open-crotch panties. In certain respects I guess I differ from other women in that I don't expect men to be my father and give me the love I never had. My father and I had an absolutely perfect relationship, and if there was any sexual activity betwen us, I do not plan to discuss that until I write my last book. Most of the women I know are invariably angry at some guy for not loving them enough. They are quick to take offense at an offhand remark. They easily feel ignored and abandoned. Not me. I always know there's more where that came from; the many men in my life keep coming back to me. I am never alone.

My most dramatic fuck at Mrs. Boothby's was an American movie star, no names mentioned. I'll just call him "Bob" and leave it at that. He's supposed to be happily married with three children, alternating between a ranch in a certain western state and an apartment in New York. Turns out Bob was in Rome the three days I was at Mrs. Boothby's. Turns out his wife doesn't give head. When I heard the knock on the door, I gave my casual "come!" It was a bug-eyed Guido. I could see his big balls shaking through the front slit in his gold bathrobe. He was whispering, "It'sa big movie star!" I thought "Sure!" When Bob walked through the door, my clit practically fell out of my cunt. Guido, with his overpowering garlic breath, said, "Give him anything he tell you."

"Okay, okay," I whispered back, agog at the god who stood before me, already half out of his clothes, the most perfect blond male movie star since Gary Cooper. Bob was even better looking than me. Hooded hawk eyes, strong Roman nose, a barrel chest matted with red-gold hair; I couldn't wait to rub my ultra-sensitive nipples in that hairy chest. His cock, normal-sized, was perfect in shape, his bush an explosion of copper wires, his legs perfectly sculptured out of living flesh.

Then, before I knew it, before I'd had a chance to break the ice and introduce myself, Bob bent over me—to kiss me, I thought—but no, he was tit-fucking me and crying out, "Diana, Diana, I love your fucking tits; my wife won't let me tit-fuck her! My fucking wife! Christ, your fucking tits! Diana, Diana, too bad you don't speak English! You cuntface, pussyface fantastic fuck!"

As shocked as I was by his assumption that I didn't speak English, I decided he was right; I didn't speak English. I couldn't afford to. I knew that sooner or later, he and his lovely, chaste wife would come to Adoro International for a fashion show, and when that happened, I would look like "someone he used to know," except that the girl he knew, of course, didn't speak English. Oh boy!

I dug my fingers into his broad, muscular back to support him in a sitting position while he rubbed his white-marble shaft with its plum-sized head in between my golden tits. I could feel both the supple outer muscle of his cock and the inner core, rock-hard and hot with blood. I pushed him backward on the bed. As he pulled my head down onto his throbbing cock, which, when erect, was bigger than I expected, I licked his tight egg-shaped balls which lay on either side of the base of his organ. He moaned with pleasure when I licked them.

"More! More!" he called out, running his strong, stubby fingers through my hair. I ran my hands up and down his magnificent chest. He was built like a wrestler, strong, stocky, hard-muscled.

I was desperate to cry out, "Bob, it's me! The All American girl you've been looking for your whole life!" But I ask you, what All-American boy will marry the whore he fucks in Rome? Repressing my middle-class needs for a movie-star husband, I dove down on his manhood, letting his swollen glans glide under my upper palate; its wet ridges stimulated his cock-head, while my tongue ran up and down his cock's undershaft and my lips pressed firm on the base of his cock, working its thick outer insulation up and down over the blood-engorged inner pipe.

My movie star cried out, "Sit on my face! Sit on my face!" and damnit, I had to pretend I did not understand.

I wanted so badly to have his fast tongue inside me, eating me out, but no, I was tragically caught in my own miserable deception. He wasn't so tragically caught, thank God. You don't get to be a superstar by taking your cues from Italian whores, do you? Bob was no dummy. I got to sit on his face after all. Using his cock as a pivot, he swung himself around under my torso. I didn't lose a beat. Presently, there was warm flesh under my tits and his teddybear crest comforted my stomach with its nest of matter hair. Needless to say, the handsomest face on five continents devoured me with maximum pleasure, sucking my nub, encircling it with the tip of his tongue, until waves of orgasm engulfed me and my juices steamed out over my labia, where he lapped them up like a hungry dog.

There was more. This wasn't just sex, you know. We weren't animals. There were human considerations. After all, I was a recent widow with tremendous financial responsibilities and a great deal of emotional complexity, according to most people I've slept with. Bob, not knowing any of this, kept sighing "Oooh" and "Aaah," like he was feasting on butter-drenched lobster bits. With his middle finger he probed my anus; with his strong hands he kneaded my buns with all the relish of a professional baker baking bread.

"Ooooh, Signor," I cried out as I came for the fifth time.

"No speaka de Italiano," was Bob's reply.

"Just like an American," I thought. "He doesn't mess with nonessentials; he sticks to basics." Meat and potatoes, that was him. Well, meat anyway. He shot his load of whipped-cream come straight into my mouth bucking like a mustang and screaming, "Jesus! Jesus!" I held on, sucking and pumping every last drop, milking his balls for all they were worth. My cunt, completely out of control, skidded back and forth across his orgasmic face.

Finally, all was still. Bob faced me with an open puppy dog expression, put his arms around me, and spoke to me as his "best little girl." The only problem was he assumed I couldn't understand a word of what he was saying. "My little angel," he began. "I know you don't speak English, so I can't tell you the way I feel about you. I love you so much. I want to marry you and run away with you. I want to divorce my witch wife Lurleen. Lurleen won't go down on me. She lets me go down on her when she's drunk, but she won't go down on me, not once in twenty years. Lurleen's too pure, too noble to be degraded like a common prostitute. I say let's run away. I know we could be happy. You've got such a delicious cunt. Lurleen has never even sat on my face!" There were tears in Bob's eyes.

I wanted to scream, "Fuck Lurleen! Let's hurry and catch the last plane for Morocco; I'll sell Adoro International and you can retire from movies so we can screw all day!" I held my tongue and played dumb. I knew I would see him again. Bob talked to me for an hour and told me the story of his life, thinking all his secrets were safe with the whore who spoke no English. After that, I went down on him again. It was even better the second time.

What can I tell you about the rest of my stay at Mrs. Boothby's except that after one day I had to use chapstick on my inner thighs. Just joking. I have to joke. Being a young widow is no bed of roses, especially when you've been given reason to doubt your capacities as a woman. As we all know, men come in various shapes and sizes with differing IQ's, bank accounts, weights, heights, and dates of birth. Their cocks come big and small; I've seen horse-cocks on men barely five feet tall and cocks that were three inches erect on rugged six-footers. My conclusion: I like cocks any way they come, as long as they're attached to a man. Some women I know claim they need at least eight inches and preferably nine to get aroused. My response to that is, if you want to fuck a cock, fine, but me, I like to fuck men; otherwise,

I'd dispense with the man and buy a vibrator. What makes a man that most special, most glorious, most exciting of animals has something to do with the arrangement of brain cells and a certain way of looking at the world. I will admit I like my men aggressive; I like them to act like men; I like them to attack. It goes without saying I like them to desire me and not the other way around. You see, if it were a question of me desiring a pretty man with a ten-inch cock, I might as well go after girls and fit them with dildos. Some of my friends have frankly informed me that I don't know the truth about myself, that, in fact, I *do* desire pretty men, as well as pretty women, that I'm the one who takes the initiative. They tell me I wait for nothing to come to me, that I'm about as aggressive as a woman can get, and a closet lesbian to boot. As I've said many a time, the only women I've slept with were exceptions to my strict rule of absolute heterosexuality. If I have lusted after some of the world's most gorgeous females, it was only to get closer to the men who were sleeping with them, too. My friends claim that I lie through my teeth. What can I say?

The climax of my stay at Mrs. Boothby's was Glorianna. It was poetic justice. Apparently, without the slightest idea that I was working at Rome's hottest whorehouse, Glorianna showed up one night, smashed on Tequila Sunrises, and paid Guido double for an hour "with the nicest girl you've got." So, without knocking, "Sister Mary Nun" showed up in my bathroom as I was cleaning myself off after a kinky marine sergeant gave me a "golden champagne shower," his principal way of showing affection. "Sister" asked me if I'd mind taking a woman.

"What's she like?" I asked, unwilling to callously refuse a needy member of my own beleagured sex until I knew the whole story.

"She is about six feet tall, dresses like und man, vit slacks and slouch hat. Her face, dark, vit dark eyes. She ist very sad, Diana. All she need, it is little attenshun," explained my Teutonic saint in the sperm-splashed religious garb.

"Is she an Italian?" I asked, curious about her nationality and occupation.

"*Nein*, she says she ist artist und citizen of ze vorld," answered "Sister." "Furdermore, she had asked Guido for ze whore who is ze most pleasing to men," she added, almost as an afterthought.

Well, this dark, sad-eyed woman sounded intriguing. You have to realize that although I run an international fashion design house, in my heart of hearts I'm still back in Beavertown where the women are short and artists are nonexistent. No matter how many kings I have dinner with, no matter how many movie stars I go down on, the ultimate in sexual excitement to me is most definitely a tall artist, so I told "Sister" to most definitely send the tall artist to me in my bath, but to please ask her to take her clothes off before she made an appearance. And, oh yes, to tell her my name was Desirée. That afternoon I had decided I needed a new name for my new occupation and "Desirée' was what the golden showers" marine sergeant and I had come up with. "Sister" nodded, bowed, and shut the door. I stripped and began to draw the water for the most sensuous bath of my holiday in Rome.

Have I described my bathroom at Mrs. Boothby's? Shoulder-high slabs of white marble paved the walls; the ceiling and the rest of the walls to a height of ten feet were gilded with gold leaf. The floor was white and gold mosaic tiles with the astrological sign of Pisces, the Fish, in the middle.

For the fish figure, the craftsman had added navy blue and silver tiles. Stunning. Pisces is such a spiritual sign. The tub was sunken into the floor! it was large enough for a small cocktail party (or cock party), which was probably why it was hung, I mean built. Lush potted

196

palms sat under the small skylight on the far side of the tub. Double racks of royal blue turkish towels stood to one side of the tub. On the other side was assembled a vast array of lotions, perfumes, and liquid soaps. The toilet occupied a small room off the bathroom I've described; the bathroom was not a place for excrement; it was a den for seduction and for fantasy.

I heard Glorianna enter my bedroom. The bedroom door shut softly. I decided to play it coy. Mind you, at this moment, I had no idea my sad, dark-eyed mystery guest was my all-time rival and thorn in my side, Glorianna. I decided that when she entered my bathroom, she would be facing the back of my head. I would be tracing my nipples with soapsuds, and my face would be covered with a mask of sudsy foam. I wanted to be seduced; I wanted to be stripped; I wanted to be unmasked. As I had planned, she came into my bathroom, took one look at the bare back of me sitting in that sudsy tub, and audibly shuddered with delight. I heard, "Oh, I'm so hungry; I want you; I've got to have you!"

"I recognized that voice at once. Yes, it was Glorianna, my employee and Grand Inquisitor, who had told me I had no idea what being a woman meant. Now, finally, I understood. Gloriana had her own definition. To be a woman meant satisfying Glorianna's lust. I was appalled and disguised. Apparently, I had been "had" by a first-class pervert. To satisfy her jealousy of me, I had almost destroyed my reputation. At first, I was mightily confused. I wasn't sure what to do. Then I got the idea. I would keep the soapsuds mask on my face, disguise my voice by lowering it, and speak in a gutteral French accent. I would then entice Glorianna into the tub with me and at the crucial moment I would drown her!

Nooooo! Down my rising heart! If I drowned her, I would ruin my Colosseum debut. There was only one solution. To absolutely humiliate her. Yes, I would stand up in my bath so that she could get a full glimpse of my magnificent body, which descended from pure globes of gold over the smooth slope of my tummy down to my magnificent pussy, a pussy that would never purr for her, dog that she was. And so, as that bull dyke begin to drool and to reach out for my bloomin' breasts with her hungry hands, I would calmly wipe the soapsuds off my face and coolly announce to her shocked and sputtering ghost of a face that she was fired from Adoro, Inc. Yes, now was the time to execute my plan.

Her voice was husky. I could tell she'd been drinking. "Hello, gorgeous," was her greeting to me, right out of a bad musical.

In my gutteral French voice I grunted, *"Bon jour."*

"Hello, Frenchie," was her predictable reply. Clearly, this woman was a boring monster, a has-been clothes-horse. According to plan, I rose up from the warm waters of my bath, confident I was better looking than Botticelli's Venus, who, in his famous painting unlike yours truly, stuck her modest little hand in front of her cunt. I could feel the soapy water trickling over the back slope of my rounded ass. I knew that Glorianna was slowly going mad with desire. I visualized her staring at my ripe behind. I knew I had her where I wanted her. I slowly turned around with a coy smile under my soapsuds, confident Gloria would never suspect until it was too late. The word is overconfident. When I finally saw her, I almost fell over in a dead faint. I wanted to run out in the streets screaming, "Life is unfair! I want out!" I really wanted to claw her to death.

What was my big surprise? Only that in my all-consuming hatred of her, I had completely blocked out my memories of her absolutely incredible body, which I saw naked for the first time when I caught Remi Scarlatti tit-fucking her. Then, as now, I was hoping that she'd look like she'd just been rescued from Auschwitz, with fried eggs for breasts. Wrong. Her nipples were the first thing. They seemed to cover the bottom third of her softly swinging boobies. They were toffee-colored medallions of suckable flesh; better yet, there were soft indentations, sweet little slits, where the nipples normally are. That meant she wasn't really turned on by me, not yet, anyway.

She raised her leg provocatively and rested her foot on the edge of the tub, watching my eyes to see if I'd look. I tried not to look. I really tried, because, like I say, women are not my thing. Then, almost accidentally, I looked, and instantly my nipples went hard and erect. Close-up, her vulva, was so fat, like a couple of enormous cocks, stuck together side by side, covered with a mist of down, the slit between them looking so lonely, just waiting for my mouth and tongue to explore it, to discover what wonders lay beneath. Well, like many people, I have never been able to resist buried treasure in any form.

Suddenly, Glorianna looked different to me. The face I had judged to be so hard before seemed classically beautiful, as her large mascared eyes filled with tears of tenderness; her flesh, too, seemed so fragile. I was confused. Glorianna was my enemy, yet I was falling in love with her. Was this the love-hate I had heard so much about? Right then and there, I decided to resolve my conflict; I made a firm decision not to have sex with her. After all, Glorianna was my employee. I needed to preserve my authority with her, even if she never found out who I was. I decided to excuse myself and have another girl sent in. Not a chance.

"Hey, you slut! Come here!" It was Glorianna, who else? I obeyed. I hated her. I was her slave. I got real close and stared into her deep black eyes. I could not help myself. When my shoulders rubbed against hers, touching lightly, I could feel the electricity. Then our breasts touched, the bottom curve of my turned-up pendants rubbing hard against her queen-sized aureoles. I found it difficult to breathe. "Kiss me, you fuckin' whore!" she commanded. I couldn't believe her mouth! It was vulgar. It was raw. I hated her, hated her power, her cheap vulgarity, her pretense at class. Without thinking, I dove for her mouth with my mouth. Her lips came down on mine with such force that I felt the air being drawn out of my lungs. Our lips and tongues meshed. She scraped and bit my lower lip like a predatory animal, holding me in a bearlike grip. I could not escape this carnivore. The question was, did I want to escape?

I could feel her hand explore me, down the curve of my abdomen, deep into the inside of my thighs. My hips thrust forward so that her elegant, well-practiced fingers could explore my swollen labia and discover that my little clitoris was throbbing out of raw desire. She discovered that slit, thank God, entered it and found my clitoris. The impact of her touch was so great I began to moan immediately, shivering with sexual excitement.

"That's okay, you fuckin' little bitch," she cooed, running the side of her hand up and down inside my streaming labia, her thumb fondling my clit, her lips sucking on my tits, her hot tongue making circles around my even hotter nipples. She pressed hard against me, grabbing all the kisses she could. I was having trouble maintaining my balance. I couldn't wait till I was underwater with her, our cunts pressing against each other, making sucking sounds, our bodies entwined as we almost drowned. I ached to rub against her silken skin and slide my legs in between her thighs, the top of my knee screwing into her vagina.

I didn't have long to wait. As Glorianna bore down on me, I fell backward into the soapy pool, taking her with me. Just as I had fantasized, we lay underwater, two mermaids eating each other out, two predatory fish feeding on each other's raw flesh in silence and in mystery. We finger-fucked each other; I pushed one of my fingers up her sucking cunt, another up her anus. She blew bubbles underwater, then began to thrash in orgasm. We surfaced in each other's arms. She was limp from release. She was moaning and crying, her eyes still shut from the sting of the suds.

"What is ze problem, *ma chérie*?" I grunted in my fake French voice, completely forgetting that my soap-sud disguise had washed off.

"I love you, you cheap little whore," she cried, sobbing out loud from the softness she had finally allowed herself with another woman, the sex she was publically in conflict with, the sex she privately adored. She hugged me, her eyes still closed, kissing me on the side of my neck with her hungry, open mouth. Then, she moved down to my breasts, devouring me all over again. "Christ, I never thought it could be like this," she sobbed, "you're the woman I've been dreaming of all my poor fuckin' life."

"Baby, baby," I cooed.

"Mama, mama," she continued in her lament. "Mama, you make me so happy. My boyfriend, he can go to hell. My father who fucked me every night the whole time I was growing up, he can go to hell, too. Mama, I just want you. I just want you." And with that, still crying, she dove between my legs, choking on the warm water we were lying in. I wrapped my legs around her neck as her talented tongue worked its magic.

"Aah! Aaah!" I screamed in orgasmic delight. Glorianna, poor baby, misinterpreted my cries of pleasure for stabs of pain. Lifting her head, she rose up and flew straight for me to kiss my lips and to comfort me. It was then for the first time, just as she cried out, "Mama!," that she saw my naked face. I have never seen such a look of terror in my life. Marie Antoinette, as the guillotine came crashing down on her, could not have looked more shocked than Glorianna did in Mrs. Boothby's bathtub that night in Rome.

I heard later that her piercing scream could be heard as far as three flights up and four houses on either side. Actually, there were two screams, each separate and distinct. First it was "Eeeeeeaaaah!" Then it was "Noooooooo!" The second cry was more torment than the first. Glorianna broke down. She was absolutely hysterical, alternating between "I can't s-s-s-stand this! I'm going to get a r-r-razor blade and slit my w-w-wrists!" and "But you're not h-h-her, are you? But you're F-F-French, aren't you?" Variations on the theme included, "Oh, Jesus! I'm r-r-ruined! I'm fucking ruined! This morning, I was s-s-sophisticated and ch-ch-chic. Now, I'm just a t-t-tramp!" Well, I guess for once I held the upper hand, hick with the hickey that I am.

"Glorianna, I think you're fabulous," I announced.

This time she looked even more shocked than before. "You d-d-do? You mean..."

"Glorianna," I said, trying to sound like the chief executive of a world-renowned fashion house that I was, "come here." She obeyed meekly; she was beginning to calm down. "Glorianna, why did you hurt my feelings by telling me I wasn't a real woman?" I asked.

"I was so jealous of you, my darling Diana," she answered. "But I didn't know I was jealous. I felt only anger and resentment and I wanted to see you dead. It never occurred to me that I was attracted to you. Oh, Diana!" she cried, "I don't know what I'm going to do! I'm so fucked up! Please help me!"

"Glorianna," I said, as tenderly as I knew how, "I was so miserable until I expressed my hatred for you..."

"Please," she interrupted, "please don't hate me!"

"Wait! Let me finish!" I insisted. "Glorianna, until I could express my hate for you, I could not express my love, don't you understand? I did not know I loved you until I knew I hated you." And with that explanation off my breast, I mean chest, I began to sob loudly, "Please, Glorianna, don't leave Adoro International. I couldn't face it without you!"

I guess that sometimes sex between enemies is the best thing that can happen. Or maybe Glorianna and I were destined to become lovers, I mean best friends. That day we made a pact to make love only to each other when we were not involved with men. Glorianna felt that if she gave in to her lesbian tendencies, she'd never be able to find Mr. Right and get married in the Episcopal Church in a white wedding gown, which had been her constant dream since she was six. And I, since I did not really have lesbian tendencies in the first place, did not want to develop them as an art form. As far as Glorianna was concerned, she was in a special category altogether. I felt that no red-blooded person, male or female, could or should pass up the opportunity to eat out such a delectable piece of ass. I mean, in this world of flux and chaos, of shifting values and the loss of meaning, there is still one constant, one absolute; the word is "cooze" and Glorianna's was the most mouth-watering of all. Sure took me by surprise, didn't she?

I decided on the spot that since I no longer had anything to prove either to myself or to Glorianna about my femininity, it was time to sneak down the back stairs and exit Mrs. Boothby's. But it was too late; my fellow whores had heard Glorianna's screams of bloody murder. Within minutes, my white and gold marble bathroom was filled with my special friends Ramona, Gerda, Anita, Valerie—with at least three of their gentlemen callers, naked as jaybirds, right behind them. I guess you could say we had an orgy. It was mostly us girls. I mean, we really didn't know the men, did we? We let them watch us and jerk off, a nice little circle jerk with come splashing all over us. I liked getting covered with come because I had a sudden taste for Gerda with the vanilla ice cream tits. I figured if we took a bath together I could offer to wash off her sperm-splashed boobs. I don't know why, I just have a thing for milk-white tits. I was fixated on her tits, but, my dear, underwater, her cunt was better than God. What a feeling of sheer cream, cream and silk and soft velvet, with Ramona, my chocolate soufflé, joining us, sticking that fantastic cooze of hers smack in my face, that incredible cunt with its gash of raspberry jam, yes, chocolate-covered raspberry jam with that special smell of musk. I was in heaven.

Then Anita wanted to join us in the tub, Anita with

her pornographic tits. I love watching Ramona nibble on Anita's clit with those sensuous Negro lips I envied so much. Those lips got so involved in that clit they seemed to be born for it. I had no choice but to bury my face in her vulva from behind. Gerda followed suit and buried her face in mine, eating me out with her pale pink tongue. We were a regular railroad train of cunt-eating cuties.

We had to tell the "boys" to find something or someone else to do. They didn't understand; we didn't expect them to. No matter; it's a wonderful thing when girls who prefer having sex with men have an occasional "girls' night out!" Little did I suspect it then, but before the week was out, the "girls" and I would share an adventure that would capture the imagination of the world!

That night, my three days were up. It was time to move on. I figured that if I became any more successful as a Roman whore, my sexual reputation might jeopardize my fashion career; after all, I hoped to sell my clothes to the middle-American housewife and mother, who definitely did not want close association with the Italian prostitutes. Which is not to say that when dressed up, the girls at Mrs. Boothby's could not outclass Princess Grace. They had perfect features, long legs, and abundant vitality. The problem is in the word "prostitute." If the English public, for instance, was convinced that Queen Elizabeth II was a call girl, a decidedly unlikely state of affairs, to be sure, it would undoubtedly demand that she resign the throne. "Prostitute" is one of those words like "Communist" which in NATO nations does no one's career a shred of good.

The fashion show was now two weeks away; I had made up my mind about one thing. I resolved that if Maxey hadn't returned from Zurich by the time I got back to the Hassler, I would take the next plane to Switzerland and find out what or who was so time-consuming. I pictured a platinum blonde with a bland face and a nothing body with a cunt that made mine look pre-pubescent. I saw a lion's mane of orange fur framing her man-eating "orchid fish," a new name for a new species of cunt, so exotic, so gorgeous, and so lethal that just thinking about it made me want to take gas.

I got dressed, said good-bye to the girls, and told a very shocked Guido, whom I'd gotten out of bed, to keep the money I'd made. He tried to block the door to convince me to stay, but I told him I had to go, I was on duty. His face froze; what could he say? I kissed him on the cheek and left. After all, there were two and possibly three pairs of legs peeking out from under the blankets on his bed.

Outside, the Roman night was full of wine and romance. I could feel it in my bones. I couldn't wait to see Maxey at the Hassler. I felt so full; I was ready to get back to work with the man I loved. My widowhood had formally come to an end.

However, Destiny intervened before I got to the bottom of the first Spanish step.

Chapter Ten

From out of nowhere, a VW van bore down on me; without stopping, two men dressed like London bankers with black suits and bowler hats leaned down from the back of the van, picked me up under both arms, put a rag soaked in chloroform under my nose, and threw me onto a mattress on the back floor. I felt the sharp jab of a hypodermic needle; I did not wake up till nine o'clock that night.

"While I was sleeping, dreaming of fucking shepherds in the mountains of Sicily, my captors mailed to *The New York Times, Le Monde, Osservatore Romano, the Washington Post,* and to all the major television networks in Europe and America the following press release: It read as follows in several languages: "Red Brigade Responsible for Capture of Diana Adoro, Capitalist Oppressor of Working Class Women. Ransom: Two Million Dollars by Next Tuesday or Adoro Will Be Shot."

The Red Brigade! The Marxist-oriented Italian terrorist group intent on taking over the country! For almost a decade, the Red Brigade had been kidnapping prominent Italian industrialists, politicians, businessmen, holding them for exorbitant ransom and sometimes subjecting them to torture and death if the money did not arrive on time. Aldo Moro, one of Italy's most popular politicians, the leader of the Christian Democrat Party, had been found murdered in the trunk of his car. Several months before my first trip to Rome, the Brigade had captured an American general, who was rescued at the last minute in a Turin apartment just as his captors had forced him to kneel to receive a bullet in the brain. With that breakthrough, the Italian police discovered what they had long suspected: the Brigade had strong ties to upper middle class students in the industrial north, post-adolescents who were heirs to generations of radical thinking in France, Germany and Russia. In Turin the police also discovered documents which led to the arrest of several key leaders of the Brigade and a large warehouse full of ammunition for the "coming Revolution." By the time I arrived in Rome there were rumors that the Brigade had recruited new members from the new crop of students and factory workers and that a new leadership had emerged.

I woke up in a former servants' quarters on the top floor of the crumbling "palace" of the Scaluchi family, a one-time branch of the Medicis. The Scaluchis, to look at them, had eaten their family fortune in pasta; one was fatter than the other—there wasn't one under 250 pounds. Mama, Papa, Big Brother Enzio, the sister Lucretzia, and the villain of the piece, the student of revolution, twenty-four-year-old Benito, named after his third cousin Benito Mussolini, "Il Duce," facist Italy's leader during the 1930s. Benito Scaluchi's dream was to lead Italy and the Scaluchi family to world domination in the name of the oppressed. The truth is, he modeled his operations on the Mafia. Local farmers, under the threat of death, contributed food and drink to the "revolution." But, as I found out later, the Scaluchis were only one small chapter of the Red Brigade. There were higher-ups. The leader of the Brigade in Italy was someone called Il Lupo, "The Wolf." His specific identity was never stated.

My room is not worth dwelling on. The floor was covered with old mattresses. The one window was nailed down and painted black and the door to the outside was guarded by two carbine-carrying members of the Brigade. As soon as I awoke, Benito Scaluchi read me the rules. In effect, unless the ransom was delivered I had three days to live. In the meantime, if I had to go to the bathroom down the hall, one of my guards would escort me. Otherwise, I would stay in my room at all times for meals and sex.

"Sex?" I said. "Sex with whom?"

"With whoever wants you, Signora," answered Benito in perfect English, adding, "This is the revolution, Signora. We have no time for bourgeois behavior patterns."

"Bourgeois behavior patterns," I thought. "This boy has been going to college." Sir," I said, "I appreciate your thinking I'm important enough to kidnap, but I assure you, sir, I'm just a dumb fashion designer."

"Shut up!" he bellowed. And with that, he ripped off my dress. "Take 'em off!" he ordered, referring to my panties. "I said, take them off! *Vestimenti*! *Tutti vestimenti*!"

What else could he have meant but my clothing, all of it? I was absolutely terrified. I had no idea where I was; my stomach felt empty, gnawing. I was sick with fear. And now I was completely naked!

"Open your legs!" he ordered. I did as he requested. Who cared? If he liked fresh cunt, I had nothing to worry about. Mine was best-in-show. Then he said something that sounded like "You like sado-masochismo?" I understood. It was the same in every language. There was only one Marquis de Sade. I was beginning to wonder if I'd ever see Rockefeller Center again. I was so looking forward to skating there the following winter under the gold statue of Prometheus Stealing Fire from the Gods. My captor called in the guards at the door, young studs who spoke practically no English. Their crotches bulged at the sight of me.

"See," said my captor. "These two boys want your body, but I in charge of you." He began to strip. He needn't have bothered. He was about five-eleven and close to three hundred pounds. "Look at me," he kept saying, "Fat man. Ugly Benito. Ugly. Fat. Benito pig."

He snapped his fingers and one of his stud guards handed him a whip which had about ten leather thongs lashed around a wooden handle, each thong with a little steel ball on the end of it. He snapped his fingers again and one of the guards left the room. There was a deadly silence. No one said anything. I thought, "Jesus, if he tries to fuck me, I'll smother to death." I had no idea what would happen next. The guard returned with my "costume," which I was ordered to don. The costume consisted of knee-high black boots with spike heels and a black Lone Ranger mask. And one other thing. There was a wide black belt with metal studs to wear around my waist. That was it. No panties.

"You put your boot on my back and you whip Benito with the whip," Benito ordered. I didn't ask questions. "This isn't going to be so hard," I thought.

As I whipped him, he called out, "Harder! Harder!" along with a reprise of "Ugly! Fat! Benito pig!" and the harder I whipped the more he got aroused, until finally I saw this hard red cock sticking out from between his fat legs. He really didn't jerk himself off. He just touched his glans a couple of times, lightly, and he came within a few seconds, pellets of white come arcing out onto the mattress in front of him. Benito had to be the most premature of any ejaculator I'd ever seen. I thought to myself,

"What the fuck is going on?" Then, out of the corner of my eye, I caught a glimpse of the most important activity in the room. An even fatter version of Benito, Big Brother Enzio Scaluchi, had been busily taking photographs of me in my S&M costume whipping Benito.

These pictures, when developed and edited so that Benito's face was not shown, were sent to all the leading newspapers, magazines, and television networks in the United States and Europe along with a tape recording they forced me to make. They must have been reading books on the Patty Hearst kidnapping. There were too many frightening similarities. I can still recall the tape recording session. After lugging in the recording equipment, Benito handed me a typed page, which I was to read into the microphone. It read as follows:

To all the customers of Adoro International. As the head of a worldwide capitalistic company which produces nonessential goods for the bourgeoisie, I confess to you that I have been using my profits to lead a wicked and debauched life, as the accompanying pictures show. I am now learning a new way of life with the illustrious Red Brigade. And so, in order to better serve the world revolution, I am now directing the officers of Adoro International to pay the two-million-dollar ransom that the Red Brigade asks for. This money is urgently needed to buy food for the hungry people of this world [the Scaluchis, no doubt]. If you do not deliver the money according to instructions, I will be sacrificed in the interests of of the Revolution. Death to Capitalistic pigs!

Once I had made this tape recording and been shown the pictures Enzio took of me whipping Benito, I knew that my career was over. I could not go back to Rome. I couldn't even go back to Beavertown. I had to start a new life in the Tuscan hills. Still, a tiny seed of hope remained. I knew that if the right man showed up, a man who truly loved pussy, I might have a chance to repair some of the damage.

On my first night, just as with Patty Hearst, different men came and went all night, fucking me in the dark. I couldn't see their faces, and since I don't really speak Italian, I could only thank God that I love to fuck so much. I never felt like I was being raped. At least it was human contact. Let's put it this way: I intended to survive, no matter how I had to rationalize what was going on. I had no intention of becoming a victim.

On the second day I thought I was lost forever. Lying there naked, I heard familiar voices, speaking Italian, coming up the stairs outside my room. When they arrived in the doorway, I could not believe my eyes! It was Remi and Baddi! "Remi and Baddi!" I called out, grateful to see two people I knew, two men who at least spoke English. "Remi! Baddi!" I cried. "I looked everywhere for you! I tried to rehire you! Glorianna and I made up. It was all a terrible mistake!" I was lying, of course, and they knew it. They just looked at me. Their crotches didn't bulge. Granted, my muff was smeared with dry come and my lipstick was smeared across my face, but the rest of me still looked pretty ripe.

Baddi spoke. "We were both here last night."

"You were?" I cried. "You made love to me last night? Really? Why didn't you tell me who you were? I would have loved to have known it was you!"

It was no use. It was macabre. A comedy of errors. Baddi spoke again. "You realize that now that you have identified us, there is no way we can let you go free."

"Why did you identify yourself?" I cried.

"Why did you fire us?" Remi answered. "Don't you know it was always our hope to become American celebrities—on behalf of world revolution, of course. You took away our one chance. I was hoping to meet Mr. Buck Johnson and learn how to make documentaries about the oppressed."

"Shut up, Remi," Baddi hissed. "She has no respect for us. None. She fired us once. She would fire us again."

"No! I won't fire you, boys! I promise!"

"Did you hear that?" Baddi remarked. "Boys. She calls us boys."

"But, Remi and Baddi," I interrupted, "you're both so good-looking, you shouldn't let me discourage . . ." But they did not want to listen to me. They were so full of themselves, so arrogant. Imagine, fucking me and not telling me who they were. Then they left my room without another word. They didn't even say good-bye.

That night neither one of them touched me. Men came and went again. I found myself calling, "Remi! Baddi?" But no one answered.

On the third day, the Scaluchi brothers, the two guards, and Remi and Baddi came to my cell. They had guns, mostly revolvers, and Enzio had his cameras. Baddi read a prepared statement: "Diana Adoro, because the ransom money has not arrived and because you can identify key figures in the Red Brigade, the Revolutionary Council has sentenced you to death by firing squad."

"No!" I screamed. "What have I done? I come from a working class family! My father was a train conductor! I've worked since I was fifteen, first at Woolworth's and then I went to Howard Johnson's. I promised I won't tell anyone who you are!" The Red Brigade had never heard of Woolworth's or Howard Johnson's, of course, and they certainly didn't believe I'd keep my mouth shut. They blindfolded me and led me down five flights of rickety back stairs. The Scaluchi Palace was so old I could smell rotting plaster. Moreover, the roof leaked. The pipes cracked. And it was a long way down to the basement room where I was to be dispatched.

Remi and Baddi wouldn't leave me alone. "This is what you get for fucking your way to the top!" and "This is the end of the Colosseum whore" and "Maybe we fuck you one more time on behalf of working classes." They were

213

beneath contempt. For the first time in my life I had completely lost my sense of humor.

When I reached the basement room, there was every rotten smell in existence, mostly from dead rats entombed behind the rotting plaster. I wished the Red Brigade had not removed my blindfold. I was absolutely terrified.

My next visitor was Il Lupo, "The Wolf," the fabled head of the entire Italian Brigade. He arrived by motorcycle dressed in a black leather flyer's uniform with a black leather cap and goggles. He was a commanding if not heroic presence and he seemed familiar. Too familiar. Was this an Italian movie star with a fading career? Was this a radical journalist? Was this a renegade member of the government? When he removed his goggles, I could not believe my eyes. It was Carlo, the Hassler doorman! "Carlo!" I gasped.

He looked at me with sadness and intensity. "This was not my idea, Diana, believe me, but yes, I approved it. I thought for sure that Maxey von Fuchs would pay your ransom." (Note: Maxey *had* paid the ransom. Remi and Baddi, the Red Brigade couriers, had intercepted it, put it in their Swiss account, and then claimed it never arrived.)

"But why do you have to kill me?" I sobbed. "I *promise* I won't tell anybody who you are!"

"This is revolutionary justice!" was Carlo's only explanation. Where was my lover from just a few days before? Where was the man who had lusted for my breasts? Where was the best doorman who had ever lived?

The climax to my stay at the Scaluchis is one which my lawyers have forbidden me to describe in detail, so I have decided to stick to my official account of what happened.

In the first place, unbeknownst to anyone but his adoring mother, Enzio Scaluchi had decided to name names, beginning with his brother Benito, whom he detested. At the very moment that Carlo was explaining to me why I must die, adding that I was defiling the Italian heritage by planning a bourgeois fashion show at the Roman Colosseum, the Italian police had already infiltrated the Scaluchi Palace and were searching the building for me.

Let's just say that at the appropriate moment there commenced a raging gun battle between police and Brigade; one of the more disenchanted Brigade members fell dead. I picked up his gun and it accidentally went off. I really know nothing about guns, do I? Where would a girl learn to shoot a gun? It was a terrible accident and by the time the police rushed in to find me cowering in the corner, Remi and Baddi were dead, accidentally shot through the back, and Carlo was grievously wounded. The two humpy guards were dead from police bullets and the poor Scaluchis would have to spend six months in the hospital recovering from head wounds before they were ready to stand trial.

I rushed into the arms of the Italian police, shaking and sobbing. Those gentlemen were so comforting. They insisted on taking me back to the station house, but Maxey von Fuchs, as it so happens, was at that very moment having lunch at the elegant Sans Souci with the head of the Italian government and the head of the Italian police, both old and dear friends of his; they had all attended the same prep school in Switzerland. When the news of my rescue was announced, a deal was struck and it was agreed that I was to be released immediately on Maxey's recognizance. An hour later, because Maxey, typically, was caught in a traffic jam, I had to face the press alone.

Postscript to my abduction: The Red Brigade trial took place six months after I returned to the States. By then, Enzio had named names; forty-five members of the Red Brigade were rounded up. I flew to Rome for an afternoon's testimony, after which I was free to meet with the international press and discuss my summerwear collection. (You see, there *is* justice in the world!) Carlo was sentenced to twenty-five years without parole in a maximum security prison outside Milan. I have since heard he is writing a book about his life, hoping it will be a best seller and he will be released from prison through the efforts of sympathetic American liberals. As for myself, the loving Italian deities, to whom the Romans are always praying, must have been watching over me.

Chapter Eleven

Shaken. Bruised. Sobbing. I was clearly a victim. When I appeared before the press to tell them my version of the kidnapping, how I had been forced to strip naked and pose for sadistic photographs, how I had been forced to read their prepared statement, I found I had become a world celebrity. And, as certain more sleazy members of the press kept telling me, on the ransom photographs that had been released, I photographed like a movie star. With or without the black bars of censorship imposed on them, my breasts were sensationally photogenic. I was horrified to hear this, not because I'm a prude, but because as far as the average American clothes-buying housewife was concerned, my gorgeous appearance would make my claims to have been "ravished" not too credible to potential customers. The photographs of me as the dominatrix had already appeared all over the world with a black bar across my tits and genitals, although the skin mags had printed uncensored photographs of me fucking the Arab, Ail Ben Gonadi, in the skies over the Vatican. Even the most liberal sensibilities, I was informed, found all of this farfetched and dismal. Most people, according to the polls, thought I had brought my problems on myself. The upshot: in that one week since I had arrived in Rome, the Adoro sales were off eighty percent. Women weren't buying. Not only that, I was already being offered contracts to star in skin flicks. The only talk shows who were willing to hear my side of the story started after midnight. The banks in Zurich, as I found out later, had advised Maxey not to risk two million dollars on a fashion show "at this time." But I was certain that if I could remove the stigma of myself as a slut I would prove them wrong. To the contrary, this was the best time for me to present my first collection. Why not? What had I done wrong?

There was only one man in Rome who could save me: my beloved Vanni at the Vatican! As soon as I was free, I called his secretary and begged for an immediate appointment. When I returned to the Hassler to change, there was still no Maxey, although he had left phone messages everywhere. It seems he had reached the press conference twenty-five minutes after I left. I had no time to lose. For my interview with Vanni, I dressed entirely in black with a midi-length, pleated, black chenille skirt, and black patent leather shoes. My stockings were black too. Sheer, transparent black. I removed every trace of makeup except for a touch of lip gloss. Of course, I still had to find some way to make a statement about my womanhood. I found it. With my hair pulled back, I wore a black patent leather rose over my left ear. A shiny black flower. It looked just a little bit evil. Exactly what I needed.

Vanni received me in his sumptuous quarters. The minute he caught sight of me he ran to me, held me in his arms, and would not let go of me. Like the solicitous father he is, he kept smoothing out my dress for me, running his hands down my back and ass. I felt so protected, so cared for. I was home.

"Oh, Father Vanni," I cried. "You must help me! I've been called a slut and a whore and no American housewife wants to buy Adoro clothes anymore. I'm going to lose everything Adoro fought for his whole life."

"You poor child. You poor child," he said, comforting me. "All you have been through. You are a victim of the godless society, the new revolution, which spits out humans in the name of progress. Diana, I prayed every night that you would survive your ordeal and come back to me. And the Holy Father prayed, too. We both prayed. Oh, Diana, you have suffered so much."

"Yes, Father Vanni," I replied, "I have to agree with, you, but you see, it's my own fault for being nice to strangers. You see, I tried to make love to all the men in Rome. Someone told me I wasn't a real woman. Then there was this Harvard psychiatrist with a twelve-inch cock, and this doorman who belonged to the Red Brigade and who got me into Mrs. Boothby's and this red-headed boy from Kentucky ... Oh, Vanni! Vanni, I don't know what I'm talking about!" Yes, I was definitely babbling like a crazy girl, half hysterical. My circuits were overloaded. I couldn't take any more of Rome or the Italians. It was all too much.

Vanni knew just how to stop me, to calm me down. His mouth sank down on mine, shutting me up, stopping my hysteria once and for all. His mouth was warm, salt-tinged, masculine in its authority. I couldn't wait to make love to him. It had been too long since I had been impaled on the cock of a man I really cared about. The clergy, however, is always full of surprises and Vanni was no exception. He brought me into his new bathroom, which, since my first visit two weeks previously, had been completely redesigned to suit the tastes of a Roman emperor. Everything, the walls floor, ceiling, and the sunken tub were white marble. An Arab screen of filigreed wood painted white had been placed over the window, which overlooked St. Peter's Square. Cloud-white Turkish towels, two inches thick, hung over ducts which could be specially heated at the flip of a switch. If I seemed a little bit shocked when I first saw the bathroom it was only because the rest of the building, even Vanni's private quarters, seemed to belong to another century. Everything was designed for office work or quiet discussion. The bathroom suggested great pleasurable soakings and a luxurious waste of time, something I had never associated with the clergy.

"In Italy marble is cheaper than wood," was Vanni's only statement. The topic of clerical life-styles was not worth discussing; by now his hands were under my dress enjoying my chewy caramel nipples. The dress, black-widow garment that it was, fell to the floor in a heap. His black clerical robes followed it. What a body! I never tired of looking at this aging athlete's muscular frame with its powerful forearms and thighs; and he, it seemed, could not keep his hands from stroking my furry mound, playing with my fur, probing for my clitoris under its protective hood as he told me he wanted to drown in my body and go straight to heaven.

"Get into my tub," he ordered.

"But Vanni, there's no water in it," I protested.

"Every since I was a little boy," he said, "I have one great fantasy for making love, better than fuck. You be the first in my new tub."

So, not fully understanding what Vanni had in mind, I climbed into the tub, hoping that more than a handful of dark sweet meat with its raw-fish coral slit between the tops of my thighs would invite him to climb in with me. Yes, I definitely needed the security of his cock inside me. But first, the surprise!

As I turned around to sit down in the marble tub, I looked up to see my very naked confessor standing over me, outsized cock in hand, with a big grin on his face.

"This is your champagne shower!" he announced. Barely had the words left his lips than a heady stream of pale amber liquid hit me between my breasts. It was warm and frothy and wickedly delicious. Vanni was treating me to a childlike act of love far more intimate than fucking, or so it seemed at that moment. For me, this was the breaking of a social taboo that says that in order to fuck, the man must always be a passionate adult and I must always be a romantic herione, at least as serious as MGM. Ha! Vanni now aimed straight at my face; my eyes smarted from the splash of acidic gold. What a daring, wonderful man! Defying convention, I opened my mouth and signaled for him to aim his sparkling gusher at the back of my throat. He complied. The natural champagne cocktail first hit my teeth with a dazzling spatter, splashed off my left cheek and then, finding its mark, hit the back of my throat. I swallowed. It was tart, acid, musty, definitely an acquired taste, and so forbidden that the intimacy of it was incredibly exciting. I wanted more. But for now the stream had run dry.

Vanni jumped into the tub on top of me and turned a gold faucet. In a second we were lovers embracing under a waterfall, the tepid liquid perfect for a hot summer's day. He turned another knob and the tub began to fill. Then he lathered me with a bar of soap the color of blond molasses, taking special care with the supple folds of my vagina I lathered his tiny nipples; within minutes they were taut and hard, sending volts of sexual electricity into his genitals. I fantasized about the pale white sea snake between his legs, hoping it would burrow into my coral cave. His hands lingered on my thighs, washing them again and again, especially on their inner recesses, which were so sensitive to the touch.

"Vanni," I said, "here in the Vatican, there's nothing of the outside world except its most beautiful furniture, its most peaceful religious art, its kindest and most sensitive men. I could stay here forever. I could dress as a nun or something. I'd never have to face the press or

Maxey or the Zurich banks. Oh, Vanni, hold me!" And with that, I threw my arms around his torso and held tight. My back was to the door. I did not see our "visitor" come in.

Vanni, smiling, whispered into my ear, "*Carissima,* we have a special visitor." I looked up, startled, to see our third party from my last visit, the jerk-off expert from behind the Renaissance screen. It was my darling "Poppa." He was stark naked, the massive Slavic athlete, big-boned and big-cocked, standing on the edge of the tub, his hands on his haunches, his cock aimed directly at my mouth.

"Oh, Your Highness," I blurted out, "I don't deserve to be in your presence. I'm a terrible person!"

"Nonsense!" he answered in his gravelly voice. "If you had not kill the Red Brigade, eventually they vould have kill you or put you in position vhere someone else vould have kill you. Your actions vere vhat ve call 'anticipatory self-defense' and you no call me 'Your Highness.' I no royalty; I tell you before—you call me 'Poppa.' That close enough to truth."

"Yes, Poppa," I answered obediently. Then Poppa sat down on the edge of the tub, his legs dangling in the water, his cock gradually rising between his legs, long and stiff and straight with a pink glans that seemed desperate for stroking. It seemed so vulnerable in that big, white, modern bathroom.

"Oh, Poppa!" I cried, at once abandoning Vanni to grasp the base of our adorable visitor's cock with one hand and to cradle his down-covered sack of testicles in the other. I could not control my upset and confusion that was mixed with so much desire. "Poppa, I'm so upset," I cried, kissing his cock, "I've been told the women of America will not buy my clothes because they consider me a slut!" I could not continue speaking; my eyes were streaming with tears. I plunged my warm mouth over his rampant, proud scepter and rolled my hot tongue around the edge of his fat mushroom-shaped cap. The man chortled like a four-year-old and held my head between his hands to better guide and caress me as I bobbed up and down on his holy rod.

"Benedicte, benedicte," he kept murmuring, translating it for me every time: "Bless you, my daughter. Bless you."

Vanni, unlike his boss, was no voyeur and not about to become one. He mounted me animal-style from behind, standing waist-deep in the tepid water behind me. I felt Vanni's muscular, hairy stomach press against the small of my back and his big hook of a cock slip into my vaginal maw. I had forgotten how thick it was, how powerful his thighs felt pressing up against the back of my legs. Being sandwiched between two strong men has always been my favorite sexual fantasy. I loved Vanni's thrusts, his need for me, his desire for my body, his hunger for my cunt. It gave me a primal animal purpose to satisfy the appetite of another human being. His raw meat pounded to a primitive rhythm, his hands reached in front of me to fondle my stiff button of flesh; it swelled to his touch as he worked his fingers into my ooze.

I ate the slippery meat of my shy Slavic protector, who, unexpectedly began to hiss out a stream of English obscenities: "Suck me, babee! Suck dick, fuckface babee!" His vulgarity aroused me to a pitch. I flicked the glans about a hundred times with my tongue and closed my wet lips around the knob, vibrating it, my cheek muscles acting as suction cups.

"Suck dick," drooled my Poppa in his low, tremulous voice which began to get louder and louder. He bounced his hips up and down, full speed ahead. His cock felt ready to burst. I rammed his meat harder and harder into my sucking trap. Vanni by this time was rocking me back and forth in my long, hot tunnel of desire. I was having trouble maintaining my balance. I tried to grasp the slick marble surface and could not. I was slipping down between two charging locomotives. The Pope began to scream as thick, hot come shot out of his chimney, coating the raw meat in the back of my throat.

"Shiiiiit!" he wailed. He bucked and rocked. I felt the first sliver of my orgasm make its way through my body. Vanni clutched at my breasts; then he began to moan. He pulled me backward as his cock went into spasm. What the hell? Life is short! I grabbed my favorite pontiff by the royal ass and pulled him forward. The three of us fell into the water vibrating like electric eels! We thrashed for breath as we clutched at each other and almost drowned in the Vatican deep. I was flesh-fed, body-entangled, cock-contained. Wonderful. About as good as a girl from Beavertown can get.

What can be better than to have a cooze that makes overly serious males get back to basics and have a good time? These men were not defying their tradition or breaking laws; they were just being men. Poppa was so happy, for a minute, at least. Afterward, lying on Vanni's opulent Oriental rugs, wrapped in oversized white bath towels, sipping Mouton Rothchild from Waterford crystal goblets eating smoked oysters, and listening to Nat King Cole records, we all let down our hair.

Poppa, his gray-blue eyes twinkling, spoke." The answer to birth control is suck. Suck better than fuck. Suck make no babies; fuck make babies. You think I am right, babee?"

"I think you're one terrific lay," I answered.

Vanni was more to the point of my visit. "We have discussed Adoro International between ourselves. We both wish you success."

"Suck-cess!" intoned the Pontiff, evidently amused at his joke.

"If you and your financial advisor, Maxey von Fuchs, would be willing to establish an Adoro Foundation and give ten percent of your yearly income to our Vatican charity for starving children around the world," Vanni, continued, "we will not only salvage your reputation, we will guarantee that you will double your income this year."

"If you can save me and the House of Adoro," I said, "I will gladly give the hungry children ten percent of my income for the rest of my life." I was overwhelmed with gratitude. I guess the Holy Father really appreciated a girl who gives good head. If I seem to be telling tales out of school in this account, it's because I have since discovered that the Pope's job is for life. I just can't wait that long; besides, no one will believe me anyway. Vanni has told me privately that the Pope will not sue for libel since he is secretly delighted to know that some people, namely me, think he has a terrific cock. Besides, what he did for me both out of gratitude for my affection and out of concern for the starving children is absolutely without precedent in the history of the Church. In a word, he saved my hide.

I stayed in Vanni's apartment with the dear Holy Father for two more lovemaking sessions. At about eleven P.M. Vanni went down to the kitchen for delicious Italian food, what else, that he'd had the cooks keep warm. Veal piccata sautéed in a light lemon sauce, polenta, which is a kind of Italian fried grits, and an absolutely delicious green salad crammed with choice nuggets of fresh shrimp and lobster bathed in a piquante vinaigrette. The wonderful thing is how Vanni and Poppa delicately stuffed my warm cunt with their portions of veal and ate me out, bringing me to a most subtle series of quiet orgasms, appropriate for the late hour.

Vanni made me spend the night. He cautioned that gossipmongers invariably had one eye on Vatican exits and entrances, hoping to see signs of sexual activity in the persons of beautiful men and women with no connection to the Vatican coming and going at odd hours.

At about eight A.M., my face hooded, Vanni and I left the kitchen entrance. He drove me back to the Hassler. With a heavy heart I kissed him good-bye and walked into the lobby. It had been two weeks since I had seen Maxey.

Chapter Twelve

Suddenly, the most elegant continental gentleman was standing over me, resplendent in a pale gray fitted linen suit, a terra-cotta crepe shirt, and a vanilla silk tie. He sported a slouch hat made of the same fabric as his suit, and his glasses, framed in a light-colored tortoiseshell, were tinted gray—a masterpiece in half-tones and shadows. Elegance married to mystery. And then it struck me. I knew this man!

"Maxey!" I cried.

"Diana!" he whispered in his low, gravelly Prussian accent, at once so commanding, so Teutonic, and, needless to say, so sexy. "Diana, where have you been?" Was he castigating me or was there a twinkle in his eye?

"Where have I been?" said I, playing the game. "Maxey, I don't know what you're talking about!"

In no time the two of us were alone in his magnificent hotel suit with its burgundy-brocaded walls and its enormous canopied bed, and Maxey was a completely different man, overtly warm and compassionate.

Why Maxey needed to be a cold Prussian general in public was beyond me. I deduced that he was toilet-trained too early; then, again, the fact that he had been sent to a military boarding school at the age of four might have affected his personality. He once told me his father couldn't have an erection unless his mother beat him across his bare buttocks with her riding crop. Maxey felt he'd been saved from psychological disaster by his English nanny, who nursed him until he went to boarding school, even though she had no milk in her tits. She also accompanied him to the military school as his personal maid, even though she had to live in separate quarters. When he was eight, it seems, she invited him to take a nap with her one fine afternoon. It was freezing cold. She suggested they get naked together under the covers. He claimed his prepubescent erection was enough to send her into her first orgasm; maybe she'd been so terrified of the burly men who'd previously taken her to bed that she'd been too frightened to let go. In any case, his extreme success the first time out was a reward factor that served to whet his appetite for more.

His nanny was long gone and Maxey still longed for her outsized breasts, ripe and creamy in the English way. He lusted for the blond-bushed cunt that offered handfuls and mouthfuls of juicy meat to the man who wanted it. And Maxey wanted it. Somehow I was and had always been the nanny he had worshipped as a child. As he turned to me, his eyes were full of gistening tears. He embraced me after taking off his suit jacket. I could feel those arms, hard from thousands of hours in the gymnasium. He was quietly sobbing, the first time I had ever seen him cry.

"Please forgive me, my darling Diana. Please. I can't express my emotions in public, but I was sick at heart that something terrible had happened to you. I wanted to take you to La Fontanella for the Fourth of July. Then

228

I saw that picture of you with the psychotic Arab and I was sure you were mashed to a pulp in St. Peter's Square."

"Arab?" I said. "St. Peter's Square?"

And then, when I was so sure the Red Brigade had murdered you, Diana—the Red Brigade is so vicious . . ."

"Who's the Red Brigade?" I asked with a twinkle in my eye.

Maxey got the joke. And the hint. He started to laugh and raced to unbutton me. "Do you realize the torment you cause me?" he said, nuzzling me with his open mouth.

"Torment? What torment, Maxey?"

"Diana, it grows like a disease until I am consumed by you. Ravenous." Then he grabbed his crotch like he had been kicked in the groin. "I can't stand the pain!" he cried.

"The pain?" I asked, being as diabolical as I could manage under the circumstances, "Maxey, are you in pain?"

"No! No! Stay away!" he shouted. "It's so wonderful to be aroused by you!" He pronounced "aroused" to sound like "soused." I wondered if he was, indeed, soused. No, apparently, there are different levels of arousal. In his case, his cock was so hard he thought it was going to burst through its skin and take off like a rocket. By now, he was screaming, "Take off your panties! No, leave them on! No, take them off! No, leave them on! No, take them off!"

To please him, I kept putting them on and taking them off, as he struggled to get out of his clothes. By the time he was down to his fashionable, tight red nylon briefs, I could see his problem: his stalwart cock was caught inside the waistband and was strangling in a struggle to get free. With a burst of compassion I helped him wrestle the underwear over and around his red-hot member and pull them down his lean and sinewy German legs, releasing his big Nordic balls. Thank God for that.

They, too, had been trapped inside those tight briefs. Now they were free to swing free and clear in the balmy Roman dusk. What majesty they had! I thought to myself, "It's too bad people are so puritanical. Maxey has such majestic balls he really should wear them hanging outside his pants, at least during his leisure hours." I fantasized designing a pair of tight, navy-blue pinstripe trousers for him with a leather penis sheath for his sizable cock and a hole cut out beneath it to let his magnificent balls be displayed. But I had to stop myself; I was thinking like a lunatic. What was the point of it? As soon as he went out to dinner, he'd be arrested—yes, even in that city of sin and swinging singles, New York City, the Big Apple. Of course, apples have nothing to do with it; it should have been called "the Big Cock." I'm not complaining; I'm grateful for all the cock I've ever had. It's just that I'd like to see more of it on display. That way, a girl can be sure who's attracted to her for all the right reasons. Now that I've inherited a lot of money, I really don't have time for men who admire my brain; I'm more interested in my primal effect on a man's basic equipment and I don't mean his heart and lungs.

I had forgotten how magnificent Maxey's physique actually was, maybe because in the past, especially in three-ways with my beloved Adolfo in our New York quarters, the bedroom was always fairly dark. There I had experienced Maxey as an imposing hulk, a brooding presence. Now, in the clear Roman light, I saw the crisp details of his physique. His skin was without moles or strange clumps of hair. It was the gold-white skin of the northern German; his flat, straight hair seemed almost beige with its fine, even mixture of white and blond. The man was somewhere in his fifties, but his body had no lumps or sagging flesh. His stomach was muscled and hard, like an eight-year-old athlete's. His buttocks were strong, pliant muscles, and his penis, perfectly formed and larger than average, was now a red-hot poker ready to burn out my insides. Maxey was pure animal masculinity. The only thing feminine about the man was his unconscious beauty and the tenderness he showed behind closed doors. Other than that, fucking a good piece of ass was clearly his great passion in life, as it was mine.

"Tell me what you want," I begged, nibbling on a tender piece of earlobe, as I let his lobbing cock through the tunnel of my inner thighs.

"Everything you do is wonderful," he said. "Wonderful." I sat on his crowbar and slid back and forth; his hot pole rubbing against my pelvic bone brought me to ecstasy. Now he was building up rhythm in his even steady strokes, his butt muscles tightening. Outside, the soft noises of honking horns and screeching brakes grew dim. The room began to glow. The burgundy brocade was a sea of liquid rubies. I was finally safe from predators with this one man in my arms strong enough to take care of me, the one man gentle enough to capture my heart.

I began to masturbate him between my breasts, coating his tool with a mixture of his glistening unguent, which was oozing in pearls from the hole in his glans, and my own honey. I rubbed this magic ointment around his bursting glans.

But I had not completely pleased my man.

"Please, please, let's fuck," urged Maxey. "I haven't seen you in so long, two weeks at least." He didn't wait for an answer. He was a man possessed. He lifted me up and brought me down on his cock, forcing my inner lips open, a hot knife cleaving into butter. Pleasure hit me with the force of dynamite, and my relationship with Maxey became much more complex as he intoned, "Bad girl. Bad girl. Don't you ever leave Daddy again."

"No, Daddy," I said. "Di-Di stay with Daddy." What the fuck, he *was* a father figure; why deny the obvious? If Maxey wanted to be my father, I was more than happy to be his little girl. I was tired of giving orders all day. A touch of make-believe incest was exactly what I needed to relax me. I had never known my real father. After my legal father's funeral, my mother told me my real, biological father was an English businessman she'd served waffles to while she was working at the Pancake House in Philadelphia, just after she'd married my legal father, who, as it turned out, was unfortunately turned on by a string of junior high school girls between the ages of twelve and fifteen. Mother told me this because my legal father, who I had always assumed was my real father, had been fucking me in the bathroom every time she went to church on week nights, and I was about ready to have a nervous breakdown. Not from fucking the man who I thought was my father, exactly, but from worrying that my mother, his wife, would come home early some night and catch us in the act. Once I found out he wasn't my real father I decided he must be pretty sick and I lost interest in him.

I could feel my cunt-walls grip Maxey's cock right up to its base. I could feel his patch of pubic hair grinding against the flesh around my clitoris, triggering nerve endings that circuited through my body. Maxey pushed deeper and deeper through my warm flesh hitting hidden spots that ignited fires and touched off vaginal spasms deep within my cunt. Boy, did I get laid! There's nothing like a middle-aged stud who likes to fuck. I bucked forward with my hips and gyrated in a circular motion, sucking him with juicy cunt-lips to drive him crazy as he ground down, pressing his pelvic bone as close to mine as was humanly possible, ramming me again and again, shouting, "Ya! Ya! Ya!" until I could resist my warrior no more. My orgasms came like machine-gun fire. I couldn't tell where one began and the other left off. I was shaking with pleasure and groaning with delight. His body was one writhing muscle, his back arched, his face red, his teeth clenched, his jaw protruding as his cock swelled up with all the ammunition of his orgasm. He was gleaming with sweat and shouting hoarsely, "More! More!" He was my warrior god, my forbidden Nazi, my magnificent Hun! Jesus, it was like coming home.

"Daddy! Daddy!" I sobbed as my wet, sucking labia let

go of his red, once swollen cock, still tremulous, still sensitive to every hair's touch and every passing breeze.

Something had happened to us. The father and daughter thing. I loved being his "Di-Di" and he loved being "Daddy." We both loved the play-acting of incest and the pretending to violate taboos. Life can really be great when you work at it. My "Daddy Maxey" was my man who could take care of me, at least between the sheets.

Later that night, with Maxey sleeping by my side, I got out of bed to read my mail, mail which I'd been neglecting for weeks, ever since my beloved Adolfo suffered his fatal heart attack in the middle of making love. Maxey had brought with him mail from my closest friends and from my dear mother, that unforgettable combination of religious devotion, human passion, and mental confusion. I decided to read her letter first. It read as follows:

My darling daughter, who is now so rich, Praise the Lord! To think you now have the blessed career you have struggled all your life to attain and for which I scrimped and saved when you were growing up in Beavertown and I was working in the tire factory sweeping up, but that's all right. Thank you for sending me the brochure for your company. Adoro, Inc., my darling daughter, but I got a terrible shock looking at the people you are associated with! I will be brief. I know how much you love men. You are the same sinner I was before I hit menopause and found Jesus. But Diana, I lied to you. Your real father was not an English businessman. Your real father was a German businessman. I told you he was English because after the Second World War, until about ten years ago, it was better to be English. Your real father was handsome and rich and he loved every woman he could get his hands on. He couldn't control his sexual appetite and I was just a girl he devoured. Of course, I couldn't tell him I was pregnant because I never had his address. Oh, Diana, I pray you have not gotten yourself into trouble.

Your real father is one of your business associates. His name is Maximillian von Fuchs! Your loving and most sinful mother, Gertrude M. Hunt.

Oh my God! My favorite fuck was my very own dad! The one man I could be a little girl with, my one security blanket, and most frequently the man I chose as my favorite piece of ass, "the ass with class," I called him. Maxey! There he was, lying beside me, snoring so elegantly, the moonlight falling on his magnificent arms. Maxey, my father? What was I to do? What psychiatrist was I to see? I could foresee years of therapy lying on a couch fending off sexually predatory shrinks who believed in letting their cocks and balls hang out. Should I wake up Maxey and tell him the news? Should I call my mother and blast her for keeping the details of my birth from me all those years? Should I take up religion and do penance for my sins? I lay in bed for three hours considering my options. I reviewed them all. Then I made a momentous decision. I ripped up my mother's letter and flushed it down the toilet. I promptly forgot everything she had written to me. I went back to bed and kissed my Maxey on his shoulder and snuggled up against him, cunt-kissing his ass. No, I would never give him up. I would never unsettle him. He was too dear to me. I resolved that he would never discover who I really was. I turned out the light and laughed myself softly to sleep, knowing I had what all my girlfriends wanted. I had the best of all possible worlds.

At noon, the news broke on the various media. Maxey was ecstatic. "Diana, wake up! Wake up! We are saved!"

The Pope had issued an unprecedented statement to the press. Its title was "Communist Plot to Discredit Savior of the Oppressed, "Diana Adoro!" In translation, it read as follows:

The Holy Father today comes to the defense of the illustrious fashion designer, Diana Adoro. Because Mrs. Adoro decided to spend millions of dollars of her income in serving the Vatican's hunger program for the world's starving children, Diana Adoro, a modern Joan of Arc, a devoted American widow and saintly Protestant working woman, has been publically defiled by an Arab terrorist and kidnapped by a subversive Communist group, the Red Brigade. The Red Brigade forced her at gunpoint to pose for scandalous photographs and to make public statements guaranteed to destroy her reputation in business around the Christian world, particularly with working women. The Red Brigade's debasement of Diana Adoro is part of the Communist plot to take over the world. Adoro clothes are among the best-designed, most fairly priced clothes in the world. I urge all working women to buy them. There is also a growing men's line of suits and shirts which I myself buy for the purpose of giving gifts. Mrs. Adoro is now planning her fashion debut as a designer at the Colosseum Sunday night. I have every intention of attending the event to lend my hand to assist this courageous survivor of our times.

It was signed by the Pope.

Maxey was jubilant. "Diana, we're saved! How did it happen?"

"I don't know," I said. "My friend Monsignor Giovanni Caro must have put in a good word for me." The fact is, I strongly suspect Vanni wrote the press release and had Poppa sign it.

"There is just one thing," continued Max. "What does he mean when he says that you decided to spend millions of dollars of your income for the Vatican hunger programs?"

"Ten percent of our yearly income," I said.

"Ten percent!" His jaw dropped.

"The Pope said that his authorization would double our business," I insisted.

"But, Diana, why did you agree to ten percent?" asked Maxey, looking bewildered.

"Because, Maxey," I said, "hunger is a worthy cause, there's a certain amount of tax write-off, and because it was the condition for his endorsement! Without that endorsement, I may as well go back to Beavertown, because no American housewife is going to buy my clothes!" And with that off my chest, I burst out sobbing.

"Never mind," said Maxey. "It will all work out. We'll get the best press people in the business; we'll create an image for you as the modern American woman: gorgeous, successful in her career, and still concerned about the world's children. As far as the kidnapping and the photographs of you go, forget it, they will only add to your legend and your mystery."

At four o'clock that afternoon, I faced the press corps. My thick hair had been pulled back into a severe bun. So much for my crowning glory. I wore horn-rimmed designer glasses with clear glass. Behind my glasses, my eyes were heavily made up. Maxey said that dark, brooding eyes would make me look like a woman of sorrow. The rest of my face was devoid of makeup. Not even lip gloss. Then he put me in the only high-necked, long-sleeved dress we sold, added a double strand of pearls, and threw in white gloves.

I read my statement: "I am grateful to the Holy Father for encouraging my work with the hungry children. Any contributions can be sent to the House of Adoro in New York, or to the Vatican, care of Monsignor Giovanni Caro. As for my ordeal at the hands of the Arab fanatic and the Red Brigade, I wish only to say that we must fight Communism on every side. I am pleased to announce that I will definitely be presenting my new collection of designer clothes at the Roman Colosseum on Sunday, August third, as scheduled. We expect the major news media to cover our show—Mr. Buck Johnson, the preeminent documentary filmmaker, will be making a film of the event for Public Television. Anyone interested in purchasing his film can contact Mr. Johnson through the House of Adoro in New York or through the

William Morris Agency. Oh, yes, one more thing. I wish to thank Poppa, I mean the Pope for his blessing; we are prayerfully awaiting his attendance at our fashion show."

That was my statement. I felt like a fucking nun. But it worked. Half the churches and synagogues around the world offered public thanks for my deliverance. For the next six months I was a household name.

Chapter Thirteen

There was only one problem. I had six days to pull off my fashion show at the Colosseum and I still did not have one original idea. I was still planning to use the gladiators, although now, because the Holy Father was planning to attend, half of them would have to wear white robes and carry gold crosses and palm branches to portray Christian martyrs who had died on the very Colosseum floor where elegant New York models were parading the latest rags from Seventh Avenue. My musical director, hearing about the martyr idea, suggested counterpointing music from great Italian operas, such as the "March from Aïda," with American hard rock. It worked. Passion attracts passion. The combined musical intensities suited the physical statement of the Colosseum itself.

Then it struck me! The idea that would make my reputation as the champion of "real" woman. Mrs. Boothby's whores! My girls! Valerie! Ramona! Anita! Gerda! I would use them in a fashion show! Armfuls of living flesh, with their brazen tits and hips without girdles and their slightly protruding tummies; in the bed the best of womanhood, yes, but in the streets, the very problem that would disqualify them from the Junior League and the kaffeeklatches in Levittown—too much lion-maned hair, too many two-inch fingernails, too many sooty, black-lined eyes looking in too many directions, too many red-slashed pouting lips open too much of the time, too many fat thighs slouching and slinking toward too many gentlemen —it would all work perfectly on stage! Women in the audience, those chic, pressed, disciplined gals, would not know who or what these creatures were. They would see mounds of pink, gold, chocolate, and vanilla flesh— breasts, hips, thighs, and vulvas filling out designer gowns for the first time in history—and with the Pope sitting there who would dare think they were whores? They would say, "Oh, I get it. These are 'real women' as opposed to the Watusi-style six foot skeletons we normally get on the runways!"

I knew it was worth taking a chance on. Why play it safe? I had never played it safe. And I had won every time! As it turned out, when Maxey approached Guido the Horse about having five of his girls take a couple of days off, the laziest stud in town asked a hundred thousand dollars for their time. Maxey said the going rate was a thousand dollars per girl per day, and if Guido didn't let them go for that, he'd find Mrs. Boothby's closed down for reasons of syphilis. Take it or leave it, Guido. Guido had no choice. Maxey knew too many Sicilians who had established themselves in Rome who could be prevailed upon to get any important job done. He also knew the old Roman families with connections in Church and state. The girls were scheduled for Sunday; Guido threw in Saturday for good measure.

Saturday. Dress rehearsal. Still shots for the press, etc. I arrived at seven in the morning. The Lucite floor had been installed the day before. It turned the Colosseum into a skating rink, except that the ice was crystal-clear.

Underneath, the supporting walls of the old prison cells and animal dens were now occupied by strategically placed lights of all colors: blues, reds, yellows, pinks. As I said, we used outside trailers for our dressing rooms. There were ramps inside and out for the models' entrances and exits. On the floor of the Colosseum itself there was a special audience section for the Pope, Princess Grace, and assorted members of French, Italian, and California nobility. In other words, except for the Pope, the usual celebrity crowd. There was a large section for the three orchestras off to one side, and a thirty-five-story scaffolding for lights adequate for any Broadway house hovered over the center of the raised stage. The physical setup was fine; in fact, splendid. Maxey was in charge of every inanimate factor involved in the fashion show; thanks to his Prussian genius for logistics, the inanimate factors were functioning impeccably.

Lulu Touché, the head of New York workrooms, a tiny Italian-American aristocrat, who always wore a loose smock and stuck a pencil in her chignon, arrived with all my clothes. Every stitch was perfect. So far, so good.

My own models, the Slink Battalion, arrived. No problems. Each girl had already been assigned her dresses. There had been two weeks of dry runs, complete with music cues, in an off-Broadway theater. The models brought my favorite New York makeup and hair designer with them, a lovely man named Mr. Wendy, who I suspected was not into women. My task for the day was to explain to the models that I had added a few changes. Where possible, I had had Lulu include copies of each dress in a size more suitable for a shorter and stockier woman. Where there were no copies, I was going to have to experiment to see how many of "Mrs. Boothby's best" could squeeze into the originals after the tall girls had taken them off. My point was I wanted to add some "mess" to the show, an off-balance element (otherwise known as "life"). In certain cases, the slinky models

241

would be trailed by the *zaftig* whores in the exact same dress; at other times I wanted the whores to deliberately show up in the wrong place at the wrong time in the wrong dress—one the audience had just seen a few minutes before. In other words, I wanted bathing suits at the cocktail parties and ballgowns at the beach. I decided that that unorthodox course would offer new insights about the same dress. I wanted to prove that my clothes looked terrific on the "sensually explicit" woman, as I called her. All in all, I was beginning to be pleased with the shape of the show and the feeling I had for my own ideas.

Enter Buck Johnson, phase two. I knew he'd come back into my life. After all, I was paying him a small fortune just to be there with his magic lanterns. I knew that once he agreed with me that a documentary film on my fashion debut would be a goldmine opportunity for him, he'd take it from there. He agreed almost immediately. He said his footage on the installing of the Lucite floor was absolutely exciting, and when he heard about the girls from Mrs. Boothby's he said he knew he'd be winning major awards. For me, his film, which he subsequently titled "Diana's Debut," meant free advertising and free publicity.

I wasn't sure whether I was ready to forgive him for walking away from me when Glorianna attacked me in his villa house in the Trastevere, but when I saw him for the first time in a week in the Colosseum, I forgot the past completely. Even from behind, you couldn't miss that black ass. The man had haunches and loins, and we all know what bulged out in front. He was an animal with an Einstein brain, and a creative artist to boot. If I hadn't already wired the Colosseum for electricity, Buck Johnson would have supplied all the current we needed.

Luckily for me, Glorianna, Buck's great fuck, was with Lulu at the Hassler coordinating signals for the following day. Clearly, I had some signals of my own to coordinate. Maxey didn't seem to be anywhere in sight.

For all I knew, he was at Mrs. Boothby's, sampling the merchandise. How could I worry about Maxey von Fuchs when I had Buck Johnson, the stud for all seasons and all reasons, a cock's length away. Let me explain. Every man worth making love to has his own special electricity. Maxey had a Prussian hardness in his very soul that was like an invisible six-foot cock. The word is phallic. The difference between a white phallus and a black phallus is the difference between skiing in the Swiss alps and windsurfing in Tahiti. Who wants to choose? I want both. The winter sun and the summer sun. The white god Thor and the black god Osiris. I worship both. And right at that moment it was summer; I was secretly worshipping Buck Johnson. Did I forget to say I was wearing lavender silk culottes, short trousers with no underwear? I am always forgetting my underwear. I wonder if it's subconscious or something. I know my ass looks delicious when the rippling of every little muscle can be seen, and felt, through the sheerest silk. Also, the slit in my cunt can easily put a crease in it, the silk, that is. Silk is very delicate. I really shouldn't have worn it to the rehearsal. I normally don't count on my pussy juices from my Von Bartolin glands to overflow my labia and cause unsightly blotches in my crotch, but during the Saturday lunch hour, I can see in retrospect, that I was putting out clear signals that I wanted to be eaten.

Buck told me later that, as I stood there looking at his ass from behind, he saw my reflection in his lens. He knew I was right behind him and he was "all torn up." He admitted, sheepishly, with tears in his eyes, that he knew he had been wrong to run away from me when Glorianna launched into me in his house. He said I had been one of the great fucks of his life, but that he hadn't been fully conscious of that until he realized he'd been masturbating two and three times a day thinking about my full, pointed breasts with their cone-shaped aureoles the color of milk and honey, the rise and fall of my tummy, and my handful of cooze. He said he'd nearly gone mad from blinding desire, and when the Red Brigade kidnapped me, he had seriously considered suicide. He apologized for not rescuing me from the Red Brigade, too, and couldn't we go somewhere and talk about all that I'd suffered and all that he suffered thinking about me and my suffering? Imagine, me having to suffer with the greatest pussy the world had seen in a generation. Buck Johnson was the greatest con-man I'd ever met and I didn't care; I loved his act. Loved it. Standing there in front of me during our lunch break, he was fully erect, his black crowbar cock threatening to rip his pants open. To avoid public embarrassment, he took off his shirt, a college football jersey, and tied it around his waist to cover his bulge. He'd forgotten he also has one of the world's great torsos. For those of us who are into eating dark meat, he displayed rare, choice, prime grade AAA. All of it.

Of course, as Mrs. Boothby's best, namely Ramona and Gerda, saw Buck out of the corner of their heavily mascara-ed eyes as they were pigging out on take-out tortellini with cream sauce, they made a beeline for him. In atypical panic, Buck turned chicken and turned around to face me. That's when lightning struck. We were a man and a woman fatally attracted to each other by mutual lust. I could see that Ramona and Gerda were prepared for an orgy. Mental preparation is all it takes. Well, I happen to be a very private person; as it so happened, CBS and NBC were in the vicinity, and Liz Smith, the New York gossip columnist, had been seen an hour earlier asking a lot of "friendly" questions. I couldn't risk another scandal.

I grabbed Buck's hand and said, "C'mon, I've got the keys to a very fast sports car." Buck didn't say a word. he came with me, which, unfortunately, did not stop Ramona and Valerie from following us. They caught up with us just as I opened the door to my rented Fiat convertible.

"Girls," I said, "this car only seats two. Sorry." With

that, Buck and I climbed in, slammed the doors, locked them, started the engine, and sped off for an hour at the Hassler.

"We're safe, pussy," he said. I smiled, knowing full well from the anger in Ramona's eyes that there would be trouble onstage during the fashion show. Yes, for everything good there is a price to be paid.

Chapter Fourteen

The fashion show. A dream come true. The Colosseum was lit like a Broadway stage. The Lucite floor shone like a glittering ice rink; the colored lights looked like Christmas. Thanks to our dramatic "attack," which was, of course, my beloved Adolfo's idea initially, and because of the publicity surrounding my ordeal at the hands of the Red Brigade and the subsequent appeal of the Holy Father, the whole world took notice. Half the audience was television reporters with camera crews. Princess Grace was there, looking as resplendent as ever. Jackie "O" sent her regrets, but the Kennedy sisters were there. Princess Caroline of Monaco was there, too, sitting apart from her mother. Pia Zadora, the emerging new star with the little girl's body and the tits, was there, too, with her Israeli millionaire husband. Liza Minnelli, of course, and at least a hundred recognizable celebrities, including "Bob," my red-blond movie star from Mrs. Boothby's; he was there with his wife who doesn't give head. When

I was introduced on stage, I swear I saw his jaw drop into his lap. And yes, the Pope was there, too, in his familiar white cassock and matching white cape. The dear Holy Father very nearly stole the show.

My clothes were sensational, if I do say so—especially my colors, my hot pinks, corals, melons, carnelians, peaches, all sexually inspired and designed to turn people on. And because the very talented Lulu Touché from my New York workroom had simplified most of my design ideas, what could have been judged outrageous turned out to be in very good taste, although many of the serious fashion critics disagreed. More on them later.

My singular and most original innovation, showing each garment on two different women, the fashion model and "the sensualist from Mrs. Boothby's," was a resounding success. Under the spotlights, "the Boothby girls," in comparison to the professional models, looked a little thick-hipped and pot-bellied with oversized boobs. It's amazing how what looks voluptuous in bed can frankly overpower a dress. No matter. In time, the audience (most of them) not only made the adjustment to living flesh, they became more interested in Valerie and Ramona and Anita and Gerda than in the professional models. It became a challenge each time a scarecrow model walked out on stage to see what a given dress could do for the well-stacked, wide-hipped creature of flesh and blood who was soon to follow.

There was one hitch. Something happened that climaxed the show and put us on prime-time news all over the world. Remember Ramona's angry eyes as I sped off with Buck Johnson the previous day? Remember how I knew that she'd get even, somehow, onstage during the show? Well, she got her revenge.

It was my most formal evening gown. Slate-gray satin, Empire design, panels of lustrous black pearl falling from the bosom to the feet. Glorianna wore it first. She looked the way a queen is supposed to look. Regal, imperious, high cheekbones, long legs. Perfect. The audience waited to see who would wear it next. Yes, my Italo-African Ramona, licorice and emeralds, her blazing green eyes singing in the very heart of jealousy. Ramona did not look like a queen, but, to her credit, she looked about as dignified as was humanly possible for her. Don't get me wrong, in the bedroom I was that woman's slave, but in the Colosseum she was working for me. When she got to the edge of the stage, where she was supposed to twirl, smile at the audience, walk back to her dressing room, and change into a bathing suit, she decided, instead on a new game plan. She stopped on a dime, right there on the front edge, right in front of the Holy Father, who was front row center. Then, she unhooked her evening gown and let it fall to the floor. She was stark naked! She didn't stop there! She got down on her haunches and began to thrust her cunt in the direction of the Holy Father's face. The audience was absolutely shocked, although I swear I saw Princess Caroline of Monaco with a big grin on her face. Ramona was not silent, either. She kept repeating to the Pope, "Hey, baby, come and get it! What's the matter? You got something better to do?" The Pope was dumbstruck. His two aides tried to hustle him away. What an outrage to the dignity of the Papacy! The orchestra stopped. Maxey froze. I, for my part, was too busy imagining how I was going to cut up Ramona into little pieces to function very well at that moment.

The Pope saved the day! He rejected the motions of his aides to remove him as quickly as possible from the Colosseum. He climbed the small stairway up to the Lucite stage, took off his white cape, and wrapped Ramona in it, embracing her as a father would a long-lost daughter. Then he turned to the audience and spoke into one of the microphones that ringed the stage.

"This is a lovely voman (woman)" he said. "God made beautiful voman. Because God love beautiful voman. Thank you, Diana Adoro, for fashion show. Much talent.

Much beautiful clothes. Much beautiful voman. Thank you. Thank you." Then he blessed the crowd, walked down the stairs, and was off into the night.

I stood there thinking to myself, "See what a good blow job will do!"

It was estimated afterward that that one gesture on the part of the Pope lost the Catholic Church twenty million people but led to twenty million conversions, so it all evened out, and I heard rumors afterward that the Pope and Ramona became "good friends." And he never did find out what an IUD was. Thank God for modern science.

The critics called my show "tasteless," "overproduced," "in bad taste," "disgusting." I got huge orders from Macy's, Gimbel's, Neiman Marcus, Lord and Taylor, Saks, Bendel's, and Bergdorf Goodman. It began to look like Diana Adoro just might stick around in the fashion world for a mighty long time.

Maxey and I fucked on the flight all the way back to New York. Under a comforter, of course, and definitely after midnight. We wouldn't want to be accused of bad taste, ever. And like I said to the ever-present flight attendant, Miss Marilyn Wood, still a stewardess, "Beulah, peel me a grape."

Postscript

After the sensational success of my fashion debut in Rome, I was free to write my own ticket. Unfortunately, I overestimated my organizational abilities. My Brazilian adventure of the following February and March, a comedy of errors, is the subject of my next account, *Diana's Paradise*. In a nutshell, I was so elated by my brilliant idea of using Mrs. Boothby's whores for my Roman fashion debut that when I went to Brazil the following February to monitor my knitwear factory in Rio, I decided it would be equally brilliant of me to import a boatload of revelers right off the streets to recreate Carnival in New York for my middle-of-March summer-wear show. As I subsequently discovered, to my absolute horror, Carnival does not travel well, especially with hot-blooded Brazilians who cannot speak English, have never experienced temperatures below sixty degrees, and who are crazy about blue-eyed blondes with big tits. In *Diana's Paradise,* I paint a picture of Carnival in Manhattan, of sambas till sunrise, of men wearing devil's horns, and women in high-heels, spangles, and not much else. I describe an ongoing near-nudity that is almost a religion, and orgiastic sex, which, in Brazil, is a companion cult to the official Christianity.

Carnival proved to be more than most New Yorkers could handle, although a good number of them handled a lot of Brazilian cunts, cocks, tits and ass before the boatload left to go back home, Ah, yes, *Diana's Paradise*. The only problem was, was Carnival the best way to sell bathing suits? What do you do when you've got hard-driving career women seated at your summer-wear fashion show, order blanks in hand, and a coffee-colored Afro-Hispanic god with black hair and ice-blue eyes walks out in a peacock headdress and a six-foot spear, wearing a khaki bathing suit with the fly unzipped and his cock sticking out? What do you do when a copper-skinned Inca goddess parades in front of the editor-in-chief of *Women's Wear Daily* in a white-pleated tennis skirt with nothing underneath but her silky black beaver with its bright coral gash? What do you do when the editor in question cannot even see the skirt, he's so busy trying to hide his hard-on? I mean, how do you sell clothes? What do you do about the impassioned Latin revolutionaries who follow your cruise ship with their terrorist bombs in the hopes of starting World War Three in the streets of New York? This, too, is *Diana's Paradise:* life in the fast lane. Too fast. I never thought the day would come when I would feel like a virgin among men and women who really knew how to use their cocks and their pussies. I never thought I'd feel deformed and deprived for not having at least one African ancestor. In Brazil, among the "old money" aristocratic families, there are always a few mahogany-colored progenitors to make their nostrils flare and their skin shine like gold and their lips become, well, that much more sensual. And what the famous Brazilian passions with their roots in the surrounding jungles can do for the development of juicy pussy flesh, oversized clits, and cocks that are the marvel of the Western Hemisphere is too much to get into here; in *Diana's Paradise*, however, I talk about my sexual re-awakening with the Brazilians, who frankly overpower the North Americans with their passion, their sensuality, their driving samba rhythms, their nudity, their voodoo, their lust for lust, their overspiced food, their extravagant spending, their ongoing revolution. The previous summer, Rome had almost defeated this simple girl from the wilds of Pennsylvania; if it hadn't been for a humpy Holy Father, I'd be back in the Beavertown Howard Johnson's. Brazil gave me a new lease on lust and taught me there is only one basis for guilt and that is not having fucked enough. And I never thought I'd be so attracted to one man—in this case, the international playboy, "Putzi" Da Silva—that I'd be willing to abandon my career and my native land to devote the rest of my life to him, he was that good in bed. His all-consuming passion for a certain European princess, with fantastic tits, no names mentioned, however, came between us and I faced the all-time crisis of my life. How could I compete with a girl who had a palace and a second language to offer him?

Then, there was "Putzi's" sister, Sylvia Da Silva, the world's most successful lesbian, who had the hots for me. Of course, I do not approve of homosexuality, but the day I saw Sylvia masturbating on her private beach I lost control of my senses. I could not help it, I had to eat her out. She provoked me with her extreme sensuality; I found it disgusting the way she stroked and pinched her own nipples with such obvious enjoyment. Nothing is worse than a narcissist-masturbating lesbian, but my lips and tongue still tingle when I recall my first mouthful of her raw meat. She possessed me. Clearly, she was a witch; she perverted my normal sexual appetites into a sweet desire for her. Such is the power of Brazil, the principal setting for *Diana's Paradise*.

When my Carnival arrived in New York, New York

was divided in its reaction. Certain normally staid people seemed to be suddenly given permission to become Latin heathens carousing in the spangled dark. Maxey von Fuchs was one. I never expected to find that Prussian pennypincher in a glittering jock strap fucking a man and a woman at the same time to a pulsing salsa beat, with the odor of marijuana in the darkened room strong enough to choke a horse. I never expected to see my arch-rival Glorianna, the object of my intense love-hate, with her obvious passion for women—who's kidding who—running stark naked down Park Avenue chasing after a great black stud who had just taken my breath away, literally. She is so jealous. Then, there is the chapter in *Diana's Paradise* where pre-teen Brazilian girls are deflowered. I cannot reveal the erotic details at this time, but the subject matter is handled in good taste. To the contrary, in how much bad taste can it be to describe human beings of whatever age who are having a terrific time? There was a twelve-year-old boy, mature beyond his years, to whom I gave a royal tour of New York, who I later discovered wanted more than the scenery. What was I to do? He really didn't seem like twelve.

For reasons beyond my control, my summer-wear fashion show turned out to be the scandal of the season and I had to go to extraordinary lengths to salvage my reputation. But, thank God, wherever I turned for help, the most wonderful people welcomed me with open arms —and legs. I'm so thankful to the human race.

All Futura Books are available at your bookshop or newsagent, or can be ordered from the following address:
Futura Books, Cash Sales Department,
P.O. Box 11, Falmouth, Cornwall TR10 9EN.

Please send cheque or postal order (no currency), and allow 60p for postage and packing for the first book plus 25p for the second book and 15p for each additional book ordered up to a maximum charge of £1.90 in U.K.

B.F.P.O. customers please allow 60p for the first book, 25p for the second book plus 15p per copy for the next 7 books, thereafter 9p per book

Overseas customers, including Eire, please allow £1.25 for postage and packing for the first book, 75p for the second book and 28p for each subsequent title ordered.